WHERE
EVIL
HIDES

WHERE EVIL HIDES

ELIZABETH BLACKMAN

iUniverse, Inc.
Bloomington

Where Evil Hides

iUniverse books may be ordered through booksellers or by contacting:

iUniverse
1663 Liberty Drive
Bloomington, IN 47403
www.iuniverse.com
1-800-Authors (1-800-288-4677)

ISBN: 978-1-4759-4719-9 (sc)
ISBN: 978-1-4759-4721-2 (hc)
ISBN: 978-1-4759-4720-5 (ebk)

Library of Congress Control Number: 2012916884

Printed in the United States of America

iUniverse rev. date: 09/20/2012

CHAPTER ONE

THE WARM, JASMINE-SCENTED BREEZE DRIFTED into the bungalow and caressed Clarisse's naked body as she lay on the bed. Her mind was awhirl with thoughts of the man who had just left. Should she have let that happen? The query did not seem to have an answer, but still it teased her. The gentleness of his touch, the whispers in her ear as they made love—all these thoughts tumbled through her mind as she drifted into a deep sleep, only to dream of when they first met, his first words, and all that had happened prior to her invitation for dinner.

"I would love to come. should I bring anything?"

"No, thanks, I have all I need. Shall we say seven thirty tomorrow?"

"I look forward to it. Thanks again."

What meal was suitable to serve as dinner for two? Seafood, perhaps, and a salad? Having made the decision, Clarisse walked slowly to the market; there was no hurry because she had a whole day to prepare a meal for the next evening. After choosing the seafood and the salad ingredients, she purchased a chocolate mousse as a compliment for the first course; a bottle would enhance the meal.

The following day Clarisse happily prepared the meal, a salad first while the seafood was cooking. When all was ready and placed it in the fridge, she had ample time for a swim. The time flew by and the night arrived. Clarisse dressed in a multi-coloured sarong that highlighted her hazel eyes. Her blonde hair was still damp from her shower, but she was ready for the night and the meal. What was there to lose? Nothing, really, only him—and would that matter much?

A knock on the door of her bungalow jolted her from the reverie. "Is that you, Jackson?" she asked.

"Yes."

Clarisse opened the door, and with a smile she ushered him in, noting again how handsome he was: tall and tanned with brown curly hair and blue eyes, and a wonderful smile. "Please come in; dinner won't be long."

"No rush—we have plenty of time." Jackson entered, handing her a bottle of red wine. "I thought red wine would be a good choice."

As they ate their meal and drank the wine, all was perfect and the conversation was light-hearted. With dinner and the clearing up finished, they sat on the swing, which hung on the veranda. As they talked, Jackson slipped his arm around Clarisse's shoulder and drew her close. The scent of his aftershave was intoxicating, and her head began to swim. She tried to pull away, but he held her closer.

"Don't be afraid. I won't take advantage—you only have to say so, and we'll stop."

"Perhaps you should. Can we just sit and talk for a while?"

Shortly after, Clarisse sensed coolness in Jackson; he had moved away and resorted to small talk. Finally he said, "I must go now. Thanks for a lovely meal; perhaps next time I can be the cook."

"That sounds lovely. I will see you then."

Clarisse stood on the veranda watching as he walked away toward his bungalow. The night, it seemed, was for him with little regard for her. Just as well that she had been careful—she probably wouldn't see him again.

Clarisse undressed and lay on her bed. The night was warm, so only a sheet was necessary, and she soon fell asleep. Later a noise woke her with a start, and she sat up, looking into the darkness.

"Who is it?"

Outside the bungalow window, a voice answered her. "Don't be frightened—it's only me."

"Jackson! What are you doing here?"

"I had to apologize for my behaviour earlier."

Clarisse reached for her robe, slid out of bed, and donned it while walking to the door.

"Well, I suppose you should come in, then."

"Thanks."

Sitting at the table, Clarisse and Jackson talked for hours, covering every topic imaginable, including where each of them was from. Jackson lived and worked in Canberra at the federal police headquarters.

"So you are a policeman?"

"Yes, I am. What do you do in Perth?"

"Oh, I am a secretary at the Alexander Library in the city."

Slowly the talk turned to love, and lovemaking, Clarisse was forthright as she said

"I have never made love to anyone before, I don't know what's right or wrong. You moved too fast, and this concerned me. It seemed all you wanted from me was sex."

"I didn't mean it to be that way. I wanted to move slowly, letting you know I enjoyed your company and that it wasn't just sex I wanted. We can make love at a pace comfortable for you."

On they talked, all the while coming closer together. Jackson placed his hand over hers, and it was warm and inviting. He skilfully let his hand move to her leg, and then he leaned in and kissed her. This kiss was deep and smouldering. Her lips parted to accept the kiss, and a fire started to burn within in her. Desire welled up and threatened to consume her.

Jackson lifted her in his arms and walked to the bedroom. Here he laid her on the bed and removed her robe. She lay there naked, feeling no embarrassment while his eyes moved over her as he removed his clothing. There was no hurry; he moved her slowly, and she let her hands slide over his chest and down his back.

"Please, Jackson!"

"Soon. I want to draw you to me completely. I need to feel you want me totally."

Jackson eased his body over, taking her with slow, rhythmic movements. A deep, searching kiss made the passion rise, and as one their climax was complete. Clarisse felt warmth she had not known before. Jackson moved to one side, still holding her, kissing her mouth, eyelids, and neck and whispering to her the language of love. Once again, Clarisse felt the passion rise within her; unafraid, she let the warm feeling claim her again, knowing this was not just a fling. He was content to wait for her complete acceptance.

On waking, Clarisse found a note on her pillow. She picked it up and read, "Thank you, Clarisse. May there be many such nights in our future."

Clarisse smiled. All fears were gone, and she felt a sense of fulfilment as she rested her head against the pillow and again slid into a warm slumber.

The rest of the holiday flew by, and too soon it was time to leave Pearl Island.

"I don't want to go, Jackson. This holiday has been wonderful. Tell me we will see each other again soon."

"It's a shame we live on opposite sides of the country, but I will call you often, and then perhaps we can meet here next year."

"Next year? What do you mean, next year?"

"As I said, we do live on different sides of Australia."

"Well, if that's your answer, then thanks for a wonderful few days, and goodbye."

It was on that note they parted, each going their separate ways. On the plane, Clarisse tried hard not to cry, but it was useless—the tears ran down her cheeks and dripped onto her blouse.

Still feeling quite used, she muttered under her breath. "How could he have done that? Surely it was just as wonderful for him as it was for me?"

Near home, she began to see things differently. What guarantees were there for a long-term romance? Jackson certainly had not promised anything, though he was kind and considerate at all times. The hours they spent together were the best she had ever known. Why did she get so angry with him? He didn't force her to do anything—it was a coming together of two people, and the enjoyment was mutual.

Jackson gave little thought to Clarisse as he returned to Canberra. He was anxious to return to his job. He had missed the excitement of the office; his job as a federal police officer gave him great satisfaction because there were always crimes to investigate and mysteries to solve. His first morning at work, he was full of his latest conquest.

"Better watch it, boy, or you'll get caught one day," a co-worker said.

"You reckon, Bob? This latest one lives almost a world away."

"So you won't see her again?"

"No, she was just a holiday fling. I'm over her already."

"You are a bastard, Jackson, but beware the feelings that remain."

Jackson did not answer his friend, but thoughts of the island and Clarisse stayed with him.

CHAPTER TWO

CLARISSE ARRIVED HOME TO FAMILY and friends, and it was lovely to catch up with them all. Her close friend Nathan was at the airport. While looking at him, she wondered if he would be as loving and compassionate if they made love. It was a tantalizing thought but one she had no intention of pursuing.

After having dinner at her parents' home, Clarisse returned to her flat. She felt tired and curled up on her bed; it had been a long day, and sleep claimed her quickly. Her sleep was troubled, though, and thoughts of Jackson filled her dreams—how tall he was, his manners, and of course his tenderness as they made love.

Waking with a start, she looked at the clock. It showed a time she remembered, a time of surrender and acceptance, in the timeless rules of love.

Weeks passed. Clarisse went to work each day, went home, cooked, and ate her evening meal. It was a very humdrum existence, and the ghost of Jackson invaded her thoughts; the memories were not as vivid now, but she still yearned for his touch.

Nathan tried to be the perfect friend, and they went to movies and had dinners out, but never thought about a life with him. The friendship was going nowhere so she decided to end the relationship.—

Free of all ties, Clarisse made the rounds with her girlfriends, in effect, and she closed down her thoughts of Jackson, Nathan, and sex. Life moved on, as it must, but her parents had noticed a difference in her. During a meal at their home, they voiced their concerns.

"What has happened, Clarisse? You've been so different since your last holiday."

"Why do you ask? I'm the same as always, aren't I?"

"No, you are not," her father said.

Her mother scolded him. "Come on, Earnest, there's no need to be so sharp."

"You meet some bloke while you were away, didn't you?" he continued.

"That's none of your business, Dad. What I did or may have done is my business, and I don't wish to discuss it."

Silence followed as they finished their meal, after which Clarisse excused herself and left for her flat.

She slammed her door with anger and threw herself on her bed, sobbing uncontrollably. "I miss you, Jackson."

How could she have fallen in love so quickly? Did it always happen like this, or was it just lust? Did she love Jackson, or was she in love with the intimacy they shared? Why did she feel so desperate that it was making her life miserable?

As time passed, the memories of her holiday dimmed. She began to go out with friends to movies, parties, and the age-old barby; it was mainly with the girls from work, and she hoped perhaps a new man would enter her life. Nathan by this time had faded into the past—he no longer moved within her circle of friends, thought on occasions she saw him and waved a cheery hello.

At one of the office parties, she met Lachlan. He was tall and handsome with dark curly hair and deep brown eyes, and he was very different to Jackson. *Stop thinking about him*, she scolded herself. *He is no longer a part of my life.*

When Lachlan, one of the men who worked at the library asked her out, she was hesitant. Later that day she declined his offer. "I need an early night, Lachlan. Perhaps at another time."

Work and relaxation became a steady but enjoyable lifestyle. It was quite some time before Lachlan repeated his invitation for an evening out. Clarisse answered in the positive this time.

"Where would you like to go?" he asked her. "A movie, perhaps, or just dinner?"

"Dinner sounds great."

They agreed to meet the following Friday, they made their farewells, and Clarisse left for home. She found herself looking forward to the date.

The week seemed to go slowly, but finally Friday arrived. She dressed carefully in a knee-length blue frock which mirrored her eyes, and she made sure her hair and makeup were right. She looked into the full-length mirror and liked what she saw.

The doorbell rang, and she opened the door. There was Lachlan, smiling at her. He looked more handsome than she remembered. A dark blue tie complemented his grey suit and light blue shirt.

"Come in; I am just about ready," she said.

"That's okay, there's no hurry."

Clarisse quickly picked up her handbag, looking around the room to make sure all was in order. Lachlan held out his hand, and together they walked out of the apartment to his car, parked nearby.

"Which restaurant are we going to?" she asked.

"I thought perhaps Romano's. They serve an excellent meal."

They chatted to each other on the way, and it took no time to reach the restaurant. A waiter met them at the door and escorted them to their table. Clarisse pondered the menu and finally selected rainbow trout with salad.

"Make that two, please," Lachlan said.

The meal was wonderful: they talked and laughed during their meal, and the wine was intoxicating. Clarisse found she was a little tipsy, and upon realizing this, she asked for a glass of water.

"Not a big drinker?" Lachlan asked.

"No, I'm not. I don't like the feeling of not being in control."

"You needn't worry—I am here, and will get you home safely."

She nodded but said, "Women should really be responsible for themselves, don't you think?"

After leaving the restaurant, Lachlan drove Clarisse home, and their conversation carried on in the car. When they pulled up outside her flat, Clarisse asked, "Would you like to come in for a coffee?"

"That would be great, thanks."

As they walked to the flat, Lachlan was very quiet. This puzzled Clarisse because he had talked so much during dinner. *Don't be silly—you are imagining it. He has been wonderful all night and is probably tired.* Clarisse opened the door, and they entered the flat. Lachlan sat on the lounge while Clarisse made the coffee. While sitting together, they talked about the evening until, feeling quite tired, Clarisse moved to the door. "Thank you for a lovely evening. Maybe we can do this again."

"I think not. I didn't come up here just for coffee."

"What did you expect? I would like you to leave now. I have to work tomorrow and need some sleep."

She hardly had time to speak before Lachlan grabbed her. His whole manner had changed. She could see hate in his eyes as he threw her down on the lounge.

She warned, "Stop or I'll scream."

"Scream, eh? This will stop you."

Clarisse felt a hard, stinging slap on her cheek. She fell backwards to the floor, hitting her head on the coffee table. Her head spun, and she felt quite sick. While she tried to regain her feet, he punched her again. The blow was so hard that it sent her reeling into unconsciousness.

Blackness claimed her, but only for a short time. When she felt him tugging her clothing, her fighting spirit was aroused, giving her the strength to hit back. She scratched at his face and eyes, but all that did was make him more brutal. He placed his hands around her throat, his thumbs digging into her flesh.

His grip tightened as Clarisse tried to breathe. While choking, she was powerless to stop him. With one hand, he proceeded to rip the clothing from her, and with each item he became angrier, his face distorted with rage.

When he had stripped her completely, she again tried to stop him from taking what he wanted. He punched her again even harder. "Shut up, you slut. Do you want me to hit you again? Believe me, I will—the sight of a woman in pain turns me on."

The evil look in his eyes frightened Clarisse, and thoughts raced through her mind. *Why has he turned into this monster? He is going to kill me!*

Lachlan forced her legs apart and savagely thrust himself into her. The pain was unbearable, and she screamed. Immediately the pressure on her throat tightened, one thumb digging into her flesh. Unable to fight any more, she fell limp beneath him. His climax came, but this was not the end—he continued to rape and beat her until she fought him no more.

By this time Clarisse had fallen into unconsciousness; she was unaware of when the attack stopped or when he left the flat. Eventually, through the pain-filled haze, she painfully dragged herself up from the floor. Every movement made her dizzy, and a gasp of pain escaped her lips. She crawled to a chair and pulled herself up until she could sit. Pain was everywhere—her face, neck, chest, and where he had so savagely forced himself into her. After a short while, she moved from the chair, crawled to her bedroom, and climbed into bed, curling into a ball and sobbing uncontrollably. With her mind traumatized, rational thought was impossible.

Should she ring the police? No, she couldn't do that—she did not want anyone to know what had happened. Blackness claimed her as she lay in a haze of pain and desperation. Here her mind took over, taking her to a place that gently soothed the body and mind.

Clarisse woke to the sound of someone knocking on her door.

"Who is it?"

"Just me. Are you all right?"

Recognizing her friend from next-door, Clarisse answered, "I'm fine, thank you."

Her friend acknowledged the answer and left.

Clarisse made her way painfully to the bathroom, looked at her refection in the mirror, and gasped. The face she saw was not hers—it was battered and bruised. Her nose looked broken, both eyes were black and swollen, her throat was bruised, and blood ran from the corner of her mouth. Seeing the mess he had made of her face, Clarisse was incensed and full of rage. "How dare he do this to me! What gave him the right?"

She changed her mind, reached for the phone, and dialled triple zero.

The officer who answered was kind and sympathetic, writing down all the relevant information, and then the woman handed Clarisse over to the officer in charge of the rape crisis unit.

"Hello, this is Detective Inspector Jan Hastings. How can I help you?"

"Can you please come to my flat? A man savagely beat and raped me last night. I didn't intend to report it, but after I looked in the mirror, I changed my mind. I need help."

"We will be there within minutes."

"Only women, please—I don't want any men near me."

"Of course. I need some information. Are you up to that now?"

"Okay."

"Have you had a shower?"

"No, I have only just been able to get to the bathroom."

"Please don't take one; wait until we get there. What is your address?"

Clarisse gave her the address and hung up.

Jan called to her colleagues.

"We have a bad sexual assault case, so let's get moving. It isn't far, and this woman sounds in a bad way. Mandy, put a call through to the ambulance service and give them the address!"

"Sure, Jan, I'll get right onto it."

When they reached the address, they raced up the stairs, and Jan tapped gently on the door.

"Who is it?" Clarisse said.

"It's the police. You called us?"

Clarisse looked through the spy hole, and as she did, Jan lifted her badge. Upon seeing it, Clarisse unlocked the door, leaving the security chain in place. Assured by what she saw, she then fully opened the door. As they entered and saw Clarisse's injuries, they were shocked at their severity.

"My name is Jan, I am the officer in charge of the rape crisis team, and my colleagues are Kelly and Mary."

"I would be happy to see you, but not in these circumstances."

Jan wrapped a robe around Clarisse and sat on the lounge with her, trying to soothe away some of the torment and pain.

"There are examinations that must be done. These will be uncomfortable, but they are essential. I know the doctor, and she is a lovely woman. You haven't showered yet?"

"No. I was about to when I looked into the mirror. What I saw made me so angry, I couldn't let such a man get away with what he did to me."

"Well done. Now, we must collect everything to do with the rape—all your clothes, the cups used, and anything else he may have touched. While my colleagues collect these items, I will get you to briefly tell me what happened."

Clarisse tried to tell all that had happened, breaking down many times, but with quiet urging from Jan, she told her story.

Jan said, "We need to get you to the hospital. They will need to examine you and take note of all your physical injuries, and they'll also take semen and saliva specimens. You will need medical treatment for your physical and mental injuries, and the hospital is the best place."

"Is it necessary? I am so tired . . . Can't I rest for a while?"

"I would like to say yes, but I can't. The monster who perpetrated this attack has left the library and disappeared, we need all the evidence to catch him. You *do* want him caught, don't you?"

"Oh yes, but he was so nice at first then he became a monster. My face feels like pulp, my stomach hurts, and I throb all over. I'd like to kill him."

"A mutual thought, but not now. We must get you to the hospital, and then we can collect the evidence that can only come from you. The doctor will be able to make sure you are not in danger of infection or any sexually transmitted diseases."

"He has taken me into hell. Please promise me you will catch him."

Jan replied firmly, "If I have anything to do with it, we certainly will."

Jan and Clarisse continued to talk while the other officers collected the ripped clothing, bedclothes, cups, and glasses; they also dusted for fingerprints. The questions finished when Jan heard the ambulance. Before the paramedics reached the flat, she helped Clarisse dress in loose clothing. Then Jan helped her onto a stretcher and stayed with her to the hospital.

After pulling into the emergency department, the medics wheeled Clarisse into a cubical. A female doctor entered, talking to Jan about the attack.

"You say it was an extremely violent?" the doctor said.

"Oh yes, one of the worst I've seen."

The doctor nodded and then turned to her patient. "Hello, Clarisse, my name is Rachel. How are you feeling?"

"Bloody awful. I ache all over. How long will these tests take?"

"I will be as quick as I can. Some are uncomfortable but necessary for your well-being. I will be as gentle as I can."

"Right now, all I feel is agonizing pain everywhere."

The doctor went to work, swiftly taking all the swabs and examining the injuries to the neck, face, legs, arms, lower abdomen, and thighs. While doing the internal examination, she spoke softly to Clarisse, calming her and trying not to let her know the disgust she felt for the man who had inflicted such terrible wounds.

Jan stayed, holding Clarisse's hand until the examination, tests, and swabs were finished.

"I know it's uncomfortable, but this will give us the evidence we need to put this depraved individual in prison for a long time."

Exhaustion had claimed Clarisse. She lay on the examination table with eyes closed, listening to the doctor and Jan speaking, their voices muffled but still audible.

"Is it the same guy, Rach?" Jan asked.

"Give me a day or two to get the results, but my guess is yes, it's him."

"Who are you talking about?" Clarisse asked.

Both women were startled; they had thought Clarisse was asleep. Holding her hand Jan spoke softly to her. "I want you to rest now; we will talk later. The doctor is going to give you a sedative. This will calm you and help you sleep."

"You won't leave me, will you?"

"No. I'll be here when you wake," Jan reassured her.

The effect of the sedative let Clarisse sink into a warm, dreamless sleep. Here she escaped the torment and the fear.

"I have to catch this sadistic bastard, Rach. He is sick. This is the worst case I have seen so far. I am sure he is capable of murder."

"I agree. He will murder someone, and probably very soon."

Jan called the station to pass on the information gleaned from the examination.

"Are you coming back now?" Kelly asked.

"I can't leave now, Kel. I promised Clarisse I would be here when she wakes. Can you return to her flat and make sure we didn't miss anything earlier? If it's slightly suspicious or out of the ordinary, bag it and take it to the station."

"Okay. We'll see you back there."

Continuing their conversation about this latest rape, Rachel and Jan tossed one or two thoughts around, voicing them only when it seemed relevant.

"You know, Doc, for all the years I've spent in the force, I have never seen a worse case."

"He thought she was dead, Jan, I'm sure of that. She was so badly beaten, the most ruthless so far."

"I must catch him. I know he will rape again."

"If you need help with medical evidence, I am here at any time."

"Thanks, Rach, I will."

CHAPTER THREE

J AN SAT WITH CLARISSE AS she had promised, her mind retracing the rapes attributed to this rapist. The attacks had happened in different locations: a high-rise flat, a house, and then a park, yet no sound was heard, no screaming or calls for help. *How does he do it?* Perhaps Clarisse would have some of the answers. The four previous victims had been so traumatized that they did not know or would not tell.

After Clarisse woke, Jan had to leave. There was work to do, and she had to crack this case and bring a violent rapist to justice.

"I have to go, Clarisse. Can I tell your parents to come and see you?"

"Please, not now. I need time."

"Okay, I won't for now, but they need to know. Promise me you will get a nurse to ring them?"

After a farewell pat on the shoulder, Jan was gone. This left Clarisse to remember the terror of last night. Her mind was clear on some points, but others were muddled.

Clarisse gingerly felt her neck and face, and they made her gasp at the touch. "Why? What did I do to make him act this way? He was so nice before . . ." she said to herself. She must have done something to make him so angry, but what? There did not seem to be any answers to her question. Round and round it went: the dinner was lovely, he was kind and attentive, and their conversation was amicable. He gave no hint of the rage that consumed him during the attack. How did he remain so charming before they reached the flat? Her head hurt, and there were no answers. The unbearable pain began again, and the shock returned, producing uncontrollable tears. A nurse came in, spoke softly to her, and administered another injection; its effect was soothing to both Clarisse's mind and body. She returned to the comfort of blackness where she could hide and sleep, the pain gone and the memory dulled as she slept.

Jan greeted her team back at the police station; everyone busy going through the items found in Clarisse's flat. "Had any luck, you two?"

"Not yet, but still searching. How is it at the hospital?"

"All the tests are done. It's who we thought. We have to hope Clarisse can tell us more."

"Do you think she will be brave enough to tell us all about him?"

"I hope so, Kelly, but she has suffered a brutal attack—much more than the last. I believe he meant to kill her. You know what that means: the next one could die, there's no doubt about that."

"This mongrel gave her a brutal beating," Mary said in anger.

"Yes, Mary, he did. Hardened as I am to the brutality inflicted by rapists, this one is frightening. She survived due to her pluck."

Jan, Kelly, and Mary made a great rape crisis team. Jan was a no-nonsense detective inspector and head of the team; she was tall with black curly hair and deep brown eyes. Though she was a hard taskmaster, her subordinates held her in high esteem. She had never married, saying her job was the love of her life. Each time she caught a rapist and had him convicted, it gave her a sense of fulfilment that made up for any sense of loneliness she might feel. It had taken a long time to gain the recognition and status she now enjoyed. Being a woman in a so-called man's profession made it hard, but she had earned the respect as an equal among her fellow officers.

The two other members of the team were Detective Sergeant Kelly Smith, Jan's second in command. Kelly was a tall, blonde-haired woman with blue eyes and a fair complexion. She was forthright in her job and a good ally; any boss would love to have her. She was married with two children and a loving husband. She was an invaluable member of the team, and her expertise in the field of sexual assault was A crime scene to her was the means to arrest a sexual predator. Her kindness to the victims and their families was beyond reproach.

Detective Sergeant Mary Lawrance was younger than her counterparts, but she had earned her place. She possessed a natural demeanour that made all who worked with her feel at ease; in addition, the victims knew instinctively she could be trusted. Like Jan, she was not married. She had dark brown eyes and an olive complexion, and her long brown hair was tied back to keep it off her shoulders.

The whole team had a bond that tied them together, even in the worst of situations. They would work day and night, until they caught the monsters.

The three officers began their search of the items found in the apartment. Would the latest correspondence shine some light on who, or what, Clarisse had been doing in the past weeks?

Kelly cast her eyes over Clarisse's diary entries. Apart from notes to friends, there was nothing of interest. Her telephone and address book were next, and there were many numbers. They would need Clarisse to tell them who they all were. "Should I ring some of these numbers, Jan? You never know, we might get lucky."

Jan shook her head. "His phone number hasn't been found in any other address books. He's a real cagey dog, this one. "What do you think, Mary? Where do we go from here?"

"I don't know, but I sure would like to get my hands on him."

The three sat down at the table and began to examine the pieces found at the flat: Slips of paper, cards from friends, a letter written after her holiday. Kelly read part of it aloud. "'Dear Jackson, I am sorry I got so angry.' Could this be our guy?"

Jan looked at the address and concluded he was too far away to be of interest in this rape or the others.

Jan said, "We have to go back to the beginning. We've missed something and must find it.

Kelly went to the evidence room and retrieved all the files from the locker. Reading aloud, she backtracked to the first attack. "This was an attack of convenience, without the extreme violence. The second victim was stalked before the attack and then he stopped her, asking for the time. The third was more violent; his victim was attacked and beaten during the rape. Did she know her attacker? The fourth victim actually went out on a date with him, so why is it she won't name him? Is she afraid to give a description of her rapist?"

"They are very good questions, Kelly. Perhaps we should question them again?" Jan said.

Kelly asked. "Do you mean right now?"

"No, we must take advantage of the fresh evidence from this new crime scene. Now there is number five, almost the same as four, though this was a vicious and sustained attack. Clarisse knew him and was happy to go out on a date. Why did he think he could get away with this crime? Surely he would know Clarisse would be able to identify him."

Mary said, "Are you going back to the hospital, Jan? Kelly and I can sift through the evidence we have. Clarisse might be awake and can give you a description of the creep."

This was the key. Here his method had changed—he must have taken time getting to know her. Did he change his appearance or hair colour? Did he grow a beard or moustache? The ideas were endless. Could Clarisse point the finger? If so, it may be just a matter of time before she led them to this depraved individual.

Back at the hospital, Clarisse was making steady progress. The physical wounds she had suffered were not as painful. Her parents had raced to the hospital and sat in the chairs next to their daughter. Her mother held her hand, talked quietly, and tried to soothe the hurt.

"Please don't fuss, Mum. All I want to do is sleep. I am so tired and ache all over."

"Can I get anything for you? Perhaps some fruit or sweets?"

If it didn't hurt so much, this query would have made Clarisse laugh. "Thanks, Mum, but it is hard for me to speak, let alone swallow."

Her father growled, "I wish I could get my hands on the bastard."

"Please, Dad, don't be stupid. We must leave it to the police."

As tactfully as possible Clarisse let her parents know she would like to rest.

Whispering goodbye, Earnest and Flora left the hospital and made their way home.

"Why won't she talk to us, Flora?"

"You heard her, Earnest. She needs space and time. What has happened to her is the most horrendous act, which can be perpetrated on any woman. We just need to be there for her."

"I know you're right, but it's just so hard to see her like this. What kind of man is he?"

"I can't tell you that. I wish I could. All we can do is let her know we love her."

Their conversation over, they drove home in silence. The house looked cold and stark to them as they pulled into the garage. Still in silence, each with their own thoughts, they entered the house. Once inside, Flora could hold her tears no longer and collapsed into a chair, finally voicing her hurt and anger. "Lachlan, what a loathsome creature! Only punishments from the dark ages should apply to him."

"I agree with you, Flora, but we must think only of Clarisse."

"What would you know, Earnest? You aren't a woman, so don't tell me what I need to do."

Earnest stayed silent, and there was only the sound of sobbing from a mother whose daughter had been brutally violated.

In her hospital bed, Clarisse let her mind return to the idyllic island, the place where she had found love. Jackson was there, and she could see his handsome face and remembered how he had made love to her with such gentleness. Their lovemaking was warm and sensual, the kisses as sips of wine, drawing them together on that night not once but many times.

The sound of a door slamming broke her reverie and brought her back into the present, back to the pain and wretchedness created by a very different type of man.

The three members of the team were hard at work. They had to develop a profile of this man. By reading through all the statements from the previous rapes, their aim was to find new clues and piece them together, hoping a profile of the man would emerge.

"We've been through all of these before. What makes you think we can find anything new?" Mary said.

Jan said, "Come on, don't let him make you a defeatist. We have to keep looking. We need one thread, just one, that could tie them all together."

"I know all that, but when I look at a woman who has been subjected to such a ruthless beating and rape, I feel so helpless."

"We all feel like that, but we have a job to do, and I suggest we all get on with it."

"You're right. Let's get to work—surely with our minds working together, plus the statement from Clarisse, it can take us closer to an arrest."

The three officers carefully looked through the evidence before them, reading anything written from friends and family, maybe hidden in them would be a clue to the case could be found. Time flew by as they worked each case, hoping to find that clue. The ring of the telephone interrupted their concentration.

Kelly picked up the phone. "Hello? No, it's Kelly. Yes, I'll put her on. It's Rachel for you, Jan."

Jan took the phone. "Hi, Rachel, have you found something?"

"No, but Clarisse is awake and wants to see you."

"Be there as quick as I can."

Jan drove to the hospital and entered Clarisse's room quietly, not wanting to disturb her if she was sleeping. Clarisse lay against the white pillow, her face the colour of the pillow. A sedative given earlier she still felt the effects, but was still able to acknowledge Jan.

"Hello," Clarisse said softly.

"You wanted to talk to me?"

"Yes, I did. Is there any news of him?"

"No, not yet, but we are all working hard. We need a quick arrest, before he strikes again."

"I find it hard to sleep, and they need to sedate me all the time. When awake, I can see his face above me, threatening me as he did during the attack."

"Try not to upset yourself right now. We have a guard outside your room, so you can rest—you are safe. We need to get your statement as soon as possible, and you need to rest. Can you do that for me?"

"I wish I could remember it all now, but I can't," Clarisse confessed.

"Don't upset yourself. I'll be back in the morning to get your statement."

"I hope I can help. I want him caught quickly. Then and only then will I rest completely."

As the drugs took effect, Clarisse closed her eyes, and sleep claimed her again.

Jan stopped to talk to Rachel for a while, and then she called her squad and told them go home but to be back early in the morning. Jan went home, and after a light meal she sat on her lounge and began going through her notes. Slowly the happenings of the day caught up with her, and sleep claimed her. Upon waking, she realized half the night had gone. She left her notes, walked to the bedroom, and lay down to sleep.

The next morning, she ate a light breakfast and made her way to the police station. Her staff was there waiting for her, and after pleasantries they set to work.

"Mary, I want you to stay here and carry on reading all we have on the attacks, to try to make some sense of them."

"Why me, Jan? I want to be out in the field catching this character."

"This character you're talking about has brutally raped five women. We will only catch him if we explore all avenues. He is an extremely devious and dangerous man. All our efforts must be combined to bring him to justice."

Mary sighed. "Well, put that way, I'll stay and do my best to find the link that will lead to his arrest."

"Kelly, you come with me; we need to get Clarisse's statement. I cannot stress enough the importance of what we do today. I believe this man will strike again, and soon."

Mary began leafing through the files, hoping she could find the one thing that would lead to his capture.

Jan and Kelly arrived at the hospital and made their way to Clarisse's ward. She was awake but obviously still suffering from the injuries she'd sustained in the attack. "Hello, Jan, have you come for my statement?"

"Hi, Clarisse. Did you rest okay last night?"

"Yes; the sedatives give me relief, helping me sleep easier."

"It will get better, I promise. Kelly is going to help me, if that's all right."

"Well, I will try to relive the horror of that night."

"While you talk to me, Kelly will be taking it down in shorthand, and then she will type it up later. Are you ready?"

"I hope so."

Painfully Clarisse started to remember the days before and the night of the rape. Many times she broke down, but slowly the story started to flow: how she had met Lachlan, how long she had known him, where they had been together, his looks, and how kind he was before that terrible night.

"Did he give you any cause to be afraid?" Jan asked.

"No, he was very attentive all the time—the perfect gentleman, if you like."

"He was always like that?"

"Yes, until that moment. But from that first blow, there was evil in his eyes. I truly felt he hated me."

"These things are very important to us, and anything unusual, even more so."

"As I said, he was the perfect gentleman."

They applied gentle pressure to help Clarisse remember everything, even what seemed to her to be nonsense. Had he changed his hair colour? Did he shave every day? How did he dress—was it casual or formal? On and on it went for what seemed like hours. Tears flowed as Clarisse talked. Jan saw the victim was nearing exhaustion and began to ease off.

Suddenly, Clarisse shouted at Jan. "No more, no more!, I can't stand this—my head aches, and I feel so dirty. Why me? Can you answer that? Can you tell me you will catch him, or do I live the rest of my life in fear?"

"I'm sorry, Clarisse. We'll stop now. We've pushed you too hard, too soon." Jan pressed the call button for a nurse; she could see Clarisse was in urgent need of sedation. The nurse appeared with the required sedative, administered the injection, and left, throwing a long, withering glare at Jan.

Jan and Kelly stayed until Clarisse was asleep, and then they left to join Mary at the station.

"What kind of man does this sort of thing? Is they born that way, or is it because of some trauma in early life?" Kelly vented.

"I guess it could be both, but that's not an excuse."

Later, as Clarisse lay in her bed, she felt very much alone, and her thoughts returned to the night of the attack. Why was there no warning? How well he had played the game—he had completely fooled her, his charm so genuine. Was this part of the ploy, get a woman to trust him completely and then loose his trap?

Clarisse was living proof that he was very adept at subterfuge, having not been caught or even recognized by his later victims. The pain surfaced again, and it was all consuming, filling her mind. She lay still, and the position eased the pain that came from deep inside her body.

Her mind had to find a place where life had been normal. There was only one place for her to go: the island and Jackson. She was swimming in the cool waters of Pearl Island, where she spent her holiday. The sand beneath her feet was soft and warm, the breeze cooled the nights, and the jasmine wafted through the bungalow.

Tears flowed as she remembered her last meal with Jackson and all the wonderful times they had shared. She was again the innocent woman, the one who wanted nothing more than an ordinary life and marriage to a man who loved her. Were her ideals too high? What had she done to be in this situation?

With these thoughts came the pain. It crashed over her, enveloping her consciousness, burning like fire. She had need for further sedation, so she pressed the call button and waited for the nurse to come.

"I'm sorry I have to call you so often," she said when the nurse arrived.

"That's all right, I'm here. You need a sedative?"

"Yes. It helps me escape from the pain and reality for a while, and I can sleep."

The nurse sat on the edge of the bed and in a gentle voice spoke to Clarisse. "If you can, my dear, it would be better if you limited the number of sedatives."

"Why?"

"The faster the police catch this man, the better. They are relying on you to give them vital clues. Please think about it."

"I don't want to go there, not now. It's too hard."

"That's all right, dear."

"Don't call me dear—my name is Clarisse."

"Sorry, I won't say it again. Just stay calm and let the sedative do its work."

Clarisse drifted into the drug-filled sleep that was so comfortable. Here she wasn't in pain and did not have to face the hurt. There was not any Jackson or Lachlan, and the assault had never happened.

While Clarisse slept and the police team was hard at work sifting through the evidence from the flat, the man who had perpetrated these brutal crimes was himself busy, already on the hunt for his next victim. He had watched many women even before he found Clarisse, but now the search was on in earnest. This next one has to be tall and slender, better looking than the last, but she had to be strong. He did enjoy it when they fought; it gave him more reasons to inflict pain. The fear in their eyes was a turn-on, and the longer the fight, the more enjoyment there was for him.

He walked the streets at night, looking at the windows and imagining a beautiful woman in each room. His hunting ground was fertile, being among the better class of homes; women were not on their guard, feeling that because of their status they were safe. This thought brought a smile to his face, and his fiendish mind began living the chase, the rape, and the setting of the scene so he would not be disturbed. There was the sense of elation as he began the ritual, making them smile while being charming, escorting them to dinner and impressing them with his manners. Then the delight of destroying them slowly, the sudden aggression, the blow to the face sending them sprawling onto the floor.

He savoured the fear in their eyes as he slowly strangled them, the pressure around their throats stifling any screams, while he ripped their clothing away until they lay naked under his gaze. He enjoyed this moment; gone was the pretence of civility, the first thrust piercing them without mercy. He followed it with more blows to the face, but all the while he kept them conscious—he needed to see their pain. The loss of consciousness irked him; he needed to make them suffer, not just during the attack but also long after the attack. Did he care if they did? Of course; not they were just pawns in his game. Clarisse deserved his aggression, pretending to be the perfect virgin, but in truth she was not new to sexual contact.

Mary and Kelly were still engrossed with the items from the flat. Their search so far had been fruitless.

Mary called out. "This might be something, Kelly."

"What is it? A name, or a letter from the creep?"

"No, a group photo of Clarisse's friends—it was taken recently. There are six people in it, but best of all the sixth is a man trying to hide at the back."

"Let me see. You're right—he *is* trying to hide. We should call Jan; she'll let us know what to do."

"You could sound a little excited," Mary said. "This could be the clue to catch this creep! Give her a call; she's looking over Clarisse's statement in her office."

"Jan, can you come in here please?"

"Why, have you found something?" Jan asked.

"It's Mary: she has just found a photo of Clarisse and some of her friends. It's a recent one, and there is a man at the back trying to hide."

"He could be just joking around. What makes you think he's sinister?"

"I don't know, but I get a bad feeling when I look at him."

"Okay, I'll come back and look at it then."

Jan made her way to the squad room, greeted her two excited colleagues, and asked to see the photo, which they all hoped would help close the case.

"See, the one at the back," Mary pointed.

"Yes, your right. Find the others in the photo and talk to them see if they know where he might have gone. I'll stay here just in case Clarisse calls."

Clarisse was in the comfort of a sedative-induced sleep that even blotted out dreams, and time slipped by. As the drug was leaving her system, she lay in a half-awake state. It was here her thoughts turned to Jackson. No man would want her now. Jackson would be appalled, and he definitely would not touch her again.

Memories of the island came to her: the balmy nights and sun-filled days, swimming in an aqua-coloured sea, the time of lying on the beach and watching others frolic in the water. It was a picture of happiness. She was happy, and Jackson had made her holiday wonderful. He had taught her the mysteries of love, the enjoyment of sex, and the closeness of a man and woman; they explored each other and enjoyed complete satisfaction.

Even if he were here, would he want her now? The rape would have lasting consequences, and she would be an outsider because of it. As she dreamt, she spoke the words. "Why do I torture myself? I must stop thinking of what was and concentrate on the now. Will my job be there when I am better? Surely my friends will see that I am not at fault. Oh, who am I fooling? My friends will snicker and make snide remarks."

As she spoke, at her office this was exactly what the conversation was about.

"I bet she asked for it. You can't tell me Lachlan could do the things they are saying he seemed so nice."

"Leave her alone, all of you. Clarisse isn't to blame he is. Have you seen him since that night? No, he hasn't been into the office; he has just disappeared."

"You're right, we haven't seen him. He was invited to dinner at my place the following night, but didn't show up."

"Does anyone know where he lives?"

The question met with silence, and then they all spoke together. "No."

The conversation ended then, and they went their own ways with their own thoughts. They had to come to their own conclusions about

Clarisse. Was she to blame? Did she deserve this terrible treatment at the hands of a rapist?

At the station, Jan was contemplating the job that was before them. Could they solve the case before he attacked again? Her phone rang, interrupting her thoughts and jolting her into the present.

"What do you want?"

"Geez, Jan, what did I do?"

"Sorry, Kelly. What do you want?"

"Can I take the photo to Clarisse? Maybe she can tell us who they all are."

"Not yet. She is still too fragile; all she needs for the time being is rest. Keep trying to find the other people for now."

"Okay, Mary and I are on it. We have identified another person in the photo, I will go and talk to her Her name is Alice, all the others in the photo are a group from work."

"Well then, we'd better find the others; maybe they will know him."

"Do start right now?"

"Yes, we do, Mary you go to the office where she worked, ask each of them to come in for a chat. Kelly, you go back to Alice and ask her how well she knew Clarisse. Also, ask if Clarisse was ever involved with a man in the office."

"Okay, Jan. What will you be doing?"

"I need to talk to Clarisse again talk this time, about her statement and that night."

Her orders given, Jan went back to the hospital. Clarisse was awake but still in pain.

"Hello, Jan, any luck yet?"

"No, but we are still working hard. How do you feel? Has the pain eased a little?"

"A little, but at times it is quite unbearable, at those times the nurses are at the ready with a sedative. One of the nurses sat and talked to me last night; she pointed to the fact that you needed my help, and I should not rely on the drugs too heavily."

"It sounds harsh, but she was right—we do need you. We have your statement, but your recollections of the time leading up to and the rape itself are essential. It's late now, I will come back Rachel wants to try hypnosis. Do you feel you could cope with that?"

"If you think it will help, I'll try."

"That's my girl. See you in the morning."

Jan left the hospital and returned to the station.

Kelly was at Alice's flat, and she knocked on the door.

"Be with you in a second." The door opened, and Alice ushered Kelly into the flat, pointing to a chair. "Would you like a coffee?"

"No, thanks. Can we just get to the questions? What do you know about the brute that assaulted your friend?"

"I told you, I have no idea who he is. Anyway, are you sure it was rape?"

"I don't follow you. Do you think Clarisse made it all up? If so, I suggest you visit her in the hospital. She has been terribly hurt and traumatized in the most vicious way possible. Your attitude is both arrogant and insensitive."

"I don't have to be insulted by you. I must ask you to leave."

"Is that so? Well, maybe a day or two in a cell would change your mind. It can be easily arranged."

"Oh no, you can't do that! I am just scared—I will help you if I can."

"Wise decision. Now, let's sit and talk about Clarisse."

They sat together at the table, and Alice began talking about the office and the staff. She looked at the photo again, shaking her head. "I don't know him. In fact I had never seen him before the day the photo was taken."

"Do you think Clarisse knew him?"

"Again, I have to say I don't know."

"Can I ask you the names and addresses of those you do know? Was the photo was staged, or was it a spontaneous snapshot?"

"From memory, it was a spontaneous photo—it was just taken, and no one was prepared for it. I only know two of them well, and they are standing together at the front: their names are Preston and Julie, and they both work at the office. I don't know their addresses."

"That's a start. We will be interviewing everyone soon."

"You think this is the Lachlan who worked at the office?"

"Could be. If he did, we will get him."

After returning to the station, Kelly finished her report and left it in Jan's office. Jan was pleased with it. Left alone with time on her hands, Kelly leaned back in her chair, letting herself ponder on

Lachlan was now planning his next attack. He felt comfortable—it seemed no one suspected him, and he was sure there was no evidence left to connect him to the attack on Clarisse or the others. The only evidence they could get would have to come from him, and to do that, they had to catch him. Smiling to himself, he began getting dressed. The new chase had already begun. She had to be tall and slender, and she should love music, going to movies, and going out for dinner. He was prepared to wait, to foster the relationship and savour the thought of the ending. The waiting was almost as good as the violent attack itself.

His thoughts were not only about rape—murder was now on his mind. Perhaps that's what he had wanted all along. The first attacks were fun, and he enjoyed the pain and fear he inflicted. Sadly, though, there was not enough time to hurt them badly. Clarisse had been a different matter, and he would need his next victim to match her spirit. He admired her spunk; she had fought like a lion, scratching him badly and making him bleed. This made it necessary to use makeup; he needed to cover the scratches for his first outing with Alicia.

This thought was like the taste of champagne. What fun: a new chase has started, and how long could he keep up the charade? With his needs growing, he licked his lips and decided what he would do and how he would do it. He must find an isolated spot so that he would not be disturbed. This one would live with pain for more than a few hours, thus prolonging his pleasure.

Away from all the hurt and the search for a rapist was Jackson. His thoughts often returned to the island and Clarisse: the night when she surrendered herself to him, the smell of her perfume intoxicating him. He lay back in his the chair and let his mind return to that night. He could feel her lips near his, the whispered words of love, and her acceptance of him as a man. The way they walked hand in hand along the beach, discovering shells and other creatures on the shore—these thoughts became words.

"Dear Clarisse, what a holiday we had," he said aloud. "Should I ring her? Perhaps not—she may have a new man in her life, one who would not appreciate a former lover."

Clarisse was slowly recovering, and Rachel asked if she would like to go home and recuperate. "No, not yet please, I can't face it."

Her flat was a place she never wanted to see again. Her parents had found a new one, but it was too soon for her to go there. The safety and privacy of the hospital was what she needed; perhaps a few more days would find her more able to cope. Still, the nightmares were very real: Lachlan menaced her every time she closed her eyes. *Oh damn, when will this torment end?* How long would he haunt her, his evil eyes glowing in the darkness, and his fiendish laugh playing loud in her mind?

"Sleep, let me sleep. Take away the memory of that night. Help me to think of better times."

Jan, Kelly, and Mary had at last caught up with each other at the police station. "First let's just compare notes," Jan said. "Mary, have you found anything that we can use?"

"Not a lot, but if we can find the bloke trying to hide in the photo, we could have a suspect."

"It's a start. Kelly, how are going?"

"I spoke to Alice. She's a weird one; at first she didn't want to say anything at all, putting me in the position of having to threaten her with arrest. That made her more compliant. She only knows two of the names but has no addresses."

"Okay for the time being we will concentrate on the man in the photo. Someone must know him. Seeing as you asked the question, Kelly, it will be your job to interview all the staff at the office. If you are suspicious of anyone, bring them in. Mary, you can go as well."

"Where will you be, just in case we need you?"

"At the hospital; Rachel is going to hypnotize Clarisse. We must help her remember his face and any other distinguishing features. It's imperative we stop this man, and quickly. Rachel thinks this might be the way."

"See you later then, Jan."

Jan drove to the hospital and entered Rachel's office.

"Ready, Rach?"

"Yes, let's go."

They made their way to Clarisse's room; she was sitting up in bed and looking a little better.

"Hi, Clarisse, are you ready to revisit the night?"

"Not really—the fear fills my mind, but his features are still blurred. Maybe I don't want to recognize him."

"Rachel is going to hypnotize you now. With any luck, you will be able to remember."

Rachel said, "Clarisse, just rest back on your pillow and watch the wheel as I count backward from twenty."

Rachel counted slowly, and it was not long before Clarisse's eyelids closed and her breathing became slow and rhythmic.

"Is she under?" Jan asked.

"Yes. You can start now."

"Clarisse, can you remember where you were when you met Lachlan?"

"At a work party, I think. It was after my holiday, and I was feeling lonely. Suddenly he was there."

"Clarisse, would it be better if I let you talk? Just remember things as you go?"

"Yes, but his face at times is distorted. I will try."

Jan and Rachel sat and listened as Clarisse told the story of that night.

"He picked me up at seven thirty. We drove to the restaurant, ate our meal, and drank a little wine; it was lovely and he was charming. When we returned to my flat, I asked if he would like to come in for a coffee. It is here my thoughts get muddled. He said something like, 'I didn't come here for coffee.' I asked him to leave, and it was then he slapped me. I fell backward, my head hit the table as I fell, and from that moment everything is a blur."

"Take your time and don't rush your thoughts. We have time; just watch the wheel," Rachel instructed.

Clarisse closed her eyes, her mind returning to the horror of that night. She felt the hands around her throat, and she started gasping for breath. She remembered the rough tearing of her clothes as she tried to fight back. Suddenly the pressure on her throat made it impossible for her to breathe or scream. "Stop, stop, I can't breathe."

Rachel spoke softly to her. "It's all right, Clarisse. He isn't here and can't hurt you."

Jan held Clarisse's hand as she slipped back into the hypnotic trance.

"I tried to scratch his face. The pressure on my throat choked me into blackness. Then a searing pain jolted me back to reality; it felt like a hot iron. I tried to scream, but there was no sound. Using my hands, I heaved against his body, trying to push him away. He laughed at my feeble attempts, saying, 'Keep struggling, slut, it turns me on. I love hurting women.'" Tears flowed as these memories became more than she could bear, making it hard for her to continue.

Rachel feared for Clarisse's sanity and asked, "Do you need to rest? It's okay, and this is traumatic for you."

"No, we must go on. I'm all right. I must go back to the night . . . I opened my eyes, and his head had lowered. I think he had dyed hair. Yes, his hair was dyed."

"Are you sure?"

"Yes, yes. The roots were almost black."

"All right, we are getting somewhere now. Are you okay, can you carry on?"

"Oh yes."

With eyes closed, Clarisse returned to the horror, into what felt like an out-of-body experience. She fought, staying focused through the pain and on the memory of his face. "His eyes were like fire, full of hate and glazed over. He's a monster and enjoys the pain he inflicts."

Jan heard the words and felt so sorry for Clarisse, but she knew she could not intervene—it had to continue until Clarisse could not go on.

"Brown eyes, brown eyes. His eyes were dark brown, almost black. Not blue at all."

"Are you sure?"

"Yes. His hair is blonde, and he was clean-shaven, except for stubble on his top lip. He's growing a moustache. His face was red with anger, his lips curled into a snarl. He's a different man, a terrible and vicious man. A searing pain inside me—what is it? Where did it come from? Now he's punching me again. All is dark. Am I still alive?"

Rachel shook her gently. "Clarisse, dear, wake up—come back to me."

Clarisse slowly returned to reality and looked into Rachel and Jan's concerned faces. "Did I tell you anything? It felt like a dream. Tell me it was a dream."

Jan said, "It was a dream. He's not here; you're safe, and we have much more information now, thanks to you." She held Clarisse's hand and patted it, making sure she was fully awake from the hypnotic trance. It would be cruel and unprofessional to leave her, considering the trauma she had just experienced in telling her story. "Is she okay, Rachel?"

"She will be, given time."

"I am exhausted," Clarisse said. "All I want to do is sleep."

"You certainly deserve it. Rachel will call a nurse, and she will give you a sedative to help you sleep."

Jan pressed the bell as they waited for the nurse to appear with the injection tray. The nurse administered the sedative and glared at Jan again.

"Why the dirty look, Nurse? Anyone would think I was the monster who savagely attacked Clarisse," Jan said. "I have a job to do: my team has to catch him before he attacks again. I would appreciate some civility from you and the staff."

"I'm sorry, but every time you come here, you upset our patient, and it is left to us to calm her, usually with a sedative."

"Please don't argue, you two," Clarisse said. "Nurse, it is imperative that Jan and her team do their work, and if I can help them, I must. The thought of some other poor woman going through what I have is frightening."

The nurse and the police officer looked at each other; both were thinking of how much pluck this young woman had. Finally Jan said, "This is the first and last argument we will have; we promise you. Don't we, Nurse?"

"Yes, we do."

Jan left the hospital and returned to the station. Her team was there, eager to hear what Clarisse had remembered. Jan walked past them, entered her office, and slumped into her chair with head in her hands, and she quietly sobbed. All the emotion of the hospital interview, and no real lead in sight, had dropped her t into a state of despair.

Kelly and Mary also felt this but knew not to intrude on Jan until she asked them.

It was not a good time for anyone; they all knew the rapist would strike again, and it was their job to catch him.

CHAPTER FOUR

MEANWHILE LACHLAN HAD SLIPPED FURTHER into his psychosis, his thoughts ever more violent. He had no need of prescription drugs—he could control his urges on his own. He had altered his persona, and as he stood looking into the mirror, he congratulated himself on the changes he had made. His appearance was completely different, his blonde hair was dyed black, and he had a sleek moustache that felt good beneath his touch. Added to this was the change of eye colour with contact lenses. Even if Clarisse had given the police a description, he was certain he had escaped again. Now it was time to search, find, and con his next victim. Her name was Alicia, a smart and talented woman who was slim with curly brown hair. This thought made him smile. What fun it would be, tearing away her sense of self-worth. He chuckled as he picked up the phone.

"Hello, Alicia, how are you?"

"Oh, it's you, Paul!"

"Would you like to go out for dinner sometime, perhaps Friday?"

"I can't make it this week; I am leaving today on a field trip with my boss, and we need to interview our clients, who live in the country."

"What a shame. Is it all right if I ring you sometime next week?"

"Yes, that would be great. I really am sorry about Friday."

Lachlan slammed the phone down. His plans for the weekend were now in tatters. *How dare she!* He needed some sort of relief. What could he do?

"I know—I'll grab a hooker off the street. Yes, that will do. When I pick her up, I'll take her to the new flat, and there I can do what I like."

He smiled in anticipation; he would do all he had done to Clarisse, but faster—no pampering at all. It would be like the first time. Still, his mind was on Alicia and how she would suffer for this rejection.

Jan finally came out of her office, making her apologies to her colleagues. "Sorry about that. I needed time to come to terms with what Clarisse told us."

Kelly shot questions at her. "She remembered something? What was it? Does she know him? Can she identify him?"

"Yes, but please, one question at a time."

"So what did she remember?"

"During the regression, she remembered his eyes and hair. His hair had been dyed, from black to blonde, and his eyes were dark brown."

"But I thought she said blue," Mary said.

"Yes, she did, but eye colour can be changed with contacts. I think she either dragged one out during the attack, or he simply forgot to put them in. Hair dying is easily done; he only needs one treatment for it to last the length of time before the attack."

"So what are we looking for?"

"Probably dark brown to black hair, and dark brown eyes. Do you have the group photo?"

"Sure."

"Who is the one that gives you a bad feeling Mary?"

"In the back row, he is trying to hide, but you can see part of his face and blonde hair."

"So he has. What do you think Kelly?"

"I think it's him."

All three looked at each other, nodding in unison. It was a carried decision, and their next step was to bring in the others from the photo. Then they could find out if any of them knew the man in the back row. Kelly rang the office where Clarisse worked, arranging for each person to be interviewed.

The interviews were scheduled for early the next morning. Jan rang Rachel and arranged for her to come in as well. Having Rachel there added a fourth dimension, with her expertise in psychology; this would help detect if anyone was lying. Jan, Kelly, and Mary went back to the files that covered the previous attacks.

"If you think it is relevant, put it to one side." Jan instructed again.

Clarisse began to feel better. It seemed after the hypnosis, her mind was clearer and she could rest. Although the trauma and the pain remained, it was less than before. At times she could sleep without seeing his leering face. As she lied back against the pillow with eyes closed, the fear gone for a moment, she slowly drifted into an untroubled sleep.

Here she was safe, and other thoughts could enter her mind. Jackson returned: their first kiss and that wonderful night when she had surrendered herself to him. It was the first time she had been able to think about the purity of love, without the memory of the deep hurt she had suffered. How wonderful he had been. Why did she get angry? It wasn't necessary. When she recovered, she would write to him and apologize.

This night was the calmest she had had since the attack, and her sleep was untroubled for a time. There was no need for a sedative, but the officer sat outside her door and the nursing staff was always nearby.

The morning dawned on what was to be an eventful day. There was expectation everywhere, and the nurse asked Clarisse if her night had been all right.

"Yes, I feel much better—still afraid, though. I wish the police could arrest him. If that happened, the morning would be close to perfect."

"Well, today could be the day. Let's all hope for that."

Jackson woke with a start, and he looked at the clock and realized he had overslept. He had a golf date in fifteen minutes with a mate. He jumped out of bed, showered, and dressed, breakfast forgotten in the rush.

His mate was waiting for him at the course.

"Sleep in, did we? Too much drinking, and flirting with the women last night? Did you strike it lucky?"

"Shut up—it's none of your bloody business what I do."

"You took her home, didn't you?"

"Yes, I did, so let's play golf, you mug."

The two friends walked out onto the course to begin their game. As they walked, they had small talk about the case on which they were working. Jackson then remembered his holidays were only a few weeks away.

"My holiday leave is due. Geez, doesn't feel like a year has passed."

"You going anywhere, mate?"

"Don't know, Alex. The last holiday was great."

"Yes, I remember—you spent half of it in bed with some woman."

"Hmm, I did, didn't I?"

With these words came the memory of Clarisse. What a woman, and it was her first sexual experience—he should have been kinder. These thoughts troubled him all day.

After dinner, he sat to watch television, but there she was: her beauty and their nights of love. Then the thoughts became words. "Maybe I should ring her. No, not now. I'll do it later."

The next day he couldn't concentrate on the work he had in front of him. Even as he drove home, her name kept popping up in his mind.

Clarisse . . . Why do I still remember her? it was such a short romance. Do I still feel something for her?

On the other side of the country, Lachlan had worries of his own. The previous night he had driven round the streets. Here women waited for clients, and he hadn't seen one that interested him. Deciding on one more turn, he cruised slowly, squinting into the darkness. There she was, the one he wanted. Slowing the car, he called out to her. "Hello, are you available?"

"Sure am. Where do we go?"

"I have a flat; it's not far."

"Okay, let's go."

He drove in silence until they reached the flat. Once there, they walked toward the building. "It's on the first floor, and not many of these flats have been let—it's a new area," he said.

"Hang on, we haven't set on a price yet. I get a hundred bucks a time."

"That's fine; I have the money with me." He put his hand on her elbow and led her to the door, opening it and stepping aside to allow her to enter first.

"What a lovely flat," she said. "It must be great to have such a place."

These words were the last she spoke. He hit her with a crunching blow to the head, which stunned and left her unable to fight. Lachlan laughed. He had her now and could do what he liked. He began ripping the clothes from her body, tossing them aside. She murmured and moved slightly, so Lachlan hit her again before continuing to rip her clothes off. Finally she lay naked. Strangely, though, he couldn't get angry—he needed her to fight.

"Wake up, bitch. Fight me."

He threw a jug of water into her face, and she stirred, opening her eyes. Looking at him, she yelled, "You bastard! You hit me. Why?"

"Fight me, you slut. Fight me!"

She tried to stand but was met with another blow. She reeled backward and hit the wall. He stood over her and laughed as she tried to fight him. "That's the way—get me angry. It helps me hurt you more."

"Why?" she screamed.

"I want you to fight, it turns me on."

She tried, but knowing she was no match for him, she let herself go limp. This decision saved her life. He could not get angry—the slut would not play his game, and try as he might, she just lay limp. He gave up, dragged her down the back stairs, and then threw her and the clothes into a dumpster.

He knew the darkness was on his side; she couldn't give a description of him or where the flats were. Anyway, she was only a hooker; the police wouldn't be interested in her. He drove to his home on the other side of town. Upon reaching home, he cursed Alicia. *She will suffer. Just wait until she is my hands . . .* These thoughts brought him some comfort as he sat on a chair near the table. He began planning what he would do to Alicia, and his growing thoughts of brutality gave him a warm feeling inside.

The morning was tense at the police station. Jan addressed her colleagues, telling them what she expected. "Lean on them. Don't give them room to move, and put the photo on the table, right under their noses."

"Why the photo? Can it do any good? All of them have said they don't know him," Kelly said.

"I know, but I don't believe it. One of them can identify him, and I want that person."

"Okay, Jan we'll do as you say. Is Rachel going to be with you?"

"Yes; I need her expertise. We will be interviewing them after you and Mary have finished."

There were three interview rooms in the station, and each officer went to one. As the witnesses started to arrive, Kelly escorted them to one of the waiting rooms. Her first interview was Alice. She called her name and led the way to the interview room.

"Sit down, please."

"Why am I here? I haven't done anything."

"Did I say you had?"

"Well, no. So why am I here?"

"Look at the photo in front of you. Look at it carefully, and tell me if you know any of the people."

"I told you before, I only know the two in the front row, and their names are Preston and Julie."

"You're quite sure about that? You do know that withholding information from the police is an offence."

"Yes, I'm sure. Why would I hide anything?"

"I had a feeling, on the day you saw the photo, that you recognized more than you were willing to tell. Therefore, I ask you again: do you know who the man in the back is? Have you had contact with him outside of work?"

Alice looked at Kelly. and tears welled up in her eyes and ran down her cheeks. She reached for a tissue from the box on the table. "I had seen him before. I was afraid to tell you. I don't know his name, but he is a dreadful man."

"You can stop with the water works—they are lost on me. What do you mean by dreadful?"

"I went out with him, and he asked me back to his flat. I refused and told him to take me home. He just stopped the car and ordered me out. His face was white with rage."

Kelly jumped up, her chair clattered as it fell backward. With fists on the table, she leaned toward Alice. "You didn't feel it necessary to tell us that?"

"No, I didn't at the time. But then I remembered the look on his face: it was as if he hated me."

"You sicken me. Had you told us that, we could have been on his tracks days ago! However, you didn't think it was important? How could you do that?"

"I'm sorry, truly I am, but that's all I can tell you. He called himself Lachlan, and apart from the anger he showed at the end, he was okay."

"Good story, Alice, but that's not all you know. What else happened on that ride home?"

"I'm afraid if I tell, he will come after me."

"What more is there?"

"I know his address."

"You know what? You anger me, Alice. How could you withhold that information?" Kelly said incredulously. She looked at Alice for some time, trying to take in what she had just heard. She could not believe that a woman, knowing all this, could stay silent. With a long withering glare, she said, "Wait here. I'll be back."

Leaving a uniformed officer with Alice, Kelly made her way to the interview room occupied by Jan and Rachel. She knocked and waited for an answer.

"What is it, Kelly? We were just getting started with Preston."

"Alice knew his bloody address—at least the one he had before he attacked Clarisse."

"What! Tell me you're kidding. She knew this all along?"

"Yep. What do you want me to do with her?"

Jan stood with her back resting on the door, trying to figure out things. "Fling her in a cell and tell her she will be charged with attempting to pervert the course of justice, withholding information, and anything else you can come up with."

"Sure, but shouldn't I go and check it out?"

"Not on your own. Wait for me; I should not be long. Go back and scare the hell out of her."

"Got it. Do you think there is any chance he will still be there?"

"No, but someone in the complex may know him."

Kelly returned to the room where Alice waited. After opening the door, she excused the officer. She sat opposite Alice and glared at her for what seemed an eternity.

"What? You look at me as if I had committed the rape, not Lachlan," Alicia said.

"Do you know what you've done? You have aided and abetted a felon. How could you do it? Clarisse is supposed to be your friend. If you had told her your fears, she wouldn't have gone out with him."

"I'm so sorry, really I am. What will happen to me?"

"Me, me, me—is that all you care about? If I had my way, you would be flung into a cell and forgotten."

Alice dissolved into tears, put her arms on the table, and laid her head down. For the first time it seemed she realized what she had done. Kelly watched her with no pity at all, thinking, *She deserves this. If she had told us earlier, we would have arrested this perverted maniac by now.*

The door opened, and Jan stepped inside, glaring at Alice with disdain. She nodded at Kelly and motioned her into the passageway. "We have finished with the others. They're okay and have told us all they know."

"So what do we do now?"

"You take Alice and have her put in a cell; we can hold her for twenty-four hours without charge. Then we will go to the address she gave us. Maybe there will be someone there who knows him."

"Is Mary coming with us?"

"No, she is staying with Rachel. I want them to go through the statements, looking for any other leads."

"Okay, let's go."

Kelly took Alice to the front desk, seeking out the young officer from earlier.

"Lock her in a cell. I'll be back later to question her further."

"Okay, Sarge, leave it to me."

That done, the two officers drove to the address Alice had given them. They climbed to the second floor where the alleged flat was, walking slowly and looking at each number.

"Here it is, Jan."

"Knock on the door; he may still be here."

Kelly knocked on the door and waited for an answer. The door on the opposite side of the hallway opened. "He doesn't live there anymore. Moved out a week ago. Don't know where though."

"Did you know him?"

"Not real well. He came and went a lot—seemed to be away more than at home."

"Does anyone else in the building know him?"

"I don't think so. He was real secretive, kept himself to himself, if you know what I mean."

"Thanks for your help. Here is my card. If he shows up, or you hear anything, can you ring me?"

"Sure, see you later."

After offering their goodbyes, Kelly and Jan walked back to the car in silence, each with her own thoughts. Jan thought, *If only Alice had come clean earlier, we may have caught him.*

Noticing Kelly's silence Jan looked at her and asked, "You okay?"

"Not really. That stupid Alice—why did she hide what she knew?"

"Fear, I suspect. Remember, we haven't seen this character."

"No, but we've seen his handy work."

The two officers made their way back to the station.

Clarisse was improving slowly: she didn't need as many sedatives and was able to walk to the bathroom alone. The hospital remained her safety net, and she had no desire to leave it. A nurse arrived with her breakfast, placing it on the table and asking in a quiet voice, "How are we today?"

"Much better now, but the pain in my lower abdomen is still there. What's causing it, do you know?"

"Sorry, I don't, but when the doctor comes, you can ask her."

"Yes, I'll do that. Thanks for my breakfast."

Later that day, Clarisse's parents arrived. They were relieved to see their daughter looking so much better.

"Hello, love, how are you today?" Earnest asked.

"Better, Dad, but the dreams still haunt me. I guess they will continue until he's caught."

"Don't worry, there's a police officer at the door; he will make sure no one gets in here."

"Mum, you're quiet today. Are you all right?"

"Yes, I am, but I worry about that evil degenerate. I hope the police are able to arrest him before he hurts some other young woman."

"They will, Mum. Give them time."

Lachlan was still furious. Why was he unable to rape the prostitute? He had her at his mercy, helpless and unable to fight back. *Maybe that's it, she wouldn't fight.* What was it that he had done wrong? He figured she was a pro and probably knew not to fight back.

What a bitch. Should have just strangled her, and no one would have missed her. Too late now. He would have to wait for Alicia. *She is going to suffer more than the others. She will experience pain like nothing she has known before.* He would take more time with this one, using more than his hands—only small things but very cruel. Just thinking about it gave him a feeling of exuberance.

On Jan and Kelly's return, Mary greeted them and asked, "Did you find anything at the complex?"

"He lived there but moved out last week. We missed him by an inch."

"Alice has a lot to answer for. What do you think, Rach?"

"She sure does, Mary. She held back information that was vital to the case."

"What's our next move, Jan?" Mary asked.

"Well, we have lost him this time, but we will stay on his tail," Jan said. "We must catch him before he has a chance to attack again."

"Where the hell do we go now? We seem to be in a maze that's going nowhere, even with the four of us working on the case. When are we going to get a solid clue about this man? We seem to be one step behind him each time," Rachel complained.

"Remember that we do have Alice. Maybe she knows more?" Kelly suggested.

Jan said, "Don't get upset, Rach, perhaps the answer lies in this pile of statements."

"I can't stay any longer," Rachel said. "I must get back to the hospital. I haven't seen Clarisse today, and she waits for me to do my rounds, so I mustn't let her down."

"Okay, Rach. Say hello to Clarisse for us."

After returning to the hospital, Rachel went to her office first and sat at her desk, her mind searching for what could give them a clue. She reflected on the injuries Clarisse had suffered and wondered how she had survived. What had happened to stop the rapist? Leaving the questions behind, she walked to Clarisse's room and found her lying on the pillows, looking a little better than yesterday.

"Hello, Clarisse, how are you today?"

"Much better, but I have a pain deep inside my lower abdomen. What is causing it?"

"It is from the rape. Your vaginal wall was torn badly, and that is why we have you on antibiotics, because we don't want any infection to begin."

"Will it heal? Will I still be able to have children?"

"We are closely monitoring it, which is why I need to examine you. We are sure you will be fine. It may take some time, but it will heal."

"That's a relief," Clarisse said. "I was worried about the pain. I do want to have children right now, but of course that depends on a man wanting me in the future."

"Clarisse, please don't let yourself believe that no man will want you. You are a lovely young woman, and there is a man out there for you."

Feeling much better after Rachel's visit, Clarisse drifted off into a dreamless sleep, until her lunch arrived.

CHAPTER FIVE

As she sat in the jail cell, Alice was fearful of what was to come. The tongue-lashing from Kelly made her think about her lies. Now it was now Jan's turn to visit her. She had entered the cell and put hands on hips as she looked at Alice.

"You're a blight on society. I wish I could put you in prison for what you have done. Do you know how serious your actions were? You have let a very dangerous man escape. Had you given us his address when we first asked, he would now be behind bars."

"I didn't know it was so important, and I was scared," Alice protested.

"That's no excuse. Let's go visit Clarisse, and you can see how he beat her, both mentally and physically."

"No! What would I say to her?"

"You haven't got the guts to face her. I'm letting you know now that we will be charging you with attempting to pervert the course of justice. One of my officers will take care of that. In the mean time, I have a rapist to catch."

Jan angrily slammed the cell door shut and went to her office. Sitting at her desk, her mind was on the time lost because of just one person not telling the truth. Where did she go from here? Someone must know and the rapist's address.

Away from all the activities surrounding Clarisse, Jackson still thought about his last holiday. He had set out to seduce her, and he had. Boy, she was a beauty, and it didn't take a lot of effort. She was ripe for the picking, and he had done just that. Then the memory of their parting, she had been so angry with him at the airport.

He still didn't feel in any way responsible for what he had done. Clarisse had joined the game, so he wasn't at fault. Still, the memory remained; maybe she would be on holiday too. This unnerved him: why was she so hard to shake? It had never happened to him before. He was the love-and-leave type, but she continued to haunt him.

The feelings he had were different. Clarisse was the only one he had ever cared about, but did he love her? Was it because he had been her first lover? No, she was what he had looked for and then left. The more he tried to forget, the worse it became, and taunting dreams flooded into his mind. After waking in the early hours of the morning, he decided to spend his holidays in Perth. If he still felt the same, he could easily call on her. He spent some time finding the address book he had written her name and address. Looking at the clock, he realized he was late for work. He would finish the search later.

"Is there an officer I can talk to?"

"What's up, Sue? Been raped again?"

"No, but I want to report some nutter out there. He says he wants to kill someone."

"Really, what's he like?"

At that moment Jan walked into the station, She held back and listened for a time, allowing the young constable to carry on with his good-hearted banter.

"It's true, I say. Why won't you listen?"

"I'll look after this, Constable," Jan interrupted. "Come with me, Sue."

Sue followed Jan to an interview room. "I haven't done anything wrong. Why are we going in here?"

"Don't worry. All I want is to ask some questions about your nutter."

"Okay, then, but I did say I haven't done anything."

"Now, where did he pick you up?"

"At the old church, where I usually work."

"Tell me about him."

"I couldn't see much because it was dark. He was well dressed and spoke politely. He had nice car and asked me to get in. We only drove a little way to his flat. I hadn't told him the price, so we settled that on the way to his flat.

"Can you tell me where the flats are?"

"No, but I can show you the dumpster he threw me in. He also hit me over the head and kept saying, 'Fight me! Fight me!' I didn't hit back and just played dead.

After much cursing and yelling, he gave up, dragged me outside, and threw me in the dumpster."

"Thanks for that, Sue. I need to talk to my staff. Would you like a cuppa?"

"Yeah, I'd like that."

"I'll send the young officer back, and he will get it for you."

Jan could hardly contain her excitement. It was him, she knew it was him. She almost skipped down the passage to the squad room, calling to her staff. "Come here, you two. I have some great news. If it's true, we may well have the clue we need to catch him. Hurry up! We have a witness: Sue just came in to tell us about a nutter who accosted her."

Kelly was sceptical. "You're sure? She's done this before, Jan."

"I know that. I'm still digesting what she had to say. I left her with a cuppa."

"We need to do a one-on-one interview with her while you and Jan listen," Mary suggested.

"I have already spoken to her, and she trusts me, so I will conduct the interview with a uniformed officer. You two listen in the next room."

"You bet. Go to it, Jan. This just might be it."

Jan went back to Sue, taking the young constable with her. They settled down at the table, and Jan began the questions. "This interview will be recorded. Sue, is that okay?"

"Yep, that's okay

"Did you have your tea, Sue?"

"Yep, thanks."

"Now let's get on with what you told me before."

"Am I in trouble? I haven't done anything wrong."

"No, Sue, you aren't in trouble at all. We just want to get your story on tape."

"I guess so. Where do I start?"

"You told us you were on your usual beat when a car drove up. Can you take it from there?"

Sue recapped her experience with the nutter. She wrapped up by saying, "That's when he dragged me down the back stairs, along the road to the dumpster, and threw me in."

"Is that the full story? Did he hurt you in any other way?"

"No, but he would have if I had fought him. He is a bloody nutter."

"Can you tell us about the car?"

"No, it was just a car."

"Could you take us to the dumpster?"

"Yes. Can we go now? I don't like police stations all that much."

Jan chuckled to herself; she knew very well why Sue did not like the police. She walked to the interview room where Kelly and Mary were waiting and motioned for them to follow outside to the car. Would this be the end of their search?

Sue gave Kelly directions to the dumpster site.

"Is this the one, Sue?"

"Sure is. If you don't mind, I'll stay in the car."

Jan, Kelly, and Mary walked to the dumpster and lifted the lid to look inside. The pile of torn clothes were there. It would seem Sue had been telling the truth.

"Sue, come here. You're quite safe."

"You're sure of that?"

"Yes, I am, so get over here now," Jan said firmly.

Sue eased herself out of the car, furtively looked around, and then walked over to Jan.

"Are these your clothes, Sue?"

"They sure are. Not much bloody good to me now—he's torn them to bits."

"Can you give us some idea which building you were in?"

"No, but he kept saying it was a new block. I can only see one new block."

Jan turned to look were Sue was pointing, and there was the only one option.

"Good for you, Sue. We are in your debt."

"Oh, that's okay. Maybe you could do a good deed for me someday."

The three officers walked toward the block, each with their own thoughts. Would he be there, or had he moved again? They entered the building and met one of the tenants on the stairs.

"Can I help you?"

"I am Detective Inspector Hastings, and we believe that a person of interest to us moved into this block recently."

"I have only just moved in myself, but I can ask around if you like."

"No, that is the last thing we want. But I would appreciate your silence about this matter."

"This sounds serious. Do I need to be extra vigilant?"

"No, just keep it to yourself, and only interact with the tenants you know and trust."

There was no manager employed at the block of units, so they decided to rent a flat and keep an officer there day and night.

"Will it be one of us, Jan?" Kelly asked.

"No, we need to be free to come and go. I think just uniformed officers should be there, but of course in plain clothes."

Mary said, "Can I suggest John? He is the one we used this morning during the interviews."

"That's a great idea, Mary. Do you know any others? We will need at least three."

"I have a friend who went through the academy with me; she would love to be in on this," Mary replied.

"Okay, we need just one more. Any thoughts, Kelly?"

"My best friend is in uniform, and she would be reliable and efficient."

The three officers drove back to the station. Jan went to report the morning's work and the idea of renting the flat. Jan knocked on the chief's door and waited for the gruff voice to answer.

"Come in! Oh, it's you, Jan. Well, don't just stand there—take a seat."

"Thanks, sir." She sat opposite the chief and told him of her plan. "I believe I know where this suspect lives. What I need from you are three officers. They would live and work in the flat we rent."

"Can you give me any assurances that this will lead to an early arrest?"

"No, I can't, but we should try."

"Where did the information come from that led you to this building?"

"Not an ideal person, but she bears the bruises left by the man who attacked her."

"Who is it?"

"Sue, the lady we all know very well."

"Come on, Jan—she tells this story at least twice a month."

"I know, sir, but I believe it. She took us to the dumpster she was thrown into. The clothes were there, all torn as she described, and she told us it was a new block of flats."

"Does clutching at straws come to mind, Jan?"

"Yes, sir, it does, but we must try. I believe this man will rape again. He is going to kill someone soon, and we need to arrest him before he does. What he is capable of is frightening, and he is accelerating each time he attacks."

The chief looked long and hard at Jan. He read the concern on her face and knew she had never been wrong before. "Okay, Jan, go ahead with your plan. If you need more officers, just ask."

"Thank you, sir. I'll get things moving, and with just a little luck we can catch him quickly."

Jan left the office and returned to the squad room.

"What did he say, Jan?" Mary asked.

"He agreed. we can have the extra officers and rent the flat in the building. I think we are on the right path—we will catch him, I know we will."

Kelly and Mary nodded their approval Kelly said, "We feel that way as well. Well done, Jan. The three of us will bring this horror to an end."

Jan sat at her desk, closed her eyes, and set out the plan that she hoped would catch the man who had created so much misery in so many lives. The three officers selected for the fray had come and gone, their instructions clear. They would work in shifts, and the only stipulation was that all changeovers must be early in the morning or late at night. All senior staff would avoid going to the flat, thus eliminating any possibility of people knowing that officers lived in the flat.

With all the plans laid, Jan decided to visit the hospital, first to catch up with Rachel and then to see how Clarisse was progressing. After entering the hospital, she saw Rachel walking to her office.

"Hi, Rach, hold up a minute."

"Oh, it's you, Jan. Come with me."

The two women entered the office and began talking about Clarisse and the other attacks. Jan's first question was about Clarisse.

"How is she doing? Is there a chance she could go home soon?"

"Not just yet—she has an internal infection caused by the attack, and it is being stubborn. We are doing everything needed to heal it."

"It will heal, won't it? She has been through enough without more setbacks."

"We are confident it will respond to treatment. She is just a wonder, that girl, and she has all the pluck in the world. She deserves only the best from here on."

"I couldn't agree more. By the way, we had some luck today. A prostitute came in shouting about some nutter who tried to rape her. She is well-known to us, but this time I believe she is telling the truth."

"Don't forget me when you get close to this bloke. I want to be there when you drag him in."

"No worries, Rach. But now I must see Clarisse. Bye for now."

Jan walked to the ward and she found Clarisse awake and actually smiling. "You're looking good. How do you feel?"

"I feel much better, and the antibiotics seem to be healing the infection."

"That's what I like to hear. Don't let him destroy the rest of your life. We are closing in on him. Won't that be a good day?"

"Just hearing about him makes me mad. I will be the first in the court to convict him."

"Good for you—that's what I like to hear from a prospective witness."

"Mum and Dad want me to stay with them for a while. Would that be the right thing for now?"

"My opinion is it would be a good move. When do you think you will go home?"

"Rachel wants me to stay for a few more days, but it is up to me."

"Good for you, love. I gotta go. Keep your chin up, and I will see you soon."

"Okay, Jan, see you later."

Left alone, Clarisse again let her thoughts return to the island. It had been such a wonderful place, and even now she could escape. Lying back on the pillows, she drifted into a deep sleep, and there were no dreams now, just a calm, untroubled sleep.

As Clarisse slept, Lachlan made his phone call to Alicia, and she agreed to go out with him on the following Friday. Now all he needed to do was make sure there were no interruptions; he would need time for what he had planned. He now owned two flats, one where he took the prostitute, and a better one on the other side of town. His plan was to bring Alicia here for a meal, and the ritual had to be perfect.

Jan sent one of the new officers to rent the flat, and he gave a fictitious name and documents. The building supervisor took him to the empty flat and asked if it would be suitable for him.

"Yes, sir, this will be fine. It's close to work and has all the amenities that my flat mates and I need."

"The rent and deposit has to be paid in advance, which comes to five hundred. I will take that now, please—wouldn't want any foul-ups."

"Okay, here is the money. Give me the keys, because my friends and I want to move in tonight."

"Here you go, son. See you tomorrow."

John left the flat and returned to the station. Jan greeted him as he arrived. "Everything go okay?"

"Yes, ma'am. I have the keys, and we can move in tonight."

"Well done. You didn't let the super know who you were?"

"No, ma'am."

"Okay then, I will leave you to it. Make sure the front doorway is covered by the camera. We are looking for a tall male; he has been described as having blonde or dark brown hair and dark brown eyes. Try not to alert him at all, keep your distance, and report anything unusual."

"Will do. Is that all for now?"

"Yes, but I will be in contact with you at all the times."

John walked away; he needed to tell the other two undercover officers they would be moving into the flat that night. "We have to make it look real, no uniforms or anything that says we are police officers. Get all you want and meet me at the flat."

"See you there," Julie said. "Oh, by the way, who's the cook?"

"Not me. Seeing as you brought it up, I nominate you."

They laughed as they walked away together to get what they would need for surveillance duty. The three officers had come from various branches of the force. John was ambitious and had slowly moved up the ladder; now he had the chance to excel. Julie was younger but was a very capable junior officer, and she wanted to work in the drug squad; this assignment would certainly help. Mia, like the others, wanted to progress in the force, but her ambition was to be in the family problems side of policing.

Jackson returned home and began the search for his notebook so he could find Clarisse's phone number and address. He tossed papers and junk out of the drawer until he found it, and then he leafed through it until he came to the page with her name and address. As he ran his fingers over her writing, a picture of the woman he had spent his holiday with appeared.

How lovely she had looked. Why hadn't he recognized his feelings before? Should he phone her, or just take a trip to her home town to see her? He would have to get leave before doing that; he would ask his boss in the morning.

Clarisse had been thinking of Jackson. She wondered if he still remembered her—probably not—but it would be lovely to see him. She was feeling much better now, so maybe she should ask to go home. She decided to ask Rachel in the morning, sure in the knowledge she could stay with her mum and dad and knowing they wouldn't mind.

With these thoughts, she lay back, closed her eyes, and there in front of her stood Jackson. How handsome and loving he looked. Perhaps his touch would help heal the physical and mental scars she had suffered.

After moving into the flat, John, Julie, and Mia joked and laughed just like any young group would. When all the furniture was in place and the rooms were chosen, they set about placing the camera in the window so that a view of the front door was visible at all times. They took a still photo and then placed all the photos on a table for comparison. When finished, the camera looked like a pot plant on the ledge. The coverage was ample, and the first constable on duty was Julie; she would take the first watch of four hours. Until they made an arrest, it would be their job to work four hours on and four hours off. All three were looking forward to the challenge.

On that first night, even during their time off, John and Mia stayed just to watch. The camera photographed each person who entered through the front door. Over the following days, they built up a list of photos. During their time outside, they met the different tenants, but under Jan's instructions they didn't try to make friends with anyone.

The man they wanted to catch was at that time working on his new victim. Unbeknown to them, Lachlan had been to the flat, but at this early stage, his photo was simply placed in the male section.

Jan came late in the evening to receive updates from her officers. She looked at the photos that were similar to the description given by Clarisse, Sue, and Alice.

"We can't make any moves at this time, but be vigilant, okay?"

"Yes, ma'am, we will."

Meanwhile, Jan had charged Alice and bailed her to appear at later date.

Clarisse left the hospital and moved into her parents' home for a while, because the infection was still healing. She thought about writing to Jackson and then decided to wait for a while. Would he be interested in her now after the attack, or would he believe she had asked for this, as many people did?

Work had not even entered her mind—she didn't think she could go back there, so maybe it was time to find a new job. These thoughts she kept to herself; once voiced, they became the truth and her mum always discouraged them.

"Don't dwell on thoughts that depress you, darling. Just think of better times ahead."

"I know you are right, Mum, but it is hard sometimes."

"Yes, darling I know, but please try."

As these thoughts filled her head, Clarisse felt she was a stranger to herself and was no longer the bubbly young woman she had been. Every sound startled her, shadows became real, and darkness was her enemy. How long was she going to feel like this? She knew it was safe here; there was still a police presence at her home. However, the fear continued. Sitting feeling sorry for herself was bad—she had to do something, and with this in mind she rang Rachel.

"Hello, this is Dr Scott."

"It's me, Rachel. I hope you don't mind me calling?"

"Of course not, Clarisse! What can I do for you?"

"You will think me a pest, but I feel so frightened all the time. I see him around every corner—he looms large like a giant."

"These fears are what I would expect after an attack like yours. Would you like me to come over after work? We can try hypnosis again; it could help allay the fears you have."

"That would be great, Rachel. Could you come over in time for tea?"

"Yes, I can—we'll make it a meal to remember. Bye for now."

Clarisse placed the receiver back in its cradle. She was happy that Rachel was coming over and called out to her mother. "Rachel is coming for tea tonight. I hope that's okay?"

"Most definitely. She is a lovely woman and has helped you so much; it would be a pleasure to have her for tea."

Still keeping watch at the flat, Julie, John, and Mia had a photo of all the tenants. They also had found where each lived. One person had his flat right at the back of the complex; he had no direct neighbours and was a loner. He was the right height, and his hair was black. They couldn't see his eyes; he averted them in the hallway when they passed. All three had become suspicious of him and watched him closely whenever he came to his flat. They reported hourly to Jan at the station, keeping her up to date with their observations. Jan and her officers were collating all the evidence to date, they had many leads, but not one told them this is our man.

Jan said, "We need just a little more time, but it seems everything is pointing to the owner of flat seven. Perhaps it is time to take the landlord into our confidence. We could then ask him the names of his tenants. Or do you think we should give it more time?"

Kelly said, "Perhaps a little more time. If it is him, we don't want him spooked."

"You're probably right, but is he stalking his new victim? If he is, then time is short. What are your thoughts, Mary?"

"Maybe given the circumstances, we should put a tail on him. We'll need to change the officers often, though."

"We don't have that many people—we are stretched pretty thin already. Let's hope we have a little more time. I might get one of the youngsters to befriend this man."

"Good idea," answered Mary and Kelly.

Lachlan did indeed have his next victim selected, but each time he asked her out, there was an excuse. *This bitch is hard to pin down.* However, he must not lose patience—he would get her, he knew he would. With these thoughts came the craving: he desperately needed relief, but he dared not make the mistake he made with the prostitute. He knew that Sue would have gone to the police, and maybe they believed her. He would have to bide his time, play along, and think about the pleasure and her pain—but for now, patience.

Rachel arrived at seven thirty, and Earnest answered the door with a smile, ushering her in. "Flora, the doc's here."

"Please come in, my dear. Clarisse is in her room; it's the second on the left."

"Thanks. I'll go and see her before we eat, if that's all right?"

"Of course. I will call you when tea is ready."

"Thanks again."

Rachel walked down the corridor to Clarisse's bedroom. She entered and found her lying on the bed.

"Hi, Rachel, come in, thanks for coming," Clarisse said.

"It's wonderful to see you so much better."

Clarisse still showed the bruises they were lighter now but the inner scars were another matter. Only time and positive thinking could heal those.

Flora called to them. "Dinner's ready."

They all sat down together and enjoyed the roast lamb and vegetables with mint sauce.

"What a great meal. You really are a wonderful cook, Flora," Rachel complimented.

"Many thanks, Rachel. Now, you and Clarisse go off and talk. Earnest and I will clean up."

"Are you sure, Mum? We can help."

"No, dear, I know you and Rachel have plans for tonight. Anything that can help you get better comes first."

"Okay, Mum. Come on, Rachel, let's go back to my room."

The two women walked toward the bedroom. It was here Rachel intended to perform hypnosis and unlock Clarisse's fears. Again Rachel spun the wheel, and Clarisse slowly drifted into the hypnotic trance.

"How are you feeling, Clarisse?"

"Fine."

"I want you to remember the night of the attack. You need to tell me what your fears are. There is no hurry, so don't be afraid."

"I see the door and asking him to come in. I made coffee and we talked. He is attentive, and everything is all right. Then I asked him to leave. He's hitting me, and now he's throwing me backward against the wall. The pain as I hit the wall is nothing, compared to the next deep, thrusting pain. He is raping me. Why did I think he was a great person? I'm trying to fight, but he punches me. Now there's blackness, but I fear he will he come back."

"The rape is over now; you are at home. Are you comfortable here?"

"Yes. I am guarded by the police, and Mum and Dad."

Rachel woke Clarisse from her trance slowly, not wanting her to be afraid.

"Did I tell you much? Could you make sense of my fears?" Clarisse asked.

"Who is Jackson? is he important?"

"Jackson, did I talk about him while in the trance?"

"You called his name many times."

"We met on the island where I spent my last holiday. I think I love him, but I don't think he loves me. Now I am damaged goods—he will probably hate me."

"Was he your first sexual experience?"

"Yes, he was. He was wonderful, he made love to me with feeling, and there was no haste. He waited until I wanted him."

"Why do you think he won't want you now?"

"Who would?"

"I would say Jackson. If he was so sensitive to your feelings then, I would say he still would be."

"Do you really mean that? I could be happy again, if he did."

"All you can do is wait. He may contact you, but if he doesn't, you will still be attractive to other men. You are a brave and lovely woman, and any man would be glad to have you."

Clarisse looked at Rachel and smiled as she asked.

"What did you say as I was waking up?"

"Just that you were a woman any man would love to have."

"Thanks for that, and for everything."

Jan arrived at the flat a little after dark, and after knocking lightly on the door, she entered. John, Julie, and Mia were there eagerly awaiting their new orders for the next few days.

"What's the go, ma'am?"

"We have to take a different tactic. Time is running out, and we need to pin this guy down soon. John, I want you to try to make friends with the bloke we suspect. Don't make any mistakes—if you feel he is onto you, back off and let me know."

"Sure, ma'am, I can do that. And I will be careful—we can't have him getting to his next victim, supposing he is the one. Do you think he *is* the man?"

"We are pretty sure it's him, but there can be no mistake."

With orders given, Jan went home and made a light meal, and then she sat on the couch thinking over the last few days and their progress. She felt she had it more or less under control, so she let the fatigue take over.

How long she slept, she didn't know, but the shrill ring of the phone woke her. She picked it up and said, "D-I Hastings here, what's up?"

"It's John, ma'am. I met the guy. He asked me to his flat for a drink. If I had doubts before, they're gone now. While he got the drinks, I saw some very suspicious looking items that would be used in a sexual attack. I believe he intends to use during the next attack. What do you want us to do now?"

"Stay put—I will be over soon."

"Okay, ma'am, we will be here. See you soon."

Jan rang Kelly and Mary, telling them to meet her at the flat. She picked up her files that held the evidence they had on Lachlan and left her flat. Then she drove to where John and the others waited.

Chapter Six

L ACHLAN HAD RUNG ALICIA AND asked if they could have dinner on the Friday night, and this time she had said yes. After putting down the phone, he sat on the lounge and picked up the bag containing the implements. One at a time he lifted them out, thinking of the best way to use them, and chuckling to himself about what fun it would be. His psychotic disorder was get worse each day; at times, he had trouble controlling himself. As he watched a woman walk by, the urge to attack her was strong. Always the non-psychotic side stopped him—the voices in his head fought each other. So far, he was safe and Alicia was only a few days away.

While all the pieces were falling into place for Lachlan, Jackson was still deciding whether to visit Clarisse. On the Monday at work, he asked his boss for a week off.

"Why? Do you have something urgent to do? Your holidays aren't due for another week."

"It isn't urgent, but I want to visit a friend I met last year."

"Well, I can't give you this week off. Will the following Monday be all right?"

"That's okay. It gives me more time to get things ready. Thanks, boss."

Upon arriving home, Jackson set about arranging a flight for the following Saturday evening. Now he had time to think about Clarisse. Would she be happy to see him, or was it all a waste of time? He remembered the island, that first night of sensual feeling that ended in a fulfilment he had not known before. He should have known then she was special: her hesitance and refusal at first, their long conversation that ended in her ultimate acceptance of him as a man. Those feelings don't come along every day. Why had he walked away? He could have at least looked back and waved. People made such flippant decisions at times, and this was his biggest.

Meanwhile the hypnosis had the same effect as in the hospital. Clarisse felt safe and free of fear, which had not happened since the attack. While having breakfast, her mother remarked on the change.

"You seem different this morning, dear."

"I feel much better. The hypnosis makes a difference; it lightens my soul, and I can think more positively. Rachel is a lovely woman and a great doctor. I always feel better after her visits."

"She must be dedicated to her work; nothing is too much trouble, and her care for you is wonderful. Do you think you will remain friends after you have fully recovered?"

"I hope so. I would also like to keep in touch with Jan, Kelly, and Mary as well; they have helped me so much and have given me strength. I am grateful."

Jan arrived at the flat, hurried up the stairs to the door, knocked lightly, and then waited until it opened. After stepping inside, she found Mary, Kelly, and the three incumbent officers. All six sat at the table, intent on what John had to say.

"His flat is laid out like this one, so a plan of attack would be easy; the implements I saw were made to inflict prolonged pain and torment."

"Are you entirely sure of this, John? We will only have one chance to catch this character."

"Yes, ma'am, I am sure. He looked spaced out at times. I wasn't with him long, but he is definitely strange."

"Okay. Now we will all look through the photos. If we all come to the same conclusion, then we must devise the plan to catch him. By the way, as I will be coming here often, it would be best if you to just call me Jan."

"Are you sure, ma'am?

"Yes, it will help maintain the subterfuge."

The officers who hadn't seen the suspect scanned the photos, placing them into two different sections, yes or no. It took some time, but finally they all had made their decision. Laid out before them were the two piles. Each of them had chosen the photo that John believed was Lachlan.

"Jan, do you believe it's going to be this easy? He's been so careful. What makes you think the case is over, and all we have to do is grab him?" Mary asked.

"No, Mary, it isn't going to be easy. He most certainly has picked his new victim—where and what he intends to do with her is the mystery."

"So what is our next step?"

"We know he likes to wine and dine his mark. Perhaps he is in the process of that now. John, you stay close to him, remember everything he says, and if possible get Julie or Mia to follow you. Be careful, you two, and don't let him see you. If he does, just walk by, showing no interest in him."

All the younger officers nodded, here it was at last: they were on his tail and had the chance to foil his terrible plans. Jan's mind and heart were racing. Was this really it? Could it be their hunt would be over soon? How wonderful that would be not only for them but also his victims. With his arrest, they could begin to heal and live normally, knowing they didn't have to look over their shoulder all the time.

Lachlan was busy with his plans for Alicia, and his mind drew pictures of how she would suffer. At times he felt he couldn't wait, but he pulled back, not wanting to make any mistakes. This had to be an attack worthy of his talents.

Alicia was looking forward to her date. There was no inkling of his murderous, inner thoughts—and if someone were to tell her, would she believe them?

Probably not. Lachlan had laid the ground well; he could still control his sanity enough for him to play his game. Should he take her to his old flat first? No one knew him there—he only used this one when he felt the need to hide. It was there he went after Clarisse; here, he felt safe and he could plan in peace. Yes, that would be best. Having made the decision, he left the office and went to his new flat.

John was at the mailbox, and he nodded to Lachlan. "Hi, mate, how are you today?"

"I'm fine. Can't stop now—things to do. I have a date on Friday with a real beauty. Can you suggest a good restaurant around here?"

"Sorry, mate, I've just arrived here, so I don't have any idea."

"Oh well. I'll use the phonebook to find a place. See you later." With that Lachlan walked away toward the building.

John looked at the mailboxes and realized there wasn't one for Lachlan, but there was one for a Paul. He knew all the other tenants; none of them had that name. Could that be Lachlan's fake identity? Thinking back, he remembered he had introduced himself as Paul. Why hadn't he noticed it then? Jan had called him Lachlan, so he must have assumed it was. He rushed up the stairs and into the flat, and he grabbed the phone and dialled Jan's number.

"Hello, can I help you?"

"It's John. I was at the mailboxes when he came home, and as we talked he told me he had a date on Friday. Also, I forgot to tell you, he's changed his name to Paul."

"Did he introduce himself as Paul when you had coffee with him?"

"Yes, he did—I just forgot."

"You forgot! Oh, John, how could you do that? This piece of evidence is crucial."

"I am so sorry. Am I off the case?"

"No! You at least know him, and we can use that. Remember, Constable, it is a matter of life and death with this maniac. Do you understand?"

"Yes, ma'am, it won't happen again."

"Believe me when I say it had better not! Okay, tell the others—at least we know now. Make sure you are ready on Friday; one of you must keep him in sight at all times. Do you understand?"

"Yes, ma'am, we will be. Can I say again how sorry I am?"

"You could, but I'm not listening."

Jan left the unit and returned to the station. She called Kelly and Mary into the squad room, and as they entered it was obvious to them their chief wasn't happy.

"What is it, Jan? You look like you're going to explode any minute."

"Young coppers . . . Sometimes I wonder how they get into the force."

"What the hell happened?"

"John forgot to tell me that Lachlan is now Paul. Lachlan introduced himself as that, and John forgot."

Mary said, "Don't be too hard on him, Jan. This is the first big case he's worked on, and he really is just a youngster."

"And that makes a difference, Mary?"

"No, but we have to understand that we all started as youngsters."

"Guess you're right. But don't let him know your feelings."

"I'm a little more professional than that, Jan."

"Let's drop it for now. We have a case to solve, and infighting doesn't help."

Jan and Mary looked at each other and nodded, they did have a case, and John had discovered that Lachlan was now Paul. They knew also that a date was set for Friday, which meant they had to be ready.

If he ran true to form, he would take his time getting to know his target; this meant he might not do anything on this first date. That assumption sounded fine, but would it evolve that way? They couldn't take any chances—if they did their job right, they would arrest him on Friday night.

The next move was up to John. He had to engage Paul in a conversation, find out if he had chosen a restaurant or if his date was going to cook a meal for them. Now, with everyone on high alert, any information gathered had to be handled carefully; nothing could be left to chance, if they were to succeed. John had to be vigilant, and any information about the restaurant was crucial. When they had that, the trap could be set.

Jan looked over the pile of files on her desk. She had worked hard to pin this case down, and now he was within reach.

"The day I can tell the women we have caught him will be a great day." As she left her office, she called to Kelly and Mary. "Feel like a drink, you two?"

"You bet—let's go to the pub across the road."

While walking together, Mary and Kelly sensed a difference in Jan: her step was lighter, and the hint of a smile crossed her face.

"You're different, Jan. You really believe that we will arrest him soon?"

"Yes, I do. If we all do our jobs over the next few days, we will close this case."

While sitting in the bar, Jan let herself believe that their hunt was almost over. It was then she remembered Rachel.

"I have to go, girls—there is one person who hasn't heard our news."

"You mean Rachel? Okay, Jan, we'll forgive you this time, but next time you will buy the drinks."

Jan made her way to the hospital and walked to Rachel's office. Through the glass door, she could see her working at her desk. "Hi, Rach, I have some news for you."

"You have? Is it about our rapist?"

"That's the one. We are almost certain we know where he lives and when he will strike."

"Why can't you arrest him now?"

"Need to catch him in the act."

"Why? We have his DNA. Why not bring him in now?"

"No, Rach, I want him too badly. We must wait until he is with a woman."

"I don't see you're reasoning. If you know him, arrest him. I will provide the evidence."

"Please Rach understand, if we wait to catch him in the act, there can be no doubt."

"What if he gives you the slip? What will you do then? If you believe he's your man, why wait?"

"Please, Rach. I know we have the medical evidence, but I have seen rapists' lawyers discredit this evidence. This one isn't getting away."

"I just hope you aren't making a mistake—the thought of another woman being raped and tortured is abhorrent to me."

"We won't make a mistake, please believe me."

"All right, I will trust you, but with reservations."

"Good for you. Rach, have you finished for the day. If so, let's go out for a meal."

"Sounds great, let's go."

At home, Clarisse was having dinner with her parents. She was much calmer now, and the serious wounds were responding well to treatment, but the bruises were still visible. Thinking of going back to work was not as frightening; in just a few weeks more, she would give it a try. Her parents had been wonderful, the new flat they picked for her was great, all her furniture was there, and it was starting to look like home. She knew life had to go on, and she had to make the move soon and not let him destroy her whole life.

She had no idea of Jackson's plans—the thought he might be coming to see her never entered her mind. Her thoughts of him were never far away, though. *Let him go. He won't ever come and visit. Perhaps it's time to close the book.* Nevertheless, thoughts of him were persistent as she wondered what he was doing and if he ever thought of her.

John sat ever vigilant at the window. Since his blunder, he wanted to keep watch all the time. Jan wouldn't find him wanting again; he would stay here as long as he could.

"You can't stay there all the time, John. You need to sleep," Julie said.

"Yes, I can."

"No, you can't. I am going to pull rank—go get some sleep."

He sighed. "Do I have a choice?"

"No, you don't. I will keep watch while you sleep for a while."

John left the window and lay down on the couch. He fell asleep within moments. He was tired and had a bigger job to do later in the day. The letterbox was where he had to be waiting for Paul.

Upon waking, he went downstairs for a short jog, making sure he had the flats in sight. His gaze took in a wide area, and there, walking from his car to the letterboxes, was Lachlan. As he approached, John made sure he was there at the same time.

"Hi, Paul, how goes it, mate?"

"It doesn't."

"What's up? You in trouble or something?"

"Or something—and I don't want to talk about it."

"You don't have to get nasty. I'll see you."

John walked off and took the stairs two at a time. He reached the flat and let himself in with never a backward glance. By his actions, he hoped Lachlan would see he wasn't the least bit interested.

John's fellow officers saw the look of disappointment on his face. Mia asked, "What's happened?"

"He's not talking," John said, frustrated.

"Never mind. Perhaps he will, when he goes for his jog this evening."

"I hope so. There's not much time left. He has to talk to me, he just *has* to."

The phone rang. Lifting the receiver, John asked, "Who is it?"

"Jan here. Did you have any luck with the name of the restaurant?"

"No, he wouldn't talk—he's in a terrible mood. I'll try again, when I meet him out jogging—that is, *if* he goes jogging."

"Keep in mind we don't have much time."

"I know, but what if he doesn't go out jogging?"

"Well, could you just go visiting?"

"Yes, that could be the answer. I'll ask if he's okay or is there something I can do."

"You try that, and I'll keep my fingers crossed."

"That's what I'll do. If I get anything, I'll ring you."

After putting the phone down, John walked directly to Lachlan's flat and tapped on the door.

A muffled voice answered. "Who is it?"

"Just me, John. Are you okay? You seemed out of sorts when we spoke earlier."

"Can you give me half an hour? I must finish something, and then I'll meet you for our jog."

"Okay, Paul, see you then."

John walked back to his flat. The others wanted to know if he had any news. He shook his head as he sat down by the table. All the while, he chastised himself for not knowing how to break into Lachlan's mind. *What's in there? If he is our person, how does he become such a brutal perpetrator? His manners are impeccable; he's pleasant to talk to, and he's very appreciative of women. So what changes? Is he insane? He has to be, or how could he do what he does?* John liked women, but the thought of rape was abhorrent.

The clock chiming broke John's reverie. It was time for his nightly jog. He put on his runners and was off down the stairs and out onto the path. Lachlan was not in sight—perhaps he was still in his flat? Regardless, John had to jog around the grounds, just as he had done since moving in. He knew Mia and Julie were watching. As he jogged, he felt someone beside him.

"Oh! Hi, Paul. Are you okay now?"

"Yes, I'm fine—just a small hiccup in my plans for Friday."

"Geez, I'm sorry about that. What happened? Did she turn you down?"

"She certainly has. Boy, it makes me mad—fucking women! They can never make up their minds."

"Haven't had much experience with them—no time really. Had to get a degree first and then take up my present job."

"What do you do?" Lachlan asked.

John thought quickly. He damn near told him he was a cop. "Business management. It pays well, and I have quite a lot of time to myself. I can work at home as well as at the office. And you?"

"I don't need to work, really. My father left a large estate, but I work at times just for fun. Can't say I like it, though."

"Lucky dog, eh?"

The two men jogged on, covering their usual course, which led them around the grounds and then back home. Upon reaching the front door, John was about to run up the stairs to his flat.

"Feel like a drink, mate?" Lachlan said to him.

"You bet, Paul. Lead the way."

The two men entered Lachlan's flat, and Lachlan offered John a beer or Coke.

"Just Coke for now. I have a heap of work when I get back to the flat."

They sat back as they drank. John felt very much at ease, but he could see Lachlan sipping a beer and watching him. That was the last thing John remembered.

When he woke, John had no idea how long he had been out to it. Sitting up he could see Lachlan had gone. Where was he? Had he given himself away? *Fuck, where is he? He must have twigged. Just as well I left my wallet home. Did he drug me on purpose? Maybe not, but he could be out on the hunt, since his date for Friday had let him down. Was he out there attacking another defenceless woman?*

John felt dizzy as he tried to rise. He was also a little nauseous, so he put his hand out to steady himself. *Damn, what have I done? Have I let this fucking monster loose?*

He left the flat and walked slowly back to his own. He opened the door and was happy to see Mia and Julie were okay.

"What the hell happened to you, John?"

"The bastard drugged me. I have to call Jan."

John picked up the phone, dialled, and waited for Jan to answer. She wasn't in her office, so the call was diverted to her mobile.

"What is it? I'm having a meal with Rachel."

"He's gone."

"Who's gone? Not Lachlan? Wait there—I'm on my way."

John waited anxiously for Jan to arrive, and the three young officers talked between themselves. Had he twigged to their assignment? Had one of them given any hint of their profession, or why they were in the flat? They could not see how he knew. This conversation continued until Jan arrived.

"How did this bloody well happen? How the hell could you let him slip away?"

"We don't think we did, ma'am. None of us gave him the slightest hint," Mia said.

"I still don't why or how he drugged me," John said.

"You're sure of that?" Jan asked.

"Yes, ma'am. But should we be here blaming each other? Shouldn't we be trying to find him?"

"Don't get fucking smart with me, you little snot."

"Sorry, ma'am, but he drugged me."

"Did he speak of another flat?"

"Not directly, but I felt he had another place. He talked about his refuge, and at the time I thought it was just talk."

"Damn it. We have two first names—is it possible we have a surname?"

"There should be a surname on the letter box."

"Well, get out and see!"

John raced down the stairs to the letterboxes, found Paul's name, and then returned to the flat. "His surname is Johnson, ma'am."

"It figures it's a common name," Jan said. "Well, all we can do for now is wait. You'd better hope he returns, John. We can't afford stuff-ups now, so keep your fucking eye on the ball."

A very contrite John nodded at his superior. "Are you sure you want me to stay, ma'am?"

"Yes, I do, so let's sleep on it. John, you stay on watch. If he returns you must confront him. You did say he had trouble with his Friday date—maybe he's out looking for a woman. What a ghastly thought."

"That could be it. The bastard drugged me so he could get away. He will be back with an excuse about the drug, I bet."

"You'd better be right. Goodbye for now. Don't let me down, any of you."

John said, "I'll walk you to the car, ma'am. He might be there. If he is, I'll tell him you're my mum."

"Cheeky young bastard, aren't you."

John didn't dare laugh. He placed his hand on Jan's elbow and apologized for his mistake.

At the car, Jan said, "Thanks, John. See you tomorrow."

"Okay, ma'am."

John returned to the flat, chuckling to himself about the mum joke. Once inside, the two girls and John sat and discussed the happenings of the day. After a while, Mia and Julie went off to bed, leaving John to watch in case Paul came back.

John dozed as he waited, and a noise startled him. He looked at the monitor and saw Lachlan stealthily walking toward the outer door. John snapped the photo, but Lachlan's only interest was getting inside the building. Picking up the photo, John saw he was carrying a satchel; this probably held the implements John had seen while in the flat. Deciding not to call Jan, he sat at his post until morning.

Paul hadn't reappeared, so John was confident he had not left his unit. As the dawn broke, he rang Jan. The phone rang for some time before she answered.

"Who the hell is it?"

"It's John, ma'am. He came back very early this morning, about 3.00 a.m. I didn't call you but have watched since then, and he hasn't gone out again."

"Interesting. Don't you think he must know he owes you an explanation for drugging you? Could be a very interesting day."

"Is it all right for me to confront him first? I'll let him know that I am not happy about being drugged. This could lead him to tell me where he went."

"Okay, John, but make sure the officers aren't seen today. It's better if he doesn't know about them."

"Okay, ma'am. Is it all right if I just go and ask him?"

"I'd say you have the right. It will be interesting to hear what he has to say."

"I'll be in touch."

As it was still comparatively early, John sat and thought about what he wanted to say to Lachlan. What would be his excuse? John was a good liar, and it would need to be a good one now. There was a knock on the door, and John opened it. There stood Lachlan.

"Oh, it's you mate! What the bloody hell was in the Coke you gave me last night?"

"I can explain, and I'm so sorry. I suffer from a psychotic disorder and need to take a drug to control it."

"Yeah, right. What do you think I am, stupid?"

"Come back with me, and I'll show you."

"Okay, but don't offer me a drink," John joked.

The two men walked the short distance to Lachlan's flat. He opened the door and then stood aside to let John enter. On doing so, John wondered

ELIZABETH BLACKMAN

if there might be a blow to the back of his head. Once inside, John stood and waited for Lachlan's explanation.

"This is what I have to take. It's a psychotic drug, and it taste's dreadful, so I mix it with Coke. I grabbed the wrong bottle from the fridge, and it knocked you out. I cannot tell you how sorry I am. I tried to wake you, but when I realized it was useless, I left you to sleep, and I expected you to be there when I came home."

"So this is your excuse, eh? Well, good enough for now, but don't ever offer me a drink again."

"Will this mar our friendship, John?"

"Not for now. I accept your apology, but I must get back to my flat—I'm expecting a visit from my mother and want to be there when she arrives."

"Okay, John, I'll see you when we go jogging."

"See you then."

John walked back to his flat, and once inside he picked up the phone and dialled Jan's number.

"Hello?"

"It's John, ma'am. I have spoken to Paul. His explanation is that he has a psychotic problem, and the medication tastes dreadful, so he mixes it with Coke. He mistakenly gave it to me. What do you think?"

"Good liar, isn't he? He had to do something last night, and he didn't want anyone to know about it. I wonder what it was."

"Have there been any reports about anyone being raped last night?"

"None that I've heard of, but it's early. If it has happened, maybe the woman doesn't want to report it."

"Lachlan wants to go jogging after lunch. I'll try to find out where he was. I think he is starting to think of me as a friend."

"Okay, John, keep it up."

John put down the phone and went to wake Julie and Mia. He told them about Paul's excuse, and both were very sceptical and snickered.

"You didn't believe that, did you?" Mia said.

"No, of course not."

While the police worked, Clarisse still could not bring herself to go back to work, feeling as she did about the gossip in the office.

"I think you should give it a try, even if it is just a couple of days," her mother said.

"I don't know, Mum. They will all stare at me, and some will think I put myself in that position and possibly asked what happened."

"You shouldn't think such things, your friends have been great and have shown only compassion."

"I know you are right, Mum. Maybe next week."

The conversation over, Clarisse returned to her room; it was here she could be alone with her thoughts. Lying on her bed, she let her mind go back into that dark place. She always felt that if she could face it squarely, she would be able to exorcise the demons. Always the first face she saw was Jackson's, her dear Jackson. How was it she could remember him without fear? Then she saw Lachlan, her tormentor, with his distorted face and evil eyes. It was at these times she could voice her thoughts.

"I can see you now. What a monster, how you enjoyed my moans of agony. Now you're pressing a thumb into my throat. I can see you, you animal. How your face has changed. Now you have the appearance of a wolf or rabid dog. How I hate you! My life is in tatters because of you. I can see now that's what you wanted, isn't it? You want me to withdraw from life. If I do, you have won, not just once but twice. Well, I won't let you win. Mum's right—I will go back to work. I haven't done anything that I should be ashamed of. You, you are the guilty one. You have forced me to live with pain and doubt. Soon will come the day when they slam a cell door, and you will rot like an animal. Then you will spend your life locked away where you belong. But not me. Slowly I will free myself from you forever."

Jan took her time before going to work, piecing together everything they knew about Lachlan. Regarding the mystery date who had let him down, her identity would be of tremendous advantage to them. Would it be fair to just ask her to put herself in harm's way? *No, this is farcical. Stop your ramblings, Jan. We just need to follow him, and he will trip himself up.*

CHAPTER SEVEN

JACKSON COULDN„T HIDE HIS EXCITEMENT. Here he was at the airport, ready for his flight to Clarisse. He had asked himself many questions about her, and always the answer came back: she was the woman he loved. As he settled back into his seat, even the race down the runway was exciting to him. The plane hurtled skyward, and he could feel his heart pound in his chest. While the plane floated on air, it fitted Jackson's mood as he thought of Clarisse; it was as if he had opened a book. His thoughts read the story of their holiday, and it was of love on an island just over a year ago.

Why did he let her go? He must be the most stupid man he knew. He should have realized the feelings he had only came once, and if not grabbed, they would float away. The plane reached its destination, and as it disgorged its passengers, Jackson found himself on the tarmac. After walking through the lounge to the car park, he hailed a cab, giving the driver the hotel name, and away they went. During the drive, the cabby asked if he had been in this part of the country before.

"No, I haven't."

"God's country, mate. You'll love it. Come to visit friends, or just a holiday?"

"Bit of both, I'd say. Looking up an old friend and maybe marrying her."

"You don't say? Well, all the best to you."

The taxi arrived at the hotel, and the cabby turned around. "That'll be five dollars."

Jackson paid the money, said goodbye, and walked into the hotel. At the desk he asked for the key to his room.

"Here you go, sir, have a nice stay."

"I'm sure I will. Thanks."

Jackson made his way to his room, entered, and dumped his luggage on the floor. Then he lay on the bed, thought of Clarisse as he rolled over, and fell asleep.

Waking with a start, he looked at this watch. It was too late to visit now, but tomorrow was another day. Should he ring first, or just go to her house? He rang room service and ordered a meal. Later he went to the bar, had a couple of drinks, and then went back to his room. His sleep was filled with thoughts of Clarisse.

Rachel was feeling just a little bit put out. She hadn't heard from Jan or Clarisse, so she picked up the phone and rang Jan.

"Hello, D-I Hastings."

"Hi, Jan, it's Rachel. Thought I'd give you a ring. Have you made any headway in the case? Do you have the suspect yet?"

"Hang on, Rach, one question at a time. Sorry I haven't been in touch, but we are getting close to an arrest. We have officers watching him as we speak."

"Where?"

"Can't tell you."

"Oh, why is that? I have been involved since day one, haven't I?"

"You are a witness. If we involve you now, the defence will cut you to ribbons.

They will say you are a biased witness. Surely you don't want that?"

"Of course not, but I do feel a little in the dark."

"Don't worry, you will be in at the end, I promise. I'll be free for dinner tomorrow night. Would you like to come round?"

"At your house? Sounds great, see you then."

While Rachel had time, she rang Clarisse. "Hello?" Clarisse's mother answered.

"It's Rachel, Flora. Is Clarisse in? I would like to talk to her."

"Yes, she's home. Hang on, I'll call her. Clarisse, you are wanted on the phone, love—it's Rachel."

"Hi, how are you?" Clarisse said when she picked up the phone.

"I'm fine. You sound much better. Do you need anything, or would you like your favourite doc to come to see you?"

"I'd love to see you. Come for lunch?"

"What a great idea! See you then. Bye for now."

Rachel arrived shortly, and Flora greeted her warmly. "Please come in; Clarisse will be with us soon."

The two women sat at the kitchen table, waiting for Clarisse to join them. Clarisse entered the room and said, "You made it then, Rach?"

"Yes, I wasn't needed, so I slipped out. They know where to contact me, so here I am, ready for a lovely lunch."

All three chatted as they ate their meal. A knock on the front door interrupted them as they were washing up.

Clarisse said, "I'll get it, Mum." She opened the door, and there he stood, her wonderful Jackson, with the same smile and cheeky glint in his eyes.

"Hello, Clarisse. I had to come and see you. I have booked a room at a local hotel. I just came to ask you to forgive me for the way I acted on the island."

Clarisse stood as if transfixed, gazing at the man she loved. The one she had yearned for and hoped would come was standing before her. "Jackson, are you really here? Touch me so I know it's true. How did you find me?"

"Don't you remember? You gave me your parents' address along with yours. Can I come in?"

"Yes, yes! Please come in. We have a lot to talk about."

Jackson and Clarisse went to the dining room, and she introduced him to Flora and Rachel. He nodded his head in acknowledgement. "Hello to you both. Mrs Stewart, your daughter is very much like you."

"Hello, Jackson. Clarisse told us she met a young man on holiday, but she never told us your name."

Clarisse said, "I'm sorry, Mum." She could not believe that Jackson was there; her mind could not grasp the fact. Suddenly he remembered the rape. He would leave once he knew the truth. *I have to tell him, but how will I do it?*

Through the wonder and chatter from her mother, Clarisse heard from Jackson,

"Is your face bruised. Did you have an accident?"

"We have to talk, Jackson. I have something to tell you."

"Rachel and I will go out to the veranda and drink our coffee,"

"Why don't you and Jackson talk in the lounge?"

When they sat in the lounge, Jackson asked, "Was it an accident, Clarisse?"

"No, it wasn't an accident."

"How did you get such bruises, I can see they have faded quite a lot, but who did it? Did someone hit you?"

"Please, let me tell you. One question at a time. When I got home from the island, I was so lonely that I didn't go out for months. At times, I hated you, and finally my friends asked me out to picnics, movies, and parties. I kept on blaming you, but it wasn't your fault. I meant to write and tell you of my feelings, but then something else happened."

"What? Please tell me."

"I went out on a date with what I thought was a nice man, but he wasn't. When we returned to my flat, he came in for coffee. When I asked him to leave because I was tired, it was then that he hit me. He punched me until I was semi-conscious, and then he brutally raped me. I regained consciousness and tried to fight him off, but he laughed and hit me again. I have no idea how long the attack lasted. When I woke, I dragged myself into the bedroom and climbed into the bed in agony. I must have fallen asleep. When I woke, I looked in the mirror. What you see on my face are the faded bruises from that night."

Jackson looked at Clarisse. He held her in his arms while her entire body shook from the emotions she had just put into words. As he held her, the rage began to build inside him.

"Do they know who it was?"

"Yes, but he is proving hard to find. The team working on the case is wonderful."

"This makes no difference, my darling. It has taken long enough for me to come to you as it is. I don't want to wait another minute. We should get married, don't you agree?"

"Do you mean you want to marry me?"

Jackson stood and held out his hand too Clarisse. "Come with me Clarisse."

Clarisse took Jackson's hand, and they walked out to the veranda where the two women were sitting. As they stepped out, Jackson slipped his arm around Clarisse's shoulder. "Clarisse and I are going to get married, Mrs Stewart."

"Oh, Jackson, that's wonderful! I know Earnest will be overjoyed."

"Is it okay for me to wait here for him to get home Mrs Stewart?"

"Yes, certainly."

Rachel said, "It's lovely news, Jackson. My name is Rachel, Clarisse's doctor. We have become close friends since the attack."

"Hello, and thanks for your care of Clarisse. I didn't know how much I loved her until she opened the door. Now we will never be apart."

"Perhaps we should ring Jan? I'm sure she would like to meet Jackson," Clarisse's mother said.

Rachel said, "Good idea, Flora. I'll go and phone her now."

"I'll come with you." The two women left.

Jackson and Clarisse stayed together on the veranda, their heads together. As they talked, Jackson held Clarisse gently. The look of love and concern told Clarisse he would stay with her always.

"Hello Jan, you'll never guess who came today?"

"I guess I won't, if you don't tell me."

"Jackson arrived!"

"Who the hell is he?"

"He is the one from the island, the one who spent his holiday with Clarisse."

"Oh yes, that Jackson?"

"It's a bit of a secret Jan."

"You're safe with me, Rach. Oh, by the way, could you come and see me?"

"Okay, I'll make my goodbyes and be with you shortly."

Clarisse, Jackson, and Flora sat on the veranda while they waited for Earnest to come home. They exchanged small talk, but Flora felt she was in the way. She told Clarisse she needed to start on the evening meal and left the veranda. It was then she heard her husband drive into the garage. After meeting him at the door, she explained what had happened earlier in the day.

"He just appeared out of nowhere, standing at the door, and Clarisse was barely able to speak."

"What's he like? I hope he's not another deadbeat that wants to hurt my girl."

"No, he is quite wonderful! Clarisse told him of the assault. Want to know his answer?"

"Of course I do."

"He walked out to me on the veranda his arm around our daughter and told me he wanted to marry her!"

"He did? Well, that's good news! It's time Clarisse had happiness, not just sadness."

"He knows that. I think he was making a point for Clarisse. He said no matter what, he still loved her."

"Well, let's join them."

They walked out onto the veranda, and Earnest could see the love between his daughter and this man. "You must be Jackson. You know you hurt my girl during her holiday?"

"Yes, sir, I do. It took a while for me to realize how much I loved her, but I know it now, and I want to marry Clarisse as soon as possible."

With a twinkle in his eye, Earnest said.

"Let me sleep on it. No, I am joking! I know Clarisse loves you, so welcome mate."

All four sat and talked for many hours. Jackson told them all about himself, though he could not reveal a lot about his work, it being of a secret nature as a federal police officer.

"You don't need a taxi, son. We have a spare room. Clarisse will show you."

Clarisse stood up holding Jackson's hand, and they walked toward the spare room.

"Can't I stay with you?" he said.

"Please Jackson you should know I am unable to have sex."

"I don't want sex—I just want to hold you, so you know you are safe."

"Okay, but we must be quiet."

Slowly they made their way to Clarisse's bedroom, where they lay in each other's arms. For the first time since the attack, Clarisse felt safe. From now on, she had a protector, a man who wanted what she wanted: a normal life and marriage to a loved one.

Rachel went back to the hospital. She was happy for Clarisse, Jackson, and herself. Her hypnosis had allowed Clarisse to face the horror fully, and a man's love had confirmed it.—With time Rachel knew Clarisse would be safe. Rachel felt the urge to ring Jan, and as she reached for the phone but was surprised by a knock on the door. Who could this be at this time of night? She looked through the spy hole and saw Jan.

"What are you doing here at this time of night?" Rachel asked.

"I need to be cheered up; this case is so draining. I seem to be rolling from one step to another, and getting nowhere."

"Don't bash yourself up about it, this bloke disguise's himself well even though the changes were cosmetic they were effective.—He also seems to predict what we're doing and when. Oh, by the way, I am living in a flat behind the hospital."

Jan said, "I will see you there. I am dying to know about this Jackson. Did you meet him?"

"Yes, I did. Now, let's get back to you, Jan."

"I am struggling to know where to go from here. The suspect we believe is our man is being watched round the clock. We are set up to follow him, if he makes a move. He gave John the slip by drugging him. He says it was an accident, but I'm not sure."

"What drug did he give John?"

"Medication he takes for a psychotic problem."

"Interesting. Can John get hold of a sample?"

"Well, he can get close to him . . . yes, I think he could."

"When you get it, bring it to me right away," Rachel said.

"Okay, I'll do that. Must go now—we both need sleep. See you later."

After letting Jan out, Rachel went to bed, and sleep claimed her quickly.

The morning light streaming through her window woke her. After getting dressed, she skipped breakfast and made her way to the hospital. On arrival she was surprised to see Clarisse and Jackson.

"Hi, both of you. Why are you here?"

"We want to know the full extent of Clarisse's injuries," Jackson said.

"Do you indeed?"

"Yes, Doc," Clarisse said. "It is the internal injuries we are most anxious about."

Rachel went to her filing cabinet, lifted out the file and sat at her desk. "Before telling you what is in the file, I must tell you that in a psychological sense, you will both have to be patient and understanding with each other—especially you, Jackson. It may take some time for Clarisse to overcome the trauma of the assault she suffered. Though her injuries were very serious, I'm confident she will make a full recovery, but it will take time. I'm sure there will be no long-term damage; in time you should have a full and satisfying sex life. The ability to have children shouldn't be a problem."

"Thanks for that, Rachel. We were a little concerned. At this time we just want to hold each other and remember how we were back on the island." Taking their leave, they walked out of the hospital, with Jackson's arm around Clarisse. It left Rachel pondering on the meaning of love. Here were two people who had found that elusive place in the sun. Even through the violence of rape, their love would stand the test of time.

John had his new orders from Jan; all he needed now was another invitation from Lachlan. Sitting in front of the monitor, he saw the man in the grounds of the building. He didn't look happy and was very agitated. John put his tape recorder in his pocket, took the stairs two at a time, and joined him.

"You look a bit hassled, mate. Anything I can do?"

"Women. Stupid, bloody women! If I could get my hands on her, boy, she would be sorry."

"What would you do, Paul? Tell me just what would you do?"

Lachlan looked at John; there was hate in his eyes as he spat out his answer. "What would I do? Well, that's the question, isn't it?"

"Why do you hate them so much?"

"Witches—that's what they are. They trick men with their wily ways and blind us to their plans."

"Their plans? I don't understand. What plans?"

"They mean to wipe us out and then take over. Can't you see? We have to chastise them and bring them under control."

John said softly, "Come on, Paul, they aren't that bad."

"You don't understand, and you never will. Leave me alone—go back to your miserable life and let me get on with what I have to do."

John left and walked back to his flat. Lachlan troubled him, and what he had said was worse. He picked up the phone and rang Jan.

"John, what's up? Anything new?"

"Can you come here now?"

"Sounds serious, John."

"You need to come now," John repeated.

"Won't he see me?"

"Doesn't matter—he thinks you're my mum, so come quickly."

John paced the floor until Jan's arrival. Mia sat at the table, too; Julie had her four hours off. John placed his tape recorder on the table and turned it on. Jan sat in amazement as she listened to the ramblings of a lunatic.

"He is mad, isn't he, ma'am? We have to arrest him now, and I don't think we can wait."

"I agree, but we still don't have enough proof. If we use this tape, he will plead guilty by reason of insanity."

"We do have Clarisse and Sue, and some DNA evidence," said John. "Would this be enough to convict him?"

"Maybe, but I would prefer to have another witness."

Mia said, "Alice went out with this man, didn't she? We should call her in. She is a potential witness, but will she do it, ma'am?"

"Geez, he has used so many disguises. With a good lawyer he will make it hard for our witnesses. Let me sleep on it, and I'll get back to you." As the police officers discussed the situation, they noticed Lachlan walking to the entrance of the building. John decided to wait in the hallway until Lachlan walked toward him, and he waved and called to him.

"Had enough for the day, mate?"

"Sure have. Sorry about the nonsense before. I'm just feeling sorry for myself. You know the girl I spoke about? Well she has gone off on holidays, she says alone—but I think she's lying."

"What a blob, mate. Why don't we go out and pick up a pair of girls? What do you reckon?"

"Not my scene, really. I like to hunt alone. See you later, John, I've got things that need to be done."

John returned to the flat with this added information. He was actually quite happy as he walked in the door. Jan wondered at the grin.

"Do you think this is a bloody joke?"

"No, ma'am, but knowing he is going out tonight is."

"He is? That _is_ news. No time to lose—we must get our pursuit team of undercover cars and officers ready. I'll get that started. You stay here, John; one of the girls can come with me now. Okay, let's go. We have a lot of planning to do."

It was about to start. Could this be the end for this brutal rapist? Everyone involved certainly hoped so. Every police officer aware of the case volunteered for the duty, knowing they all couldn't be involved. It was up to Jan to choose the team. This called for a series of unmarked cars, in the first instance at every connecting road near the flats. When they knew which direction he was taking, the cars (linked by radio) could move as he drove along the road. In total there were six cars and twelve officers. After the first call, each car made ready to take over from the lead car. The atmosphere in the cars was electric: everyone was alert and ready for the call for action.

The only officer not in the cars was John. Jan had left him with orders to get into Lachlan's flat and get a sample from the Coke bottle. He also had a radio and could follow the pursuit to know if Lachlan turned back toward the flats. Standing at the apartment door, John could feel the tension in his own body. He picked the lock and entered the apartment. He had a high-powered torch, so it wasn't necessary to use the light. He walked to the fridge and retrieved a small sample from the Coke bottle and returned to the flat.

The crackle of the radio let him know he was safe; Lachlan was still on his way to the destination. Once inside, John called Jan on the radio, letting her know he had been successful. Jan acknowledged his details and told him their position, and then he closed down his radio.

Lachlan had a smirk on his face. Unknown to the police, he had received a call from Alicia. She had invited him to her home for a late dinner, as an apology for the broken dates. While he drove, the ideas for the evening played in his mind. First enjoy the meal and play her game, and then his game would begin. These thoughts would have been frightening to a normal person, but Lachlan was far from that.

Lately, he had been reading a book on sadism. This volume had given his disturbed mind the perfect ways of inflicting ultimate pain while enjoying it. Yes, Alicia would regret her earlier indifference to him.

At home, Clarisse didn't know what was happening—all she could think of was Jackson. *What a man! He dismissed my thoughts of being a lesser woman because of the attack. His words speak of love and place the blame squarely where it belongs, on the inhuman man called Lachlan.* He was kindness itself; she loved how he made love to her, without the inclusion of intercourse. Speaking softly while letting his hands play over her body, he gave her long, lingering kisses until she could not bear any more, and then he gave her and himself sexual satisfaction.

She watched him as he slept. How handsome he was; his curly brown hair lay damp on his forehead. She moved slightly, waking him.

He looked at her with his sparkling blue eyes, which danced mischievously. "Hello, my angel. Why are you awake?"

"I wanted to look at you—you are so wonderful. I never expected to see you again, and after the rape, I believed no man would want me."

"Please, my darling, you must stop blaming yourself. You are just as lovely and unblemished to me as you were on our holiday."

Through her tears, Clarisse looked at him, taking in all the features that had drawn her to him from the very beginning.

He said to her, "Love is strange, don't you think? It took me almost a year to realize I loved you, but you loved me right from the start."

"Oh, Jackson, if you knew how much I loved you . . . I don't know how to show you. I've loved and missed you every day since we last saw each other."

"Why don't we get married here, and then have our honeymoon on the island? Maybe we could get the same bungalow."

"That's a great idea!"

"Do you think we can make the arrangements in time?" he asked.

"I'm sure we can. Let's tell Dad and Mum in the morning. We may have to wait until that rapist is caught—they will probably need me for the trial."

"They may not catch him for months. I can't wait that long. We'll ask the police tomorrow if we can leave after the ceremony."

Jackson pulled Clarisse close to him. Gentle feather-like kisses started the warmth in her body again, and he held her to him while his hand traced the outline of her face. Then he gently touched the bruises that remained, kissing each one in turn. In his mind he was wiping away all traces of a monster.

Flora and Earnest had watched their daughter slowly come to terms with the horror and anguish of her ordeal. They knew her progress was because of Jackson. His love of Clarisse was taking away all the hurt and humiliation. They both liked him very much, and he had worked wonders. By letting their daughter know he loved her, the past months did not matter. They watched as he held her hand, the gentleness of his touch, and the look of love in his eyes: they sparkled whenever he looked at her. Flora and Earnest's job was almost over: they could confidently leave their daughter's happiness to Jackson, knowing he would watch her well.

Back at the flat, John waited for someone to call. He was anxious about the chase and whether it was working. Were they still behind Lachlan, and was he still going to his destination? Almost at the thought, the radio crackled.

"Hi, John you there?" Jan said.

"Yep, what's up?"

"We are still on his tail. Just thought I would let you know."

"Thanks, ma'am. I was getting worried."

"Sit tight, mate."

John sat at the table and started playing patience, a card game he loved. It was going to be a long night as they waited, and he hoped it would be a fruitful one.

Jan sat in the passenger seat of the police car, watching and waiting for any word of their quarry. When they pulled out into traffic for their turn to follow, it looked as if he had a definite destination in mind. From what she could see, he hadn't looked back or used his mirror. She deduced he was not aware they were following. Intersection after intersection went by, and he didn't deviate from the main street—it was evident he knew where he was going. Jan turned at the next corner, and another car took over. She then waited for the radio call; it crackled into life, and a voice reported their progress. Kelly told her all was well, and Lachlan was still heading east and showing no sign of knowing they were there.

Jan signed off and voiced her thoughts. "This must be the last night. We cannot let him wriggle off the hook this time. The amount of effort and time and all the officers that are involved—surely they will win."

Mary's car had taken over from Kelly, and they continued to follow, always heading east. All was going well—until another car cut them off. Mary slammed her fist on the horn.

"Bloody idiot! Can you still see him, Ken?"

"No, I can't. You have to pass the bloody car in front. We should pick him up again."

"I hope so. If not, we've blown the surveillance."

Mary swerved past the car in front. Both officers strained to see if his car was there. "There he is! Speed up a bit, Mary, and get right up behind him."

As their car took station behind him again, Mary heaved a huge sigh of relief. They hadn't lost him, and the chase continued.

As they followed, Lachlan was voicing his plans for the evening. "How will I pace this? Do I make my attack tonight, or play the gentleman? If I play the concerned friend and let her know the other dates were not a problem, it would put her at ease, and I could progress. This time I need seclusion—I have to find a place where I will not be disturbed. Would her flat fit my needs? Should I use my other flat? Time, I will need plenty of time if I am to get the gratification my body needs."

These thoughts played in his mind as he drove. He had no idea the police were following him. He slowed the car to read the house numbers. *There it is,* he thought, and he turned into the driveway.

The police car pulled to the curb and stopped. They heard Lachlan as he slammed his car door, made his way to the front door of the house, knocked, and waited for a response.

"Oh, it's you, Paul! Come in. Did you find the place without too much trouble?"

"Yes, it was quite easy. How are you?"

"I'm fine. A friend called in unexpectedly and is joining us for dinner. I hope that's all right?"

Lachlan could not believe what he was hearing. *What a bitch! She has done it again!* He felt he could just grab her by the throat and strangle her. How could she do it? Once again, his plans were thwarted by a woman. "No, that's fine," he lied. "We can go out another night."

"Oh, that's good. I thought you might be quite put out, considering the broken dates."

"Never mind; we will have our date soon, and I assure you it will be memorable."

Alicia introduced her friend Kyle to Lachlan, and then all three sat down to a delicious meal. There was much banter as they ate, and Alicia was impressed with Lachlan's charm.

"Where do you work, Kyle?" Lachlan asked.

"I work at the Australia Bank, Paul. It is a good job with plenty of scope for advancement, and I love it there. And where do you work?"

"I'm between jobs at the moment, but I was the accountant for a mining company."

"Come and see me, if and when you decide to go back to work. I'm sure there would be a place for you there."

Alicia listened as the two men talked. The night was going well, and her feelings toward Paul were growing. *He really is a nice man.* The meal finished, and Kyle made his excuses, saying he had had a long day and needed an early night.

"It was nice meeting you. Perhaps we can do this again?" Kyle said to Lachlan.

"Sure thing, Kyle. Have a safe journey home."

"Yes, Kyle, do take care," Alicia said. "I'll see you later."

Kyle walked to his car, looked back, and waved to Lachlan and Alicia. The new police officers waiting at the curb watched the car pull out and drive off.

"You sure this is the right car mate?"

"Well there was only one car so it must be him."

This left Lachlan free to drive home without the surveillance team.

John was still waiting for some news about the surveillance. He looked out of the window and saw Lachlan pulling into the complex car park. *Good God! How did he get back here without a police car behind him?* John stood stunned. Composing himself, he turned on his radio. "Ma'am, are you there? Please pick up?"

"John, what are you doing on the radio? We need to keep it clear—you know that."

"He's here! Ma'am, he's here!"

"What are you on about? A car is still following him."

"No, they aren't. I don't know how it's happened, but he's here, and there isn't a police car in sight."

"Damn, what the bloody hell's gone wrong? Just wait until I get this bunch together."

The radio crackled, and Jan called the surveillance team. Her words shocked them all. "Meet me back at the station now! All of you."

Fortunately, John had turned off his radio and put it in a drawer. A knock on the door startled him. "Who is it?"

"It's Paul. Can I come in for a while?"

"Not right now, Paul. I'm just stepping into the shower and then making an early night. I'll see you when we jog in the morning."

"Okay, see you then, mate."

What a disaster. All the hard work done by the team—torn apart by the use of officers from a different section. These officers, while good at their job, were not up to date with the urgency needed to catch this psychotic fiend.

Jan sat in her office until all the team were present. She marched into the room where they were, stood with her hands on hips, and glared at the police officers she was to address. "How did this happen? How could you mistake a car?"

"Remember, we're new to this case. We were told to follow him until he stopped. We did that and pulled to the curb to wait."

"You were given details of his car and the license plate number. Were you looking at all, or just goofing off?"

"All I can say is I am sorry like everyone else. Am I right in saying you know where he is now?"

"Yes, we do, but I wanted him caught with the woman in the car! Do you know where she is?"

"Still at home, I suppose."

"No more smug answers," Jan warned.

"Well, she is at home, isn't she?"

"That's enough from you, Ken! Your superior officer will hear about your attitude."

"We did as ordered, and the woman is safe."

"If she is, you are the luckiest police officers I know. I say that because if he had taken her, we would be looking for a body. Do I make myself clear?"

"Geez, ma'am, we are really sorry. If we can help turn this situation around, we will."

"Everyone but Kelly and Mary, please get out of my sight. You failed this job, and I hope you won't let that happen again."

Kelly interrupted in the defence of the officers. "Come on, Jan, we are just as much to blame. We could have made the instructions clearer."

"How much clearer could they have been? If one of you had been in that car, you would have made sure his was the only car in the driveway. You would have taken down the plate number and waited for the second car. This is where it all fell apart. I am so glad I left John at the flats. Had he not been there to tell us Lachlan had returned home, we would have blown the whole case by stopping the wrong man. We could have pulled over the other guy; he is supposedly a friend of Alicia's, and I imagine he would tell her, and bingo—we would be left with nothing. We would have had no alternative but to arrest Lachlan, and as soon as we did that, he would hire a smart lawyer who would call it entrapment, and he would be free. Well, let us call it a night. Fortunately John managed to get a sample of the drug Paul is using, so the night wasn't entirely wasted. Come on, girls, let's go home. Tomorrow is another day."

Once inside his flat, Lachlan exploded. He threw a chair across the room; it bounced and hit a vase, which in turn smashed, and a small piece of glass flew up and stuck in his leg.

"Bitch! What a bitch!, Now look what she's done! I could kill her right now. You're just a bloody, rotten bitch, and like all of them, you need to die."

It was here he remembered where he was. *Damn, did anyone heard me during my tirade?* All seemed quiet, so he believed he hadn't been overheard. He took the medicine bottle out of the fridge and poured the prescribed dose; after a few moments he felt calmer. He then mumbled to himself and removed the glass from his leg, putting a piece of tape over the cut to stop it bleeding.

Rachel was unaware of the dramatic night. She had waited for Jan to arrive for their promised dinner, and her absence could only mean one thing: duty must have called her. Rachel decided that going to bed early with a good book was the best idea. After taking a shower, she slipped between the sheets and began to read. A steady knocking at her door interrupted her reading.

"Who is it?"

"Only me, Rach," Jan said. "Sorry it's so late, but you know police work."

"Come in. By the look on your face, it hasn't been a good day."

"Can I be frank? It's been a bastard of a day and evening."

"Got time for coffee?"

"You bet—hot and black."

Sitting at the table, the two women talked for a long time. Jan told of the fiasco regarding Lachlan, and her disgust for the two officers who followed the wrong car.

"We almost blew it, Rach."

"But you didn't, did you?"

"No, but . . ."

"No buts, Jan. You know where his next target lives, he is being watched by the three officers at his flat, and John is becoming friendly with this degenerate. Am I right?"

"As always, your words make me feel better, and yes, you are right, it will be better in the morning."

"That's my Jan. Keep your chin up."

"I will, and now I must leave. Have to be up early."

"Is anyone expecting you?"

"No, I live alone."

"Well, use my spare room. I'll wake you when I leave for work."

"Thanks, Rach."

Rachel showed Jan the room, went to a drawer, pulled out some pyjamas, and offered them to her.

"Don't need them, Rach—I like to sleep naked," Jan said.

"If you say so, it's all right with me."

Both women made their way to their respective rooms. Jan was asleep almost as her head hit the pillow. For Rachel it was not so easy. Thoughts of Jan filled her head: how she did her job, her no-nonsense attitude, but also had a sweet feminine side.

Rachel loved this side of her, and the way she could empathize with the women who had suffered. It was as if she knew what they were thinking. She had watched as Clarisse entered the hospital, and Jan stayed until the sedative soothed the torment. Even then, Jan kept her promise to stay until Clarisse woke and then let her know why she had to leave. Yes, she was one great police officer and was becoming a very good friend.

On waking, Jan made her way to the station. She needed to find out where it all went wrong the previous night. Kelly and Mary were already there, and after the usual greetings, the three officers walked to the squad room.

"Now, let's look at the operation as a whole. What went wrong and why?"

Kelly said, "Listen, Jan, just because we didn't pick up the rat, we do know more today than yesterday. Don't we?"

"Yes, we do, but I want more. I want *him*."

Mary asked, "How did John feel when Paul returned? I bet he was dumbfounded."

Jan said, "That is the biggest understatement of the year: he couldn't believe his eyes."

"Has the sample of the medicine been sent to the lab?" Kelly asked.

Mary stated, "Yes, it has; we should know soon what it is and what it treats."

"I stayed at Rachel's place last night," Jan said. "Didn't want to be alone. She is an all right lady, don't you think?"

"Yes, she is. Her interest in the case is great, and it's always nice to have a medico in our line of work."

"Well, I'm going to my office; I need to make sense of last night and where we go from here. Can you both write up statements about it for me, please?"

"You bet. See you later, boss."

John dressed for his jog around the complex. After leaving the flat, he walked to the stairs. He was hoping Lachlan would join him, and he had to know what had happened the night before.

A voice came from behind him. "Hey, John, hold up, mate."

"Oh, it's you, Paul. Thought you weren't coming. Let's go."

They didn't talk much as they jogged, but John felt Lachlan wanted to tell him something. The silence was electric until Lachlan spoke.

"Let's sit for a while. I can't talk when I'm jogging."

"Okay, mate."

Both men sat on the bench, wiped the sweat from their faces, and began to talk of the preceding evening.

"I've found a great girl. I had dinner with her last night."

"What's she like?" John asked.

"She's a beauty, but the night was stuffed up. One of her male friends dropped in unexpectedly, so I had to share her for the evening."

"You sound pissed."

"I had plans for the night, and he destroyed them, so yes, you could say I'm pissed."

"Don't be like that," John said. "There's always next time. Just imagine the fun you and she can have then."

"Oh yes, it will be fun, I assure you."

John did not like the look in Lachlan's eyes. There was a hint of madness in them, and his demeanour spoke volumes. John was becoming afraid for the woman. *I think he means to kill her—I'm sure of it.* He turned away so Lachlan would not see the look of disgust in his eyes. "You sound as if you are going to do something out of the ordinary?" he said.

"Oh, you can rely on that. We have a date in a week, and everything will happen then."

"As much as I like to talk, I have to go to work. See you tonight, okay?"

"Okay, John, see you then."

John entered his flat, leant against the door, and placed his head in his hands. "He's mad. Something must be done, and quickly, or we are going to have a dead woman on our hands."

Changing into his ordinary clothes, he went down to his car and headed for the restaurant where he had arranged to meet Jan.

"God damn it, Jan. We have to get this guy. He's nuts, and I mean it."

"What's happened, John? Tell me."

"While jogging, he talked about a woman from last night. I believe he means to kill her. If you could have seen the look in his eyes . . . We have to do something, and fast."

"I hear you, John, but you know we can only get him while the attack is happening."

"What the hell do we have to wait for?"

"I want this degenerate so bad, do you think it's easy for me? Time is of the essence. Did he tell you when he would see this woman again?"

"Yes, he said a week."

"Well, that's your job: stay close to him. If he says he's going out, try to invite yourself. If that doesn't work, let me know, and we will have a car follow him. I can't express enough how urgent this is. Please come through for me, mate."

"I'll do my best, but it's hard. All I want to do is arrest him and put him where he belongs."

"I know the feeling, but we both should get back to our respective duties. By the way, what do think about a promotion to my squad?"

"You mean that? Boy, that would be great!"

"I'll see you later, then."

Early the next morning, Clarisse and Jackson told her parents about the plan for the wedding. "We would like it to be here so all our friends and family can attend, and then we can have our honeymoon on the island where we met. We think it's the right choice for us.

"You haven't asked me yet," her father said.

"Oh, Dad, always the joker, aren't you?"

"Of course, love. Your mother and I are thrilled. Wherever you have the wedding is fine with us."

Breakfast was a happy one; the four people at the table talked and laughed as they ate. Clarisse's life had certainly turned the corner from despair to happiness. There were still scars, but with all the love around her, they would fade.

"Oh, by the way, Mum, we are going to see if I have to wait for the trial."

"Surely not—they haven't even caught him yet."

"We know that, but we must ask."

Waving a happy goodbye, Jackson and Clarisse set off for the police station. On arrival, they joked as they entered the station.

"Hello, Constable, can you tell me where I can find Jan?"

"She's in her office; I'll let her know you're coming."

As they walked toward her office, Clarisse told Jackson how wonderful Jan had been.

"She has been kindness itself. Her job is her life, and she is able to use forward thinking and stay one jump ahead of the game." She knocked.

"Hi, Jan, is this a good time to come calling?"

"Any time is good time when it is one of my favourite people." Jan said. She looked up in amazement as Jackson entered her office, and then a broad grin crossed her face. "So this is your Jackson."

"Do you know him already?"

"I sure do. Say hello to one of my cousins."

Clarisse was shocked. "Your cousin? Really?"

"Yes. If only I'd known before. Now I know why you loved this Jackson so much. How's the job with the federal police going?"

"Remember Clarisse I mentioned it when I first arrived, sorry I didn't tell you before, but security and all that."

Clarisse said, "Jackson and I have some questions to ask you, Jan, but maybe we can discuss them during dinner at home."

"I couldn't think of anything better. I'm busy now with the case, but I'll see you tonight."

"Okay, Jan, we'll see you then."

As soon as they had gone, Jan rang Rachel, letting her know about the latest news on Jackson and Clarisse. "I couldn't believe my eyes when they walked into my office. One of my cousins is Clarisse's Jackson!"

"A great surprise, I would say. They are due here soon, and Jackson wants to know how he can help with her rehabilitation."

"He's a good man, Rach, and he loves her very much. It might have taken time, but he's made up his mind now."

"I have to go, Jan," Rachel said. "They've just walked in." She hung up and addressed the couple. "Hello, you two. Jan just told me the news, but I can still congratulate you both and tell you how happy I am."

Clarisse replied, "It was quite a shock to find that my Jackson was Jan's cousin, but when I think about it, they are alike, don't you think?"

"Yes, they are."

"Enough about my cousin, you two. I want to know all about Clarisse's injuries and how I can help her, both mentally and physically," Jackson said.

"You believe in getting straight to the point, don't you? Well I believe with your love and understanding, Clarisse will make a complete physical recovery, but the mental scars may take a little longer. Since your arrival she has faced most of her demons and has handled them extremely well."

"Thank you, Rachel. I can call you that?" Jackson asked.

"Yes, of course, Jackson. Now, let's go to the canteen for lunch and a chat."

Clarisse said, "Yes, let's do that. And by the way, Jan is coming for dinner tonight at my house. Will you come as well?"

"Barring unforeseen circumstances, Clarisse, I would love to."

Alicia let her mind return to the evening with Paul and Kyle, but it was Paul she thought about the most: how handsome he was, the way he dressed, and how he was so courteous to Kyle. He could have been angry, but he just took it in his stride. With this in mind, she found herself looking forward to their date on Wednesday. She thought about the meal and what she would cook for dinner. Perhaps a stir-fry; it was always well received by a guest. What would she wear? Something daring, to catch his eye? All of these thoughts brought her pleasure. *Such a handsome man, and he has chosen me. This date will be special.*

CHAPTER EIGHT

LACHLAN ALSO HAD HIS MIND on the coming date with Alicia. He didn't think anyone he knew was aware of her address, so this would be the best place for their union. With what he had learned about sadism, from the books he had read and his own style of giving pain, the anticipation made him tremble with excitement. He must control himself—the internal injuries must be as bad as the external. He could use any implement he wanted, but the beating beforehand was the part of the attack he enjoyed most. The crushing internal injuries had to have a lasting effect and remain long after the bruises had gone. Some people would say he was mad, but was he? He laughed, cried, and loved just as other people did.

He then began to think of Clarisse again. He was ready to bet she was finished as far as men were concerned. What man would look at her now? He would have liked to inflict more pain, but she had stopped fighting. He now knew that he had to keep them conscious, and then they would feel pain for the whole time. As he thought this, he chuckled to himself. Wednesday was just a few days away; this is when his fun would begin.

A sharp knock on his door interrupted his thoughts, and he jumped to his feet. The chair clattered over onto the floor.

"You okay, Paul?"

"Yes, John. You startled me, that's all."

"Are you busy? It's just that I am going for a jog and hoped you might join me."

"Not just now. I have a headache and am going to lie down."

"Okay, mate, I'll see you later."

John walked back to the flat. Julie and Mia were about to go to the station for further orders.

John said, "Can you stay here, Mia? I need to see Jan."

"Sure. Some new developments about our man?"

"Yes, there is."

John pulled up at the station and went straight to Jan's office. He knocked lightly before entering.

"Hi, John, anything new at the flats?"

"No. Have the results for the substance from his flat come back?"

"Not yet, but probably later today. Tell me what's on your mind," Jan said.

"He's really insane. We must watch him all the time. I believe the next time he goes out, he will kill."

"I tend to agree with you, but where should we watch? The number of cars is limited."

"My thoughts are that he will go back to the girl's place. It's the perfect place for an attack."

"Why do you say that?"

"Well, it's on a main road with lots of traffic noise, and it's in a high-profile suburb. Even if people heard the noise, they would assume it was from a party nearby.

"Bloody brilliant. We need only to have one car somewhere near her home. This would mean only one officer on watch, probably four-hour watches. In our job, we need to cover all our bases."

"You don't think it will be that easy?" John said.

"No, I don't, but we have to look at all scenarios. You will learn this as you progress in the unit."

"Will the chief go for a stake out anyway?"

"Yes, Constable, I will. Clever little bloke, isn't he, Jan?"

"Yes, sir, he is."

"Make all the arrangements, Jan, and then show me your plan."

"Yes, sir, I'll do that."

With that, the chief of detectives left the office, leaving Jan and John to talk about his idea, which officers they would use, and where and when to put the plans into action. It would need to be soon because John was convinced Paul was ready to attack.

John felt at home talking to Jan; she didn't make him feel inferior, and she listened to his ideas and gave them credence. He liked being in the crisis team, and as the only male, he hadn't felt out of place. He knew there would be times when he would need to stay away. Women who were terribly hurt and traumatized would only want female personnel around.

Jan called Mary and Kelly into the office; they all stood around the table and laid out the plans. "What's he doing here Jan; he isn't part of the team?" Kelly asked.

"John has developed a good rapport with our suspect and has an idea about when and where Paul will strike next. Sorry I didn't tell you before, but I feel he will make a positive addition to our team."

"Why?"

"I won't answer that now, the decision has been made, and I would appreciate your loyalty."

John said, "I'll leave if I am not wanted, Jan."

"No you won't, John—you are here to stay. Now, let's get on with the job."

The four officers looked at each other and nodded. They began working on the most appropriate steps to deal with John's plan.

"We will have to cover the roads around the flats and have a car outside the woman's home. I think three officers to staff that car, plus us as backup for any unexpected scenarios that might arise."

Kelly asked, "Do we know where he will strike?"

"Not really, but John has befriended him, and he will try to find out when and where he might strike. Mary, I'm putting John in your capable hands. We must get to the woman quickly—it will be your job to keep her calm. John will grab him and handcuff the sod."

"How will we know where he is and who he's going to attack?" Kelly asked.

Jan glared at her. "I've already told you that, Kelly. For God's sake, listen, will you?"

"Sorry, Jan. I'm still coming to terms with John joining the unit."

"Get over it. John, go back to the flat and try to engage Lachlan in a conversation. Try to find out if what you suspect is right."

"Okay, ma'am. See you."

As John left, he knew he would be the topic of conversation. The other two women on the team were not happy.

"Well, team, let's get to work. We will use John's idea as a benchmark. He believes Paul will attack the woman at her home. We have only two days to prepare—I know that because of John's information. He has knowledge of the criminal mind, and that is rare. His work getting to know the target, and the ability to know when a person is lying or hiding details of himself, is exceptional."

Later, Jan was working in her office when a frantic call came in from John.

"It's tomorrow night!"

"That soon?"

"Yes. I've been jogging with Paul. He's having dinner with the girl tomorrow night. We have to move fast."

"Good job, John. Just stay where you are. We will start the planning here."

"Okay, ma'am, I'll see you later."

"John, you don't have to call me ma'am anymore."

"I don't? Well, okay."

Jan hung up and addressed her officers. "Well, girls, this is it. The date is tomorrow night at the address from last week. We can't proceed on the assumption that the attack will come on his first date alone with this woman. We all know he has graduated from the outright attack; he now likes to play the game, just as he did with Clarisse. Mary, get close and hold John's enthusiasm in check. He will want to grab him right away. If, as I suspect, it will be the first date, we must wait, but if there is any hint of violence or noise, get in fast. Kelly, you will be with me. We will stake out the flats; everyone will have a radio, and if it is necessary for any one team to act, we all will. The two officers at the flat will remain indoors on call. I will ask the Chief for two more people; they will be parked a little way from Mary and John as backup."

John sat in the flat, his heart pounding. *The time is here, and soon we will have this bloody lunatic in custody.* He felt good about his promotion to the squad, though his fellow officers couldn't understand why he wanted to work in the sexual assault team. To John it was the ultimate sign of trust: the work he had done, getting Paul to trust him, filled him with a sense of achievement. He could now study psychology, which would help him understand the trauma a person felt after such an attack.

His manner henceforth would let the victim know he understood and would be able to accept him, without fear. Here lied the challenge: traumatized people needed just that—a safe environment to heal, and people they trusted near them. This was what he aspired to in the future.

Jan left the station to see Rachel, bringing her up to date with the case. Rachel's work and care for all the victims made her part of the team. Upon entering the hospital, Jan observed the doctor wasn't in her office. She asked a staff member, who pointed to the dining room. Jan could see Rachel sitting alone, eating her lunch. For the first time Jan really looked at her, and in doing so, she wondered why she hadn't married.

At that moment, Rachel looked up, saw Jan, and motioned her over to the table. Jan sat down and relayed the latest news.

"We may have him, Rach."

"Oh, Jan! Are you really that close?"

"Yes, we are. The meeting for his capture is tomorrow night."

"Will you nab him then, or wait until he attacks, as he did with Clarisse?"

"That will depend. I will have two officers very close, and Kelly and I will be the backup. We will move in when we hear any noise of an alarming nature."

"Give him to me for a few moments, Jan. It would be my pleasure to slap the creep around a little," Rachel said with a gleam in her eye.

"I am having trouble keeping all this from Jackson. If he gets a sniff, God help him."

"He is a nice bloke, your cousin. I particularly like the way he treats Clarisse. He has lifted her spirits and made her feel human again. When I look at them, the love just flows. They don't hide their emotions, do they?"

"I'm biased, but he *is* a nice bloke. I nearly fell over when I realized Clarisse's Jackson was my cousin. I'm sorry, Rach, but I must get back to work—there's a lot to do before tomorrow night."

"Go to it, Jan. I look forward to his downfall. By the way, the result from the flat is in. It's only a sedative that controls the symptoms of psychosis."

Jan returned to the station. She remembered her thoughts about Rachel's marital status and it teased her, but there was no answer. She walked into the squad room and acknowledged the members of the team, both old and new.

"We need to finalize our plans for tomorrow night."

"Yes, ma'am," they replied.

While the team put together all the action for the arrest, Flora was busy deciding what to cook for the evening meal. There was quite a cross section of people coming; Jackson and Clarisse wouldn't be any trouble, but what would Jan and Rachel like? She decided to ring Rachel and ask.

"Hi, Rachel, its Flora. Can you tell me what you and Jan would like for dinner tonight?"

"Hi, Flora. Well, what about the universal favourite, a good roast?"

"That sounds about right. Yes, that's what I'll cook. Bye for now."

Jan had finished all the plans for the following evening, allocating different job to the police officers. Having finished all she had to do, she picked up the phone and rang Rachel.

"Hi, Rach, do you want me to pick you up tonight?"

"Yes, thanks, Jan. What time will you be here?"

"Give me fifteen minutes."

"Okay, see you then."

Jan picked Rachel up, and they drove to the Stewart home.

Flora greeted them at the door. "Hi, you two. I'm so glad you could come. Everyone's here and waiting in the dining room."

"Thanks, Flora."

Clarisse went to greet Jan and Rachel, and during this time Jackson and Earnest were alone.

"I bought a ring today," Jackson said. "Can you tell me if Clarisse will like it?"

"It is a lovely ring; I'm sure she will love it. But why ask me, Jackson? You should have shown it to Flora—she has a better eye for such things."

"I did it this way because you and Clarisse are close—plus I need to suck up a little, don't I?"

The two men were laughing as the women walked into the room. "What's the joke?" Jan asked.

"Nothing, just a male joke, is all."

"I bet, knowing Jackson, it probably wasn't quite right for the female ear."

Everyone took their seats at the table; the food, presented in self-serve dishes, looked delicious. The group enjoyed a great meal and friendly banter.

Jan said, "This all looks and smells so good! You are a great cook, Flora."

"Thanks, Jan, but the proof is in the eating, so let's tuck in."

The meal started, and so did the banter around the table. Jan gave a small hint about the following night, no one quizzed her, and the happy chat continued. Rachel gave an opinion for when they caught the perpetrator. Jackson also had his own ideas about him, but with each word spoken, Clarisse became paler, being unable to bear any more.

She spoke in a loud voice. "Do we have to talk about him? I want to forget he exists. Please, can we change the subject?"

Everyone stopped and looked at Clarisse. They could see she was visibly upset. Her face was a picture of agony and fear.

Flora said, "Oh, my dear, I'm so sorry. Of course, consider it done."

"Thanks, all of you. I know I'm a pain, but the less I hear about him, the better I feel."

Everyone stopped talking about the case at Clarisse's request. During the lull in the conversation, Jackson took Clarisse's hand and stood up.

"As you all know, Clarisse and I met over a year ago on holiday. It took a long time for me to realize I loved her. When I was sure of my feelings, I decided to come here and find her. Now I am taking it further by asking Clarisse to be my wife. We have spoken about it before, but tonight it is official. My dear Clarisse, will you marry me?"

"Oh, Jackson, I love you, and of course I'll marry you!"

Jackson took a small box out of his pocket. Then, holding her hand, he placed a sparkling diamond ring on her finger.

"It is so beautiful!" she said.

Everyone at the table wished the couple good luck. Jan and Rachel kissed them both, and Flora and Earnest admired his strength and the love he had for their daughter. They knew he would always look after her. Love and goodwill filled the room while two people who loved each other kissed to seal their love.

Earnest then remembered they had a bottle of champagne, and he left the room and returned with bottle and glasses. After filling each glass he said, "Please be upstanding and drink a toast to Clarisse and Jackson." All those present stood as one for the toast. "Clarisse and Jackson, may your love and life always be blessed."

The evening flowed as the happy party talked about every subject. Everyone enjoyed a wonderful evening, and there was no hint of what was just over the horizon—an event that would test them all to the limit.

John had walked down the hallway to visit Lachlan; he knocked but received no answer, and he wondered where the rapist had gone. *The film should be able to tell me what time he went out.* He played the film through and discovered Lachlan had left very early that morning carrying a small bag. Where was he going, and why the bag? Maybe he was visiting a friend. John then noticed the logbook, and to his surprise no entry made for the time, he left. Walking to one of the bedrooms, he knocked and waited for an answer. A sleepy voice called from the room.

"What?"

"Do you realize what time it is? You were meant to be on duty."

"Oh damn, is it very late?"

"It sure is—you've missed Lachlan leaving the block!"

"I'll be right out."

The door opened. Julie looked at John and knew instantly she was in trouble.

"Please don't tell Jan. I'm so sorry, and it won't happen again."

"No, I can't do that."

"Why not, John? I'm really sorry."

"You let the team down, and I have to tell Jan."

Tearfully Julie returned to her room, dressed, and made ready for her shift. She was angry with herself. While dressing she thought about the consequences—she had to tell Jan. Having made the decision, she finished dressing, took up station at the window, and began her shift.

John had made toast for them, and they sat and ate their breakfast in silence, after which John left the flat to see if Lachlan had returned home. After he left, Julie rang Jan.

"Hello, ma'am, it's Julie. I overslept this morning and missed my shift."

"What! Does John know?"

"Yes, he does."

"Stay at your post; I will be over later. We will speak about it then."

Jan, Kelly, and Mary were engrossed in all the evidence they had collected during the case. They knew they had enough circumstantial evidence to gain a conviction, but they did not feel it was enough—they needed to catch him just before or during an attack. Jan had told them of Clarisse's reaction the previous evening.

"She actually shivered when we spoke of him. I don't want her pushed too far—we need her testimony."

"Has she become hesitant?" Kelly asked.

"Yes, she has. I don't think she would admit it, but she is still suffering from the horror of the rape. Jackson has made a difference, but he can only reassure her so much. The mind is a tricky thing, and Clarisse's mind is still very troubled."

"Do you think any of the others would testify?" Mary asked.

"We can hope, Mary, but they haven't shown any enthusiasm to date."

"I wish they would; it sure would make our job easier."

"We have to remember that they have also been traumatized, and this is what makes rape cases so hard to prosecute. Rapists know this; it is only when they are caught in the act that a conviction is certain."

"Bloody hell, Jan, why did we decide to work in this section? All the others are somewhat easier."

"Now, both of you, we took on the rape crisis unit because we wanted to make a difference, and we have done so. You are both fine officers, and I couldn't do without you, so just hang in there. Soon it will be our turn to gloat, when he faces court and is put away for many years. We will be the winners, so chin up—our turn is coming. Now, I must go to the flat; a young officer has messed up our surveillance by oversleeping, and our perpetrator has gone."

"Oh no! Do we have any idea where he has gone?"

"No, we don't. Now we are blind until he returns. I must go—see you both later."

CHAPTER NINE

A S HE LEFT THE BLOCK, Lachlan looked up to John's window. Seeing no one, he got into his car as he drove off, thinking. "Maybe I should have knocked on his door, and then I would have his company for the journey."

Pushing that feeling aside, he drove on. His destination was a small town close to the city; his mother lived there, and he wanted to see her. It only took half an hour to reach the town. Pulling up outside his mum's house, he left the car and walked to the door. He walked in without knocking. His mum was sitting at the table; a man was sitting there with her.

"Who the bloody hell are you?"

"Don't be like that, Lachlan. He lives here now, and I'm not so lonely."

"I wasn't talking to you, Mum. Can't he answer for himself?"

The man said, "My name is George, and what your mother does is no concern of yours."

"Is that so? Mum, tell him to go. I want to talk to you."

"No, son, I won't. He is here to stay, and if you object, then that's too bad."

"So that's how it is? I am leaving so you can fornicate with your lover like a prostitute. Rest assured, I won't be back."

With that he walked to his car and set off for home, his thoughts awhirl. How could she betray him like this? Of all the women in the world, he believed his mum to be above all the sinful lusts of the flesh. His anger grew as he drove, and then there in the distance he saw a woman just walking on the road with long black hair, a slim figure, and dressed in jeans. Stopping, he leaned across the passenger seat and asked if she wanted a lift.

Looking into the car, the young woman liked what she saw. This was her biggest mistake as she answered, "You bet! Thanks for stopping. How far are you going?"

"Back to the city, but I have a stop to make. I have my eye on a block of land and just need to see it again before I make the deal. By the way, my name is Paul."

"That's fine—I'm just grateful for the lift. My name is Sandy."

He couldn't believe his luck. Here she was, and grateful to be in his car! His mind spun with ideas of what he would do. At a crossroad, he turned left. He knew he had to keep up the charade. In the distance, he saw a sign advertising land for sale.

"This is the place! I won't be long." Walking into the bush, he decided this was the place to attack and not be heard. "Can I ask you a favour?"

"Sure, what do you want?"

"There are two blocks; they intersect at the corner, and I would like you opinion as to which is the best."

Without a second's thought, she followed him into the bush. After they had walked for some time, she asked, "Is it much farther?" A blow from behind sent her hurtling forward into unconsciousness. Paul made sure she wouldn't wake before he returned; he walked back to the car, retrieved a small bag, and then made his way back to the woman. He looked for a perfect place to live out his fantasy. Taking three pieces of rope, he tied them to tree trunks, and then he carried her and placed her in such a way that he could tie both hands to one rope, then each foot to the others. This left her spread-eagled with her hands pulled tightly, making it impossible for her to move. He then sat and waited for her to wake up; he couldn't do anything until she woke. He hoped she would fight him—she looked the type with quite a muscular body.

Slowly Sandy regained consciousness and looked around her. Through the haze she saw him. "What's going on? Is this some kind of a joke?"

"There's no joke here. Don't try to move—you can't. I need to satisfy my sexual needs, and you're going to provide it."

"No, please! Don't hurt me! If you let me go now, I won't tell anyone. Please! What have I done to you?"

"Hurt you? Yes, I am going to hurt you. You will beg for release before I've finished."

Sandy tried to free herself from the ropes, She twisted and turned, all the while cursing him. She felt like a caged animal, one that had no way of freeing itself.

He came close to her face, as if to kiss her, and she tried to bite him. Slowly but surely, she was doing all the things that triggered his psychotic urges. He toyed with her before starting to rip the clothing from her body.

"Don't, please don't! I'll do anything you want, just don't rape me!"

"Sorry, darling, this is going to be much more than just rape."

It was then that Sandy thought he meant to kill her. If this was so, was there anything to gain by fighting him? She closed her eyes and turned her face away from him. She fought back tears as he continued to rip her clothes away. Soon she lay naked under his gaze.

"Now, fight me, bitch, or you will die in the most horrible way."

"You're going to kill me anyway, so why fight?"

"I'm not going to kill you. Where did you get that idea?"

"You said this was more than rape, didn't you?"

"Yes, but I didn't intend to kill you. If you don't fight me, though, I just might."

Lachlan became so excited. She was a fighter, as he thought. Each time he hit her, she struggled and spat at him.

She was in a great deal of pain, and it seemed to be everywhere. Then she felt a sharp object he forced into her; the first thrust almost sent her into unconsciousness. The pain was excruciating, and she screamed and her body shuddered. Her screams went unheard as they echoed in the stillness. The pain deep inside her, was like fire, and with each thrust it threatened to consume her.

"Stop, please stop! I can't take any more," Sandy screamed.

Silence was her only answer. Another deep thrust sent her tumbling over the edge, and she could no longer fight. The sky turned black, and the pain came from her very being. Blackness claimed her, giving her the relief she so sorely needed.

After regaining consciousness, she had no idea of how long she had been in the pain-filled stupor. The ropes still held her, but she was able to look around. She couldn't see him anywhere and hoped he was gone.

Sandy pulled at the ropes that tied her hands; with each pull, it became slacker. Finally, she was able to free her hands, and then she tried to sit up. Pain racked her body, and again she almost fainted. Gathering all her strength, she pushed with her hands until finally she was able to sit upright. Pain was her companion and threatened to hurl her back into unconsciousness. Knowing this, she had to work through the pain to free her legs. After what seemed forever, she was free. Her clothes were still there, torn but still a cover for her naked, bloody, and bruised body. Rising to her feet, she wrapped the torn clothing around herself. Each movement sent sharp pains all over her body, and she almost fainted with each step, but she continued.

After reaching the road, she could see that her tormentor's car was gone. She looked in both directions, fearing he might still be watching. Sandy started to walk. She couldn't see any houses, but even so she kept on, and each step was agony. As she walked, the sound of a car reached her. Fright sent her into hiding at first, but then she made her way back to the road. She had to find help, so she bravely took the risk. The car stopped, and a woman came over to her, shocked at Sandy's state. She turned and retrieved a blanket from her car, and wrapped it around Sandy's shoulders.

"Oh, my dear girl, who are you, and who did this to you?"

"It's my fault I got into his car didn't I, my name is Sandy."

"No, it isn't your fault. The man who did this to you must be an absolute animal. Let's not talk about that now. I must get you home and ring an ambulance."

Sandy was too sick to reply; she accepted the help meekly. There was only one thought in her mind: get to a hospital and her mum. Arriving at her home, she helped her inside and called the ambulance and police. It would take time for them to arrive, so she made Sandy as comfortable as she could and made her a cup of tea. Sandy lay on a couch, her lips were so sore she could only sip the contents of the cup slowly.

"Can I have a bath? I feel all dirty; a bath would sooth my body."

"No, my dear, you can't do that. The paramedics said you must wait, by the way my name is Caroline."

The wail of a siren cut through the pain. Sandy knew it was the ambulance, and she at last felt safe, even though her attacker must be far away by now.

The paramedics lifted Sandy onto the stretcher and placed her in the ambulance. One of them recognized the MO, and he asked his partner, "Remember the flyer that was sent to us from head office? You know the one about the serial rapist?"

"Yeah, sure. Do you think it could be him?"

"It has all the characteristics of his work. We should ring the city police and find out. If it is him, we may need to take her to the city hospital."

"What a mongrel. He might as well have killed her; she is so close to it."

They rang the city police and explained to the officer the circumstances of the rape.

"Bring her to the city hospital," the officer said.

Jan was in the office when the phone call came. She listened to the paramedic tell his story, and she was convinced it was the work of their suspect. Her next task was to ring Rachel—she needed her to be there when the ambulance arrived.

"Hello, this is Dr Ford."

"It's me, Rach. He's done it again, and from what I hear, this woman is close to death. Where did we go wrong? We should have caught him."

"Don't be too hard on yourself, Jan. Where did it happen?"

"Somewhere out in the country."

"In the country? Why would he be there?"

"Don't know, Rach, but they say the attack follows his MO to the letter but more violent. I must go now—I will be at the hospital soon."

After putting the phone down, Jan sat for a time, her mind could not comprehend this latest attack. Why in the country? Where was he going? What had gone wrong? Coming to her senses, she drove to the hospital. Rachel was waiting for her, and both waited for the ambulance to arrive.

They heard the ambulance in the distance, and it was only a short time before it drove into the bay. The paramedic stepped out and acknowledged the two women waiting. "Who is the doctor?"

"I am Dr Ford."

"She is in a bad way, Doc. If I were you, I'd get in there quick."

Rachel did exactly that, and after climbing into the back of the ambulance, she was appalled at what she saw. Sandy's condition was indeed grave. Rachel felt it necessary to sit down and gain her composure, and then called to her waiting staff. "Take her straight to intensive care, and quickly."

"Okay, Doc."

Jan could see how badly beaten the woman was, but there were injuries she could not see and could only imagine. Rachel's tone let her know it would be touch and go for this young woman. Jan turned to the paramedics and motioned them over. "How bad is she?"

"Worst I've ever seen. It was lucky the woman found her; she was on a side road that's not used much."

"Can you give me her name and address? I will need to talk to her: where and how she found the woman will be important."

"Everything is written down in our log; you can copy it all from there."

"Very good. It seems you thought of everything. Now, which ambulance service are you from?"

"Laton. It's a small town about half an hour from the city."

"What made you ring us before taking her to your local hospital?"

"We had a flyer sent to us about a serial rapist; it gave full details of his MO, and this attack fit them all, so we decided to bring her here."

"Thank you so much for your care of the young woman, and also for your observations and knowledge. I feel your actions will save her life."

"We must get back to Laton, just in case there is an accident or emergency."

"Once again, my grateful thanks. We may need you if we get this animal to trial. I can only hope it is soon."

"We'll see you then."

With that the ambulance drove off. Jan entered the hospital to wait for Rachel. While waiting, she rang Kelly and Mary, asking them to join her. That done, all she could do was wait. She knew Rachel would do everything necessary and keep all the evidence intact for court.

It seemed an age until Kelly and Mary arrived. When they did, all three sat in the café. Jan ordered coffee for them all, and they sat in silence. Jan didn't talk for a while; the others could see she was extremely upset, and her eyes told a story of failure and disappointment. Finally, in a stunned voice she asked.

"How did this happen? Why was it so late after he had left the flat?"

"We don't know but will find out. Do you want us to go and ask the officers at the flat?"

"No, not now. I need you to visit the woman who found Sandy. From there, get her to show you the crime scene, and tape everything off ready for forensics; they will need it undisturbed. Stay with them and phone me as soon as you have anything to report. The woman's name is Caroline." Jan gave them the woman's address. "It isn't far from there to the crime scene. Is that clear? Don't let me down—we need all the evidence we can get, and we have to arrest this merciless bastard. I will stay here until I can see the poor girl. Damn, this bastard makes me sick. Why can't we catch him? How can he do this? It seems he just slips away all the time."

"You can't blame yourself," Kelly said.

"Can't I? this time I'm not going to wait. He has raped and beaten his last woman. I'll arrest him after I have talked to Sandy. I say this in the hopes she will survive and isn't too badly traumatized by the viciousness of the attack."

The two officers collected their gear, and after saying goodbye, they left to carry out Jan's orders.

Jan waited for Rachel to come and give her the report on Sandy's injuries. It seemed hours before she came. She beckoned Jan to follow her, and they talked as they walked to Rachel's office.

As Kelly drove, she voiced her disgust at the rapist. "What an animal this bloke is!, I can't wait for the day when we catch him."

"You and me both, Kel, I wonder if this poor woman is going to make it?" Mary said.

"With Rachel as her doctor, she has every chance. Did you see her?"

"No, but everyone there looked very grim. They said it was worse than Clarisse, so it must be bad."

The conversation ended as they drove, each with their own thoughts and feelings about this latest case.

Back at the flat, John had watched Lachlan return, and he noticed his flushed face and dishevelled appearance. *Where has he been? He's been gone quite some time. Must have left very early.* Unfortunately, John did not know the exact time. He decided to ring Jan to let her know Lachlan's time of arrival and his appearance. He rang Jan's personal phone; strangely, there was no answer, so he rang the station.

"Duty Constable here. How can I help you?"

"It's John from the rape crisis team. Can you tell me where Jan is?"

"She is at the hospital; you should be able to contact her there."

"Thanks mate. Catch you later."

Why is Jan at the hospital? What had happened? It was then he remembered Lachlan's flushed and dishevelled appearance. *Has he attacked again? Should I ring the hospital? Yes, I'll do that.* She picked up the phone and rang the hospital.

"Mercy Hospital here. How can I help you?"

"I am an officer from the rape crisis team. Is there any chance of me speaking to D-I Hasting?"

"Oh yes, she is with the doctor now. They are discussing a patient who came in this afternoon."

"Would it be possible for me to speak to her? It is quite urgent."

"Not at the moment—they are very busy."

"How bad is the patient?"

"Very bad. That's all I can say."

"Thanks. I'll call later."

John sat with his own thoughts. He looked out of the window with a blank stare. As if stung, he jumped to his feet, opened the door, walked down the passage to Lachlan's door, and stood just looking at it for a time. Then he knocked.

"Who is it? Just go away—I'm busy," Lachlan said.

"It's John. Can I come in?"

"No, are you deaf? I said no! Just go and leave me alone."

Put out by the tone in Lachlan's voice, John turned and walked back to his flat. Just as he opened the door, the phone rang. He reached out and picked it up.

"Is that you, John? I want to speak to John."

"Yes, I'm John. What do you want?"

"What time did your jogging mate go out this morning?"

"I don't have to answer that. Who in blazes do you think you are?"

"Just an interested party. Just answer my question?"

John slammed the phone down angrily. *Some people. Just who do they think they are?* Yes, he was the keeper and had failed on this day. Why didn't he get here earlier? If he had, would the newest attack have happened? He had relied on a colleague. *This is my fault, not hers.* Who ever it was, the depraved individual down the hall had brutally raped another woman.

As he was blaming himself, the phone rang again. He stared at it for a time and then lifted it out of its cradle.

"Hello, this is John. What can I do for you?"

"It's Jan. Do you know if Lachlan is at home?"

"Yes, he is. I just came back from his flat; he wouldn't let me in. Then somebody rang me and asked if he was home and where he had been. I just hung up."

"I know about the non-entry in the log John, Julie came and told me. Do you know what time he got home?"

"He pulled into the car park about an hour ago."

"How did he look to you?"

"He was flushed and quite dishevelled. Why?"

"We are thinking of arresting him, so don't let him leave under any circumstances."

"My pleasure, Jan. How is the woman who was attacked?"

"It will be quite a while before we can question her, if ever. Don't leave the unit, and make sure he doesn't leave, either. I will be over in an hour, and we will know our course of action by then. The poor young girl has been beaten and raped so savagely that she is very close to death. Never in my career have I ever seen anything like it. Don't let him leave."

"I promise I will knock on his door every so often, just to make sure he is still there. There's a chance he will let me in, and then I can watch him firsthand."

"You do that. We must get him this time. Was he carrying anything when he went to his flat?"

"Yes, he had a small bag. Is it important?"

"It could be. Just stay there, and I will see you soon."

Jackson placed the phone back in its cradle; he was feeling stupid about his phone call to John. He wanted to be involved in the case, not only for Clarisse but also for Lachlan's latest victim. He would apologize to Jan, who had trusted him with the information. Walking into the kitchen, he made a pot of tea for himself and Clarisse. Earnest and Flora had gone out leaving the two lovers alone, so he called Clarisse.

"Cuppas are made, darling."

"You spoil me, Jackson. It should be me getting them, not you."

"No, my love, I could never spoil you. I love you so much, anything I do for you gives me pleasure."

Clarisse put her arms around the man she loved. She felt so lucky to have him with her. Even though thoughts of Lachlan still made her apprehensive, Jackson's presence kept her safe. With her injuries almost healed, all she prayed for was Lachlan's arrest. She knew that with Jackson's love and strength, she would be able to give evidence at his trial and then watch as they convicted him and locked him away.

"You're deep in thought, my love. What's going through your mind?"

Clarisse smiled at him. "Just how much I love you."

They sat drinking their tea, and then they walked out into the garden hand in hand. They lay together on a blanket in the sun, and all thoughts of Lachlan and his menacing ways slowly receded from Clarisse's mind as she rested in Jackson's arms.

Kelly and Mary reached the home of Sandy's saviour, Caroline. The woman greeted them as they arrived. "Are you, the two officers from the city?"

"Yes, we are. I'm Kelly, and my colleague is Mary. We know your name is Caroline; is it okay if we use your first name?"

"Oh yes, that's fine. We should go to the place where I picked up Sandy. Where the attack happened is a little way from the road."

With that agreement, the three women drove to the site; as Caroline had said it wasn't far. Reaching the spot, Caroline told the officers she would prefer not to see the sight. "I'll just wait here for you. Seeing Sandy was enough for me."

"That's fine; we shouldn't be long. We just have to rope off the site, and then we'll wait for forensics."

Kelly and Mary walked to the crime site in silence. It wasn't long until they saw the scuffed-up dirt and the ropes, which lay where Sandy had dropped them.

"How did he know this area, Kel?"

"A local, I reckon. Someone who has lived in the area."

"You're probably right. If so, perhaps he has family here?"

"I hope so—my God, I hope so!"

With that, they set about taping around the trees and then made a line up to the road. They photographed everything in the taped area; at each photo site, they placed a numbered card. They heard a car coming toward them in the distance, and they nodded to each other as the van came into sight; it was the forensic team.

Mary greeted them. "You lot made good time. Everything is taped off, and we have taken photographs of anything suspicious."

"That's great, Mary. Hi, Kel, what's the scene like?"

"Lots of evidence for you. Some of the victims' clothes are still there, and there's a small bag, probably what he carried the ropes in."

Their job done for the time being, they drove Caroline home. Once there Caroline offered them a tea or coffee.

"Coffee would be great. We will need all the sustenance we can get, as it could be a long night."

They knew they could not stop long, and after drinking their coffee they made their way back to the crime scene. They heard a car approaching; when it drove up and stopped, they saw it was Jan.

"Hi there, you two. know I can't do anything, but I just had to see this place."

"It's pretty isolated," Kelly said. "Mary and I think he could either be a local, or he has lived in the area at some time. What do you think?"

"As you say it, is isolated, but we won't know too much until all the evidence is in. I want this bastard, girls. I want him so bad it makes my head ache. He's not getting away this time, believe me."

The police officers stood staring at the scene before them. The forensic team was hard at work, and any tiny piece could be relevant, so they had to work carefully. The medical officer called out.

"Hey Jan, can you come over here? Don't step inside the tape though."

"I'm not stupid you know."

"That's debatable, don't you think?"

"Well maybe."

Jan reached the spot where the evidence was: she looked down at a perfect shoe print. It was quite indented, and a second print, not as clear as the first, was nearby.

"He must have carried her?"

"That's my guess Jan. He probably knocked her out back near the road and then carried her here. Is she very badly hurt?"

"Yes, I'm afraid she is. Her injuries are extensive, both internal and external. This individual is such a sadistic bastard, so please find all the evidence we need."

"It will be my pleasure. Now, I must make a cast of the footprint while the others collect the other evidence. See you later, Jan."

Jan walked back to Kelly and Mary, and they headed back to her car. Before leaving she told them to stay where they were while she went to get a statement from Caroline.

"She's a very nice lady, Jan, and very easy to talk to. Her evidence and knowledge of this area could be vital," Kelly said.

"Okay, I'll see you back at the station."

Jan drove off, leaving her team at the site. She pulled up outside of Caroline's house, walked to the door, and knocked.

"Come in. You must be Jan. The other officers said you would come by when you arrived."

"Yes, I'm the leader of the rape crisis team. As you already know my name, can we start from when you first saw Sandy?"

"I usually don't use that road. I had been to see a friend, and as I drove, I saw a figure in the distance. When I got closer, she tried to hide, but as I got even nearer she walked out again—it was as if she was resigned to the fact it might be him returning."

"Did she say that?"

"No, she couldn't speak at all. She literally fell into my arms. I held her close; and she was shaking with tears running down her face. What a beating she had taken . . . I could see she was badly hurt, and I spoke to her, trying to sooth some of the fear as I led her to my car. I found it hard not to cry. After getting her into the car, I drove home as quickly as I could, and by that time she was unconscious. I went into the house and rang our local ambulance. My thoughts were telling me to be quick, and after the call I went back to Sandy, in the car.

"She was conscious when I reached her, and after opening the car door, I eased her legs out first and then turned her sideways so I could lift her out. Every movement was agony for the poor girl. Placing her arm around my neck, I lifted her up and walked her into the kitchen, then into the lounge. I helped her sit and then lifted her legs so she could lie down. I didn't wiped her face or body—they told me this could wipe away vital evidence. All she wanted was a bath, and I had to say no.

"I covered her with a blanket and then made a cup of tea; I held the cup while she sipped the liquid. I have never seen anything like it. She was so terribly hurt, it was hard not to cry. Then in the we heard the wail of the ambulance. I turned to tell her it wouldn't be long, but she was again unconscious and remained that way until the paramedics moved her onto the trolley. She was afraid at first when she saw the men, but they calmed her fears and told her she was safe; their tenderness as they moved Sandy was wonderful. When they left, I sat down and cried for some time. I have never seen this sadistic, brutal side of life. How could a human being do what he did to this lovely young woman?"

"I understand what you're saying, but it happens all too often. As you can imagine, I see it all the time. But this one is appalling, even for me."

"Are there times in your job that you feel you could kill the person who commits a crime such as this?"

"Yes, but always in silence. Well, I must get back to the hospital; there should be some news by now. Will you come into the station tomorrow so we can get your statement while it's fresh in your mind?"

"Yes, will 9.00 a.m. be too early?"

"No, that will be fine. I'll see you in the morning."

With that, Jan drove back to the hospital. As she drove, the horror of the last two attacks played in her mind like a bad record. After pulling up at the hospital, she walked into the emergency department, but Rachel wasn't there. *Maybe she's in her office,* Jan thought as she walked to the door. A nurse told her Rachel was still in surgery.

"Do you know how things are going?"

"No, but it could be a while—the patient was in a terrible state."

"I know, believe me, I know. I have a phone call to make; I'll use Rachel's office. If you hear anything, please tell me."

"Will do. We should have some news soon; let's hope it's good."

Jan sat in Rachel's office, picked up the phone, and rang John.

"John here, what can I do for you?"

"It's me, John, is he still there?"

"Yes, he is. When are we going to arrest him?"

"As soon as the others return."

"How is his latest victim?"

"Not good. Keep watching him—he mustn't get away this time."

"Okay. How are you going to approach the building?"

"I'll ring you as soon as I know Sandy's condition."

Jan had just put the phone down when Rachel walked into the office. She looked tired and strained, and she slumped into a chair and looked at Jan. "Oh, Jan, how do they justify what they do? Even animals don't act this way; they only hunt for food, not perverted sexual desires."

"Do you think you've managed to save her life?"

"Yes—for now, at least. It will be a while before we know about the long term. She has been traumatized badly, both mentally and physically. Her injuries are horrendous—don't ask me to tell you right now, because I can't. Later, maybe."

Jan walked over to Rachel leaned down, and held her in a warm embrace. "Come on, love, hang in there, I'm sorry I can't stay now, but I will come back later."

"Is there much evidence? Can we get him this time?"

"You bet, and as soon as Kelly and Mary arrive, we are going to arrest him."

Jan moved to the door and opened it—the two had arrived. Both could see the pain on Rachel's face, and Jan's look was one of sheer determination.

"Things are pretty grim, eh?" Kelly asked.

"They are more than that, Kel. The poor woman is just clinging to life, but with care and the grace of God, she will recover," Rachel replied.

"We will go now, Rach. I'll phone John, and the arrest will follow."

"Go get him for me, and look away if someone gives him a thump, won't you, Jan?"

The three police officers left Rachel with the difficult job of keeping Sandy alive. Jan had rung John and the station; there would be ten officers in the team to arrest Lachlan, four of whom were SWAT officers, and they would be the first to enter the flat. John and Jan would be outside the door; Mary, Kelly, and the two young female officers from the surveillance team would be at the back under the window.

After parking their vehicles in the street, they split into their groups. The four SWAT officers along with Jan climbed the stairs, and John was waiting for them. The others joined Kelly and Mary outside. Once they were all in place, a SWAT officer knocked the door in, and they all followed him. They found a very startled Lachlan sitting on the lounge.

"Stand up!"

Lachlan did as ordered. As he stood up, he looked at John on the landing. "You're a cop, you bastard?"

"Yes, I am, and proud of it. I get to arrest scum like you."

"And what am I supposed to have done?"

"You'll find that out later. It is all in the charge sheet."

As Jan read Lachlan his rights, he began to laugh. "You can't pin anything on me—I'll be out by morning. What a joke you all are."

The officers dragged him out of the flat and down the stairs. When they reached the van, he was hurled head first into the back. They slammed shut the door and locked it. All ten officers breathed a sigh of relief. The arrest had gone well, and they congratulated each other before heading off to the station. They locked Lachlan in a cell while Jan talked to her boss.

"We've got him."

"Now you have to prove it. I hope there won't be any slip-ups From what I hear, he almost killed your most recent witness."

"Yes, she is, but if Rachel has anything to do with it, she will recover and be able to give evidence. Plus there is a lot of physical evidence at the scene, and with Clarisse and Sue's testimony, we should get a conviction."

"Well, Jan, I don't know of a more competent police officer than you, so get him for us," the Chief said.

"I'll do my best, and in this case, that means nothing less than life in prison for this animal."

Jan left the Chief's office and walked to the squad room. The police officers involved in the arrest were waiting for her there. While looking at them all, she felt a sense of pride. They had done a great job, and she felt compelled to tell them this. "I want to thank you all. I won't put one officer above another, but the work you have done in this case has been exemplary. In addition, I thank you the SWAT officers who helped in the arrest. Between us we have stopped the reign of a vicious rapist. Now our job is to convict him. We have a lot of evidence, and there is more to come, but we must not become complacent—these cases are not easy to win. Let's get him."

After telling her staff to work hard, she returned to the hospital. Upon arrival she made her way to Rachel's office, and when she opened the door she could see Rachel was obviously upset.

"What's wrong? Don't tell me we've lost her?"

"No, Jan, she is still with us and is responding well to treatment. My tears are for just that. I know we have a long way to go, but I am optimistic of a recovery. Two hours ago I wouldn't have been able to say that."

"Oh boy, you sure know how to scare people. Now can you tell me about some of the injuries?"

"Sorry, Jan, not now; it is still too raw. Come back tomorrow, and we will talk. Also, Sandy may be able to talk as well. I'm not completely sure about the latter."

"Okay. I have to go back to Lachlan's flat and sweep the place for evidence. I'll see you tomorrow. Oh, by the way, I'm leaving an officer. Can you show him where Sandy's room is?"

"Sure, I'll do that."

Jan returned to the station, picked up Kelly and Mary, and then drove back to the flat.

The officer left to guard the unit quizzed the three officers. "I am not allowed to let you in—these orders come from the top."

"It's okay, I *am* the top." Jan showed the young officer her credentials, as did Mary and Kelly. "You are relieved for the moment. We have to sweep the room for evidence. You can't go home, but you can relax; if you want a drink, here is the key to our flat."

The young officer left, and the team went to work. They had to search every cupboard, drawer, box, and piece furniture. Any items found were to be relevant, bagged, and sealed. This was a long and demanding job, but a very necessary one.

Jan looked at her watch and was surprised at the time. "Hey, you two, it's almost 11.00 p.m. You'd better go home; I'll finish up here and make sure everything is locked."

"Do you want us to drop the evidence bags at the station?"

"No, I'll do that. See you both in the morning."

With her colleagues gone, Jan sat at the table. Alone with her thoughts, she remembered his attack on Clarisse and the evidence that followed, and this sparked another memory. *There is another flat somewhere. Maybe more evidence is there!* She picked up the bag filled with papers and began her search. Separating each piece, Jan scanned them all. Finally, there it was: Lachlan owned a unit on the other side of the city. A sense of elation excited Jan; they could fill more gaps once they searched this place.

After checking Lachlan's unit, Jan felt quite tired. She picked up the evidence bags, locked the unit, and said goodnight to the young officer. She made her way back to the station, let herself into the evidence room, and locked the bags in one of the lockers. Then she left the station and went home. As she climbed her stairs, her weariness almost crushed her. *Why am I so tired? Maybe it's relief, not fatigue.* On reaching her floor, she was surprised to see Rachel standing at her door.

"Rachel, why are you here?"

"I couldn't be alone tonight. I hope you don't mind?"

"No, of course I don't. It was just a shock seeing you here. Come on in."

The two women entered the flat, and Jan put the kettle on to make coffee. While it boiled, they sat at the table and talked.

"Let's not talk about the case—I just won't to relax for a while," Rachel suggested.

"Sure, Rach. Anything in particular? Or maybe we could just laugh."

Rachel grinned at Jan, and the tiredness started to lift. Jan returned the grin, and a new subject came to the foreground. This subject they never talked about, but each had known in their own way that they had feelings for each other. Should they discuss such a topic when each was so exhausted, or leave it for another time and place? As they looked into each other's eyes, it was as if the words had been spoken, and something new was about to begin. The whistling of the kettle broke the silence, and Jan made their coffee before she sat back down at the table.

"You can stay the night, Rach. Has the hospital got my phone number?"

"They sure have. When I left, I told them not to disturb me unless Sandy was in trouble. She was sleeping when I left."

"Is she going to be okay?"

"I think so—but didn't we decide not to talk shop?"

"You're right. Let's go to bed. We can look at it all in the morning."

Back at the police station, Lachlan wasn't feeling as brave as when first arrested. He looked around at the four blank walls, and finally he had to face the fact that maybe he wasn't who he dreamed he was.

Gone was the pretence of infallibility. He became the scared man he was, though he tried to tell himself that none of the women would testify against him. This didn't work, so he hid inside his disturbed mind; at the time, he wasn't aware that this was his only defence. The women he had tormented, raped, and beaten would tell their stories, and in time he would be alone, with only his thoughts for company.

Morning came, and to all the people involved in the case, it was to be of great significance. Now they could begin the task of convicting a criminal. Both believers and non-believers of Lachlan's guilt felt a sense of relief. His friends would not believe him capable of such fiendish crimes, and they looked forward to the trial and a positive outcome for him.

The police knew he was their man, and a conviction would be quick in coming. Only the women involved had moments of doubt they faced their fears—and the thought of facing their tormentor. He had caused them such pain, fear, and mindless terror. This was a lonely place, as it was at night they saw his brutal face and evil eyes.

Jan woke and looked at the face that lay on her arm. How lovely Rachel looked, her features relaxed in sleep. *Should I wake her?*

It was as though Rachel heard the unspoken words and opened her eyes. "Is it morning already, Jan? What's the time?"

"A time we both shouldn't be here. It's six thirty, Rach."

Rachel jumped out of bed and into a shower, and then she dressed, not waiting for coffee, and returned to the hospital. After opening her office door, she saw the nightshift charts and read over them quickly. She saw there had been no change reported about Sandy. While carrying the notes, she made her way to Sandy's room. The IV still flowed into her arm, and the machines kept up a steady hum, showing her heartbeat was steady and regular. Rachel sat beside the bed and asked the nurse about the night. "Has there been any change at all?"

"She woke once, but I don't think she saw me. She only moaned and closed her eyes again."

"How much morphine is she getting?"

"Only the amount you set last night. It seems to be enough for her pain."

Rachel leaned over and smoothed the hair from Sandy's brow. *How could anyone do this? He has a lot to answer for, but it will never be enough for what he did to this lovely young woman.* Rachel knew that the girl faced a long, hard road to recovery.

"If she wakes, can you have me paged? I will be here all day/ I hope to start her treatment for the mental scars quickly, but I have no desire to cause more pain. Take good care of her."

"I certainly will. All the nurses have given up days off, so at least one can stay with her at all times."

"That's wonderful! Can you pass on my gratitude to all of them?"

"Yes, Doctor, I'll do that. Will I see you later?"

"I will be in my office, so call me at any time."

Rachel walked back to her office and began reading the charts of other patients. With time on her hands, she lent backward in her chair. Her thoughts were of Jan and the look in her eyes as she woke. Was it love, or just appreciation for her dedicated work with the rape victims? There was no answer at that time, and both would be too busy to explore what it was.

Clarisse woke on this day knowing Jackson had to return home. His holiday was over, and his boss couldn't extend his leave. The federal police were very busy and needed Jackson back.

"I'm sorry, angel. I will put in for a transfer as soon as I get back."

"I will miss you so much. Please come back home soon."

"I have more time off due, but I can't take it now. I will talk to my boss and get the remainder of my leave. The job they want me for shouldn't take too long. I'll surprise them all when I tell them I am getting married! Right now, darling, we must leave for the airport; Jan is going to be there, too. What a send-off—the woman I love, her parents, and my cousin! This will help me leave."

"I know all this, Jackson, but I am going to miss you. You are my rock, and I feel safe when in your arms. When I think of them arresting Lachlan, and the trial . . . I will need you, darling."

"For that I will come back. I could never let you face that without me. Come on, my love, let's go."

With that, everyone climbed into the car and set off for the airport. Jackson tried to call Jan but received no answer. After trying for some time, he gave up and expected she would be there when they arrived. The car purred along, and Clarisse and Jackson sat with their arms around each other. They spoke gentle, loving words to each other as they neared the airport and Jackson's departure.

Jan had forgotten her cousin was leaving that morning; her job took up all of her mind and time. She went to the hospital to see how Sandy was, and she stood looking down at this lovely young woman. With each second she became angrier. She left the hospital and drove to the police station. Her staff was waiting for her, and everyone was eager to begin the interrogation of the suspect; Jan acknowledged them all and then started organizing the different areas, to begin making their case against the prisoner.

"John, I would like you to work with Kelly. I want you both to search the new flat."

"What new flat?"

"Oh, I didn't tell you, did I? Sorry, John, but when you all left last night, I remembered someone saying he had another flat. I think it was you, John. Didn't he tell you about another place where he lived?"

"Of course! It's just as well you remembered—I had forgotten."

"Here is the address. If you go and search it now, it could yield more clues for use at the trial."

"Okay. Let's go, Kelly. I can't wait to see what is there," John said.

With that the two officers left to carry out their assignment. Jan turned to Mary and beckoned her to follow.

"What are we doing Jan?" Mary asked.

"We are going to question our prisoner. Does that sound like fun to you?"

"It sure does—it's time he was faced with the fact that his reign of terror is over."

They walked to the interview room, sat down, and waited for their prisoner to enter. As he entered, there was still the hint of the arrogance he had shown when he was arrested. The officer with him sat near the door. Jan looked at him long and hard, and she noticed a hint of panic in his eyes. No one spoke for a full minute.

"Sit down," she ordered.

"Why?"

"Because I told you too. Now do it!"

With a shrug of his shoulders he sat down. Jan let the silence hang between them as she leafed through the list of charges laid against him.

"How will you like prison?"

"I'm not going to prison. You haven't the evidence to put me there."

"Keep thinking that, but believe me, you are going. We have the evidence and the witnesses to convict you. I haven't made up my mind as to what I should call you. Perhaps just Lachlan, or maybe Paul. What do you think?"

"My name isn't Lachlan. It's Paul."

"Well, right now I couldn't care less what your name is. But I *do* care about the women you tried to destroy. I know Sandy was your last victim. I went to see her in hospital this morning, and she is doing fine."

"Sandy? Who the bloody hell is she?"

"She is the one you thought was dead, isn't she?"

"I refuse to say any more until a lawyer is provided for me."

"That's fine with me. Officer; please escort this piece of filth back to his cell."

"With pleasure, ma'am."

Wrenching him to his feet, the officer shoved him toward the door, opened it, and slammed the prisoner up against the doorway. Lachlan gasped with pain.

"Did that hurt? Oh, I'm sorry."

"Don't apologize, Officer. He'll get used to a lot of pushing and shoving in prison—he might as well get used to it now. What do you think, Mary?"

"I'm with you, ma'am."

Jan and Mary walked away talking to each other, and Jan gasped when she looked at her watch.

"Oh damn! I've missed seeing my cousin off. He left an hour ago for the eastern states. He's not going to be happy with me. Clarisse should be home by now; I'll give her a ring."

Jan dialled the number and waited for an answer. The phone rang out, so she left a message. Then went back to the hospital, and upon walking to Rachel's office, she found it empty. *Where is she? Probably doing her rounds, to check up on her other patients.*

Jan decided to go to the cafeteria and have a light lunch before visiting Clarisse. She ate a sandwich and drank her coffee, thinking about missing Jackson's flight. A hand rested on her shoulder, and when she looked up she saw Rachel standing above her.

"Have you time to join me, Rach?"

"Just for a moment. I have just left Sandy; she is still critical, but there are signs of improvement. When I look at her I'm full of rage. Who does this man think he is?"

"Well, he's not as cocky now. He's hidden behind a lawyer for now, but he won't get away this time. There was a wealth of evidence at the scene and more in his flat. I also found deeds to another flat, and I sent Kelly and John to search it."

"It all sounds positive. I hope it all goes to plan. I can't stand the thought of him being acquitted."

"He won't. We can use the time we have before trial to get all the victims together—Clarisse and Sandy's evidence will be crucial. We have a cast of the shoe he was wearing at the scene of Sandy's rape. Well, I must leave now. Can I see Sandy before I go?"

"Sure. I'll walk with you to her ward."

Clarisse returned home and listened to Jan's message. *I am so glad she's okay. We all understood at the airport.* Clarisse tried to ring her. After she called the police station, they told her she returned to the Police station but was expected back soon. Clarisse left an invitation for Jan to join them for dinner, and she hung up.

"I hope that's okay, Mum?"

"Of course, dear. It will be nice to see her again."

I wonder why Jan is at the hospital. Maybe just to see Rachel. She hoped there wasn't anything wrong. Only a short time was spent thinking about Jan, because her mind drifted to Jackson. He would be halfway home by now, and she missed him already. *It is going to be a lonely night without him.*

As she lay back in the chair, her mind filled with thoughts of Jackson and his love. She must be the luckiest woman in the world. As she pondered this, the phone rang.

"Hello, Clarisse here, how can I help you?"

"It's Jan. Thanks for the invitation and the understanding about the airport. I can't come tonight—the whole squad is going to be busy."

"Has something happened? Has he attacked again?"

"I can't tell you at the moment, but I can say there has been a break in the case."

"I understand. I only ask that you give me time to compose myself if I am needed."

"I will do my best. When is Jackson coming back?"

"He thinks about two weeks."

"That's good. With any luck, he will be here for you at trial. I must go for now. I'll try and see you tomorrow."

"Okay, Jan, I'll see you then."

Clarisse stood silently with the phone in her hand. She mused on the conversation she had just finished. *They have caught him!* She knew they had. The case would start to move.

Her silence puzzled Flora, who asked, "Is everything okay, dear?"

"I think they've caught him, Mum."

"Did Jan tell you that?"

"Not in so many words, but it was inferred."

"Will you be all right to give evidence, love? It will be very traumatic for you."

"Oh, Mum, I think it will be some time before that happens. But I want Jackson back—I miss him already. What will it be like if he isn't here?"

"He'll be back, love. He won't let you face that on your own. You can talk to Jan when she comes tonight."

"No, Mum, she is too busy."

"Why don't you have a rest, darling? You look tired."

"I think that's a good idea. Wake me for lunch, please."

Clarisse lay back on the bed, and as she drifted into a deep sleep, she felt Jackson's presence lying next to her. "I love you so much. Please come back soon . . ."

Flora gave her a gentle touch to wake her. Jumping with fright, Clarisse asked, "Who is it? What do you want?"

"It's me, love. Jackson is on the phone, and he wants to speak to you."

"Thanks, Mum. Jackson, are you home already?"

"Just walked in the door, darling. I had to ring to see if you were okay."

"I'm fine, but I must have slept longer than I thought. How was the flight? I miss you so much. Please come back as soon as possible."

"I miss you too. The plane trip seemed to take me so far away from you. The next two weeks are going to be hell. I must go now, love. The boss has called me into the office for a briefing. Remember, I love you, and we will be together soon."

Clarisse returned the phone to its cradle and walked into the kitchen. Flora had made salad sandwiches for them both. The two women chatted as they ate, but their thoughts were not the same. Clarisse's mind was on what Jan had said, and Flora worried about the trial and how her daughter would cope if Lachlan was in custody.

Rachel had not left Sandy's bedside. She watched the machines as they worked, and in her mind she was afraid they might stop. *Why does this have to happen? Why is it some people think they have the right to destroy a fellow human being in this way? Do they have any rational thought, or is this type of brutality in their mind all the time?* Sandy stirred and tried to open her eyes; a moan of pain came from her lips, and she tried to sit up.

"Please, Sandy, don't try to sit up. Just lie quietly. Is there anything you need?"

"Where am I?"

"You're safe in the hospital. We have guards outside your room, so just try to rest."

"Who are you?"

"I'm your doctor, and my name is Rachel. Are you in much pain?"

"Some, but not as bad as last night."

"We have inserted an infusion drip; this is feeding enough morphine to make you comfortable. Is there anything else you need? Perhaps a cup of tea or coffee?"

"Not now, thanks."

Rachel could see that Sandy had once again slipped into the comfort of drugged sleep. Rachel reached a hand to her own face and felt a teardrop on her cheek; this surprised her because she was the consummate professional and should be able to control her emotions. Whatever the reason, the tears fell, and Rachel wasn't able to control them.

The silence in the room was broken when a nurse entered. "Are you all right, Doctor?"

"Yes, Nurse, I'm fine."

Rachel stood up and left the room, making her way back to her office. Upon reaching her sanctuary, she let the tears flow. To Rachel there was no reason for her to be so emotional. She felt the need to talk to someone and rang Jan.

"Hello, this is the front desk. Whom do you wish to speak to?"

"Is it possible to speak to Jan?"

"I'm sorry, she is in the interview room with a suspect. Can I take a message?"

"No, that won't be necessary; I'll call back later. Thank you."

CHAPTER TEN

JAN WAS IN THE INTERVIEW room, and across the table sat Lachlan with his lawyer. Kelly was also there at Jan's side. Their suspect sat with a smirk on his face and looked at the two police officers with disgust.

"You lot are a joke; you'll never get me on any charge."

"Don't talk, Lachlan," his lawyer said. "Leave the talking to me."

"Why? They don't have any evidence."

"Shut your client up, will you? If not, I'll have to gag him," Jan growled.

"You know that you can't do that, so why threaten?"

"I want this criminal locked up for a very long time. We *do* have the evidence, so keep him quiet."

The lawyer said, "Come on, Lachlan. Let's listen to what they call evidence."

"Okay."

"Now, for the tape, could you give me your correct name and address?" Jan asked.

"Lachlan Johnson, U/5 King St. You already know that, so why ask?"

"You do have another address. Where is that?"

"I don't have another address."

"Liar. You do, so give it to me."

Lachlan sat with arms crossed looking at Jan. His mind was racing. How did she know? He hadn't told anyone, so how?

"Answer me—what is that address?" Jan repeated.

"Do you have another address, Lachlan?" the lawyer asked.

"No, they are making it up. I only live at the address where they arrested me."

"If you don't tell me the truth, you will have to find another lawyer. I can't defend someone who hides the truth."

"Well, piss off then. I don't need you. Go on, get out!"

With that, the lawyer stood up, made his apologies to the officers, and walked out.

"Well, its back to a cell for you. Feeling a little stupid right now, are we?" Jan pressed the buzzer, the door opened, and the duty officer entered.

"Yes, ma'am?"

"Take this piece of filth and throw him into his cell, please."

"With pleasure."

They wrenched Lachlan bodily from his seat and returned him to his cell. Here he knew he had made a mistake. He hated women, especially that Jan. *Just wait till this is over. Boy, will she be sorry. It will be very easy to just kill her. Rape is too good; it's a feeling for her, and she would probably enjoy it too much.* He would just tie her up and beat her to death. These thoughts seemed to comfort him. *Oh yes, she will be sorry.*

Walking out of the interview room, Jan was happy at the way the interview went. *He is so sure we don't have any evidence. We will keep it that way, and given time he will convict himself.* After entering her office, she looked through his file. There was new evidence from forensics as they continued their work. The cast of the footprint matched a pair of runners from the flat; the clothes he had worn yielded more DNA for comparison to the semen and saliva taken from Sandy. Sandy . . . She should go and see her. She hadn't heard from Rachel this morning and wondered why. *Probably busy. We'll catch up while I'm at the hospital.* She gave her team new orders and left for the hospital.

As she entered, Rachel was in the lobby and gave her a wink. Jan continued on to Sandy's room. A nurse sat by her bedside and nodded at Jan as she entered the room. Lying back upon the pillows was the young woman who had suffered the most horrific of experiences. Her face beneath the bruises was pallid, and the morphine dripped steadily into her system, dulling the intense pain. Jan sat on the chair near the bed; she had eyes only for this young woman. She placed a hand lightly over hers and hoped the love and concern would flow through to her. Sandy stirred and opened her eyes.

"Who are you?"

"My name is Jan; I head the rape crisis team."

"Please get him, please get him!"

"We will. Now, just rest and leave him to us."

Sandy closed her eyes, and as she did Jan saw a tear run down the girl's cheek. She took a tissue and wiped it away. Anger filled Jan's heart, and the need to make sure the monster who had done this would never see the light of day. Jan felt a hand on her shoulder; it was warm and comforting.

"Oh, Rachel, I can't help it! It would be very easy to just kill this perverted monster."

"Our thoughts are exactly the same."

"Sorry I haven't rung, but we have been very busy. We arrested him last night and interviewed him today."

"I know—I rang earlier, and they said you were busy. Will you get a conviction?"

"Yes, we will. He acts so smug and thinks we don't have the evidence."

"*Do* you have the evidence?"

"We do, and as time passes more is found. He is going nowhere, I promise you."

"Have you time for a coffee, Jan?"

"Yes, but I need it to be a quick one."

"Okay, let's go."

The two women went to the cafeteria and talked as they sat at one of the tables. Rachel asked if Jan could come for dinner that night, and she answered in the affirmative as they finished their coffee. After leaving the cafeteria, Rachel went to her office and Jan headed back to the hospital.

Later in the day Clarisse rang Jan, who told her of the arrest. A shiver went through her. All she could think was that he had savagely raped another woman. Maybe she could visit the girl when she was a little better. With this thought in mind, she rang Rachel.

"Dr Scott here."

"Hello, Rachel, it's Clarisse. How is the young woman?"

"I can't say anything right now—maybe later. How did you know about her?"

"I don't know a lot, but Jan told me a man had been arrested and charged. I guess I just made the connection."

"It's okay, but don't talk about it to anyone, please."

"I won't, but if in time I could visit her, I would be grateful."

"We'll see. I must go now, love. Say hello to Flora and tell her I look forward to another invitation for dinner. Bye for now."

Clarisse sat looking at the phone for a time. Her mind went back to the first time she had opened her eyes after the attack. She knew the girl was safe but wanted to tell the latest victim her life would go on. *That doesn't always happen, though. How badly is she hurt, and how long will it take before she is healed?* Clarisse felt the tears fill her eyes and run down her face. All the fear and self-loathing came back. She shivered at the thoughts in her head. *Will this keep happening to me, or will it fade? How silly of me to think all the scars were gone.*

Flora entered the room to find her daughter in tears. She placed her arms around her and asked, "What is it, darling?"

"He has done it again. Another young woman is in hospital, torn apart by that mongrel."

"How do you know that? Did Jan tell you?"

"Not in so many words, but the inference was there."

"Don't let your mind get ahead of the facts. Calm yourself until you know for sure."

"I know you're right, Mum, but I feel bad. I hope Jackson comes back soon—I need him and miss him so much."

"He'll be back soon. Now, just lay back and have a rest; I'll get you a sedative to help you sleep."

"Thanks, Mum."

As she walked away, Flora felt a pang of uncertainty. *Will she cope with what's ahead? She will be facing him in court as she gives her evidence.*

Clarisse's voice startled her, as she called for the sedative. "I need that tablet, Mum. Can you bring it, please?"

"Flora hurried to the cabinet, got the tablet, and called out, "Sorry, love. Got lost in another world for a time."

"You're worrying about the trial, aren't you?"

"Yes, I am. It will be hard on all of us, and I hope it is soon, because then we can start living again."

"How do you think Dad will take it? He will hear all the evidence from me and this latest case."

"He will cope. It will be hard, but the reward will be great. They will lock him away, and some sort of peace will come for us all."

Flora looked down at her daughter and could see her eyes had closed. *My dearest daughter, why did this happen to you? Why did this man think he had the right to rape and beat you?* She would never understand the human mind, it was a mystery to her.

Jan's phone rang, startling her. She picked it up and asked, "Hello, this is D-I Hastings. How can I help you?"

"Are you Jan? I would like to speak to her."

"Yes, it's me. How can I help?"

"It's Caroline here. You met me the night Sandy was attacked."

"Oh yes, how could I forget. How are you?"

"I'm fine, but I can't get an answer from the hospital. Could you tell me how she is?"

"I can't tell you much, but thanks to you she is alive. If you hadn't found her, she may not have made it."

"Oh, thank you so much. Since giving you my statement, I haven't been able to sleep. Perhaps I will now."

"If you give it a few days, you should be able to visit Sandy, but ring the hospital first."

"Yes, I'll do that. Thank you again, Jan. Bye for now."

Jan put the phone down and was thinking of the poor young woman in the hospital. After seeing her earlier in the day, the hate for her attacker grew stronger. She picked up his file and began to read all the evidence they currently had: there were DNA matches, the shoe print, and statements from all the people concerned. *He won't be so smug when he hears all this in court. With luck he might plead guilty. No, he won't do that—he's too cocky.* The phone rang again.

"Detective Inspector Hastings. How can I help?"

"I am Lachlan's mother, Mrs. Johnson. I believe you have charged my son with aggravated rape, abuse, and causing bodily harm. Is this right?"

"Yes, it is. He will go to trial in the very near future."

"My boy wouldn't rape anyone—he is a good boy."

"That he maybe to you, but believe me, he's also the man who sexually and physically, and with malice, attacked several women. The last is so badly beaten she may not live. If you doubt my word, come and see me, and I will show you the evidence."

"I can't and won't believe you. I will see you at the trial and laugh as he is acquitted!"

"That's entirely up to you, Now, I must go—I have work to do."

Jan sat in amazement at the mother's call. Surely she must have known her son wasn't normal? While she sat at the desk, a young officer knocked and entered.

"Hi, Jan, thought you might like to see this."

"What is it?"

"When that call came in, I checked the area code. It's Laton."

"Well, another piece of evidence. Could Lachlan have been to see his mother? The case just gets better all the time. This piece could be the clincher. Thanks for that."

The desk officer left and went to the front desk, leaving Jan to digest this latest part of the puzzle. Now she had the added proof of where and why he would be in the area where the rape had occurred. How she hoped Sandy would be able to tell them her story; she would know everything, and the attack happened in daylight, so there would be no problem for her to identify him.

Lachlan would have plenty to say, and if she remembered all that, the case was almost over. But how long would it be before Sandy could tell them? Her bruised and battered body, along with the mental scarring she had suffered, meant it would be some time before they knew her story.

Rachel walked into Sandy's room. The machines still whirred, and her heartbeat was slow and rhythmic. All the outward signs were good, but how were the mental injuries? Rachel took a step out of the room when a voice called to her.

"Where am I?"

"You're in the hospital, Sandy. I'm your doctor."

"How long have I been here?"

"Not long, but you have slept most of the time. We have to keep you sedated."

"I was raped, wasn't I?"

"Yes, my dear, you were. But don't be fearful—we have a policeman guarding the door at all times. We have done this to aid in your recovery, so all you need do is relax and let the healing begin."

"Have the police arrested him?"

"I can't answer that, but Jan will be in soon, and you can ask her."

"Is she nice, this Jan?"

"Yes, very. She has been with the rape crisis team for a long time, and her work is her life."

"That's nice . . ."

The silence told Rachel that Sandy had drifted back into a drugged sleep; the best thing was she had spoken. Rachel made her way to the office and phoned Jan.

"Hi, Jan, just thought I would let you know that Sandy woke and spoke to me."

"She did? Well, that's great. And how is the poor girl?"

"Still critical, but I think the worst is over. How are you? Getting any sleep?"

"Not much. The mind just goes round and round."

"Are you free this evening? If you are, we could have a meal out."

"Sounds great, but I will have to get back to you later. Is that okay?"

"Certainly. I'll wait for your call. Bye for now."

Jan put the phone down and then just sat and looked blankly at the wall. Everything that had happened in the past four or five weeks was taking its toll. Even feeling the way she was, Jan knew she could not rest now. Closing this case had to happen before she could rest. Still, a meal out with Rachel would give her a boost and take her away from all the horror of the last few days. Deciding to accept the invitation, she rang Rachel and arranged the evening.

Then she picked up Clarisse and Sandy's files. She knew it would be their evidence which would put him away. One file fell open at the section where Clarisse was telling her story. *Life is funny sometimes—how could anyone ever guess that a rape victim could actually be in love with my cousin? The wedding will be wonderful, and Clarisse will find that even after such a traumatic experience, life can be beautiful again.*

Lost in her own thoughts, Jan didn't see John walk in. He stood by her desk and finally gave a quiet cough. Jan jerked her head up and looked at John. "What in blazes do you want?"

"Sorry if I startled you, but I have a request."

"And what would that be?"

"Can I be in the team that guards the latest victim at the hospital?"

"You are prepared to put in extra time? I say this because you could be called out if any other rape occurs. And by the way, lose the uniform—I have your detective badge here; put it in your pocket after you've changed."

"Jan, thank you. A dream of mine has been filled. When do I start at the hospital?"

"Right now. I will send someone to relieve you later; tell the constable on duty you are taking over, and you can even flash your badge if you wish."

"I'll do that, and thanks again. Just think: I'm now D-C John Barton." With that, he left Jan's office, changed his clothes, and made his way to the hospital.

Jan still sat at her desk reading the information in the files, and suddenly she thought, *Why isn't there any information about Sandy? Surely there must be parents or siblings out there.* Jan called out to Kelly, asking her to see what she could find out. *It is funny though: Sandy was attacked almost three days ago, and there hadn't been contact of any kind.* Leaving her desk, she walked to the front desk.

"Hey, Joe, do we have a contact number for Sandy's parents?"

"No, we don't. Do you want us to follow it up?"

"I've given Kelly the job, but if you have time to help, it would be appreciated."

"No worries, Jan. I'll see what I can find."

Jan returned to her office once again to ponder on the case she had to put together. She had no room to make a mistake, so everything she did had to be double checked. It was then she thought of Clarisse and her hesitancy when they last talked. Leaving her office, she drove to the Stewart house, and as she got out of the car Flora called to her.

"Hello, Jan, how are you?"

"I'm fine, Flora. Is Clarisse home?"

"Yes, she's inside. I think she's lying on her bed reading."

"Thanks. I'll go find her, if that's okay."

"Certainly, my dear."

Jan walked into the house and made her way to the bedroom. Clarisse was asleep with a book resting on her chest. She looked so peaceful that Jan hadn't the heart to wake her. She went back out to the garden. "She's sound asleep. I won't wake her; tell her I stopped by, please."

"Was there something special you wanted to talk about?"

"Yes. We need to get her evidence for trial. It will be a while, but she needs to be prepared."

"I won't tell her all that, just that you came to visit. Bye for now, Jan."

"See you, Flora."

Jan drove off and looked at her watch. She could see there was time to stop in at the hospital. As she entered the corridor where Sandy's ward was, she saw John, who was sitting on the chair just outside the door. He stood up when Jan addressed him. As he did, he put his finger to his lips to signal that Sandy was asleep.

"How is she, John?"

"There hasn't been much improvement. The doctor came about fifteen minutes ago, and she was frowning when she left."

"Sounds like I should go and talk to her myself. Keep up the good work."

Jan walked away, heading for Rachel's office. As she turned a corner, she almost collided with her.

"Geez, nearly knocked you flat, mate!"

"You did! Have you been to see Sandy?"

"Yes, that's why I was coming to see you."

"Let's get a coffee, and I will fill you in on her condition."

They chatted as they walked to the café; Rachel ordered and paid for the coffees and then sat opposite Jan.

"Okay, let me have it," Jan said.

"She isn't doing as well as I would like. Luckily there is no infection, but I am having trouble with her mental state, and that worries me."

"We have time, Rach. I can delay the trial by charging our suspect with another rape, and this will allow us to keep him jailed for a long time."

"Thank goodness for that. In my opinion, it will be another four weeks before Sandy is well enough to talk, let alone give evidence."

"Don't worry, it will all work out. By the way, Rach, what about tonight?"

"Is my place okay? Say, eight o'clock?"

"See you then."

In the meantime John returned to his seat outside Sandy's door, and he heard a low moan. He leaped to his feet and walked to her bedside.

"Are you all right? Can I get a nurse for you?"

"Who are you? Are you him? Why are you in here? I don't want you near me!"

"I am a police officer; we are guarding you while you are so ill."

"Get a nurse. Go away, please!?"

John pressed the call button, left the room, and waited for the nurse to arrive. It wasn't long before the nurse came, and after looking at John's face, she asked, "What is it, John?"

"Sandy wants some help. When she moaned, I went to help her, but she asked me to leave."

"Don't take it personally; this is a common reaction for a woman who has suffered as she has done. I'll attend to her; you could take the chance for a coffee. I won't leave till you return."

"No, I'll stay here. Thanks anyway."

Lachlan sat in a cold jail cell. Here he was, alone with his thoughts, and they did not paint a nice picture. To himself he could tell the truth, and as it played through his mind, fear crept in. *Do they have the evidence they say, or is it a con?* He had been careful. His thoughts then turned to Sandy. Was this his mistake? He knew that she could identify him and everything he had said; he had also left the ropes. *Why did I just leave, not knowing if she was still alive? She looked dead; there was blood all over her, and the ropes still held her tightly. She must be dead. That leaves Clarisse and Sue. The others won't say anything, and even if they did, they don't know me.*

Would Clarisse point the finger? Yes, he felt she would. *Bloody slut. How can people believe anything she says? She's the one to blame, leading me on and then making me fight for what was my right. Damn woman—they think nothing can touch them, and then when it does, they screamed foul.* If he could get out of here, he'd put an end to their lies, and then at the trial he'd tell the world what they were. Chuckling to himself, he began to believe that he would be fine. *No one will believe those sluts—they will believe me. I am sure they will see the victim is me, not them. It was they who lured me into unnatural sexual depravity.*

My mother won't believe any of it. Yes, my mum will save me. She will tell them it was the women, not me. She must be coming to see me, but they won't let her because they are frightened. They know she will make them set me free. Still he mumbled to himself while the thoughts echoed through his mind will they be able to convict him.

Meanwhile, his latest victim was fighting a life-or-death struggle. She was under constant watch from both the hospital staff and police. Her dreams were nightmares: he was there all the time, and the only time he got pushed into the background was when the doctor raised the level of morphine.

Rachel spent a lot of time with Sandy, even when she was asleep; she spoke gently to her in a soothing manner, telling her she was safe and her wounds would heal. Whenever she stirred, Rachel would touch her hand and softly massage it until sleep calmed Sandy again.

As Rachel sat at her bedside; she heard a disturbance in the corridor. Leaving Sandy, she walked out of the room, where a woman stood arguing with a nurse. Walking up to her, Rachel asked who she was.

"I'm Sandy's mother. Where is she? I want to see her?"

"Could you show me some identification, please?"

"Why? I've told you who I am."

"That isn't enough, so please show me something that identifies you."

"No, I won't! Just take me to see her, or I'll phone the police."

Noticing the argument John walked down the corridor toward them.

"What's up, Doc? Is this person giving you trouble?"

"She won't show me any identification."

John turned to the woman who was creating all the fuss.

"If you are Sandy's mother, it would be better if you just showed your driver's license. It's that simple."

Looking long and hard at both she turned on her heels and walked away.

"I wonder who she is, Doc."

"Don't know, but I'm going to ring Jan. There's something about her I don't like, let alone the fact she refused to identify herself."

"Okay, Doc. I'll go back to Sandy's room."

Returning to her office, Rachel wondered about the behaviour of the woman. She picked up the phone and dialled Jan's private number.

"D-I Hastings here."

"It's me, Jan. A woman walked into the hospital and demanded to see Sandy. I asked her for identification, but she refused."

"Was John there?"

"Yes, he was. He ordered the woman to identify herself, and after he did that, the woman just walked out."

"Describe her to me, Rach."

"Very ordinary about fifty light brown hair, brown eyes and quite short. Why, do you know her?"

"No, but a woman very similar to your description, came here to visit Lachlan."

"Very suss, don't you think?"

"Don't let her in to Sandy's room. She is trouble, and I believe the woman is Lachlan's mother."

"His mother? Well, she won't get inside the hospital again, let alone Sandy's room. Thanks, Jan."

"No problem. I'll see you tonight?"

"Yes, of course. I'll see you at my flat. Bye for now."

Rachel returned the phone to its cradle and then sat thinking. The nerve of the woman! No wonder she didn't identify herself. Rachel walked back to Sandy's ward and told John of Jan's orders about the woman. Having done that, she went into the ward and she made sure everything was in order, and then she made her way back to the duty desk.

CHAPTER ELEVEN

CLARISSE PICKED UP THE PHONE, and as expected, the caller was Jackson.

"Hello, darling, are you all right?"

"I'm fine, Jackson, but I miss you so much. Just as well we only have a week to wait until we are together."

"I have some news about that."

"Please don't tell me you can't come?"

"No, of course not. I am being transferred over there!"

"Oh, how wonderful. When? Will it be soon?"

"I'm doing the paperwork now. I should be there next week. Do you think I could stay with you?"

"I'm sure Mum and Dad won't object. This is so exciting! I will see you every day and be in your arms every night."

"After one more week, you will be in my arms always. Do you think we could arrange a wedding in a week?"

"Yes! I can't tell you how happy I am. To be with you for life almost makes me cry."

"I must go, sweetheart. I need to tie up some loose ends, and then I am free to come to you."

"I don't want you to go. The next week will be the longest I've known. Bye, my love. See you in a week."

Clarisse called excitedly to her mother.

"Where are you, Mum? I have some great news."

"In the kitchen, dear. What's all the excitement?"

"Jackson will be here in a week, and he wants us to get married then! Can we arrange a wedding in a week?"

"Well, that *is* news! I'll start making plans now; it will have to be a back garden kind. Do mind that."

"No, Mum, I just want to marry him as soon as possible, so anything you do is fine with me."

Flora looked at her daughter and wondered at her newfound strength. Since Jackson's appearance, Clarisse had healed both mentally and physically. There were still days when just a thought could send her into a flood of tears, but Flora now believed she would have no trouble when she had to give evidence.

Rachel had given her a full physical, and her report was very good. She hadn't been so sure about the mental scars, but she agreed that Jackson's love would ease them in time.

Rachel entered Sandy's room hoping she might be awake. Her blonde hair glistened with dampness, her small and rounded face was still pale, and her breathing was slow and consistent. All looked positive. *She is going to live.* Rachel sat on the chair next to her bed. She lifted Sandy's hand and cupped it in her own. It was warm but slightly clammy. Her thoughts were all about Sandy, and what life would be like after such a brutal attack. She knew that there was a lot of work ahead, for both of them.

Sandy broke the quiet; she moved and pulled her hand away from Rachel.

"Who are you?"

"I am your doctor. Remember when you first came in? I introduced myself."

"No, I don't recall much at all. I can only remember his eyes, the pain, and his laugh. I knew he wanted to kill me—it was terrible."

"I know, my dear, but here you are safe. There is a guard outside your door."

"Did he come in here earlier?"

"Yes, he did, but you told him to leave. He is a nice young man and is very concerned about you."

"Can you tell him I'm sorry? But he mustn't come in again."

"Certainly, but now you must rest. Let the sedative do its work, and I'll come back later."

Rachel left the room and stopped to talk to John.

"I heard her, Doc. I'll just stay here and guard her."

"Good for you, John. See you when I come back."

The day was over, and Rachel drove home. What should she cook for dinner? She really didn't feel like cooking, so take away was the way to go. There was a Chinese restaurant nearby that would do. Her order was for fried rice, garlic prawns, and chicken chow-mien, it didn't take long, and it was no time before it arrived home.

Jan parked her car at the curb and waved as she approached. Rachel acknowledged her by waving through the window. Jan entered Rachel's home and sat down at the table, and the two friends helped themselves to the food. They chatted while they ate, mostly about Clarisse and Sandy. Both knew it would be these two whose evidence would be crucial in the upcoming trial.

"How is Sandy?" Jan asked.

"There are signs of improvement, but she is still very ill. Can we not talk shop tonight? I just want to forget for a while."

"Okay, let's just curl up on the couch and watch a funny movie."

"Great idea, Jan, let's do it. I have a box of chocolates and a bottle of white wine, so let's enjoy ourselves."

Clarisse's life had definitely taken a turn for the better, with a marriage and life with Jackson to look forward to. As she sat out in the sun, her arms wrapped around her knees, she knew all these positive affirmations would help when she had to give evidence at the trial. The trial . . . Was she ready to do that? She hoped so. *He will be in the court.* This thought brought back memories of that night, and a shiver went through her. As she again felt the heavy blows, of falling and the agonizing thrusts during the rape, could she do it?

"I must. He *has* to be stopped. Jackson, all the police officers, my parents, and Rachel will get me through."

Armed with that fact, and with Jackson returning in a week, made her smile again. She looked up as the sun shone brightly, and Clarisse came to a place where her strength would carry her through.

Flora had been watching her daughter realizing she was working on her strength. From what she saw, her daughter had turned the corner and was ready to face the world again.

Choosing not to disturb her, Flora returned to the kitchen and the wedding cake she was baking.

John sat outside Sandy's door. He had chosen to stay even though his shift was over, due to the strong feelings he had for the patient. This lovely young woman who had been hurt so badly by an evil predator was new to him. His career in the force had always been his ultimate goal, and now all he wanted to do was to help Sandy recover. If that meant staying on duty a little longer, it was a cheap price to pay.

As he sat, his thoughts went back to the beginning of his inclusion in the rape crisis team. To him this was what he wanted, and he had fitted in from the start. Here he could care for the people who were hurt by sexual predators, and at the same time he could find evidence that would put a criminal away.

Jan was a great boss to have. She made her orders clear and what she wanted. If one followed them, life was easy. Her knowledge of rapists was extensive; just to listen was to learn. John heard Sandy cry out, and unlike the first time he beckoned a nurse.

"Sandy's woken up."

"I'm coming. Why don't you go in?" the nurse said.

"Sandy doesn't want me to."

The nurse went to Sandy's bedside. "Are you all right, love?"

"Who were you talking to at the door?"

"Just the police guard. Now what do you need? Are you in pain, or do you just need to talk?"

"No, I'm all right; it was just a sharp pain that came with no warning. Is the doctor here?"

"No, she has the night off, but I could fetch one of the other doctors."

"Don't do that. I'll wait for Rachel—she is my doctor."

"Is there anything else you want?"

The nurse looked down at Sandy and realized she was asleep. It was clear it would be a long time before she recovered fully. Leaving the room, the nurse nodded to John and went on her way; she had plenty to do for the other patients on the floor.

Lachlan sat in his jail cell looking at the four walls. He must get out of here. *Why did they put me in a cell like this one? I haven't done anything wrong.* Doubt began to fill his mind. *What if they do know what I've done?*

Then a picture of Clarisse swam before him. He hadn't done anything to her. *What was a slap here or there? She had asked to be raped—begged him. As for the last one . . . Well, if you didn't want to have sex, then you shouldn't have got into a stranger's car. Maybe it went a little too far, but who cares? They don't have the evidence. If they did, they would have charge me with her rape as well. They are saving that—they'll stick me with that when they fail to convict on Clarisse's so-called rape.* Slowly his mind was descending into madness; reality was a long way away, and he knew they couldn't convict someone who was insane.

While these thoughts swirled in his head, the cell door opened. A police officer and a doctor entered his cell. The doctor opened his bag and took out a syringe. "I am going to give you an injection that will ease your psychosis."

"No, you're not."

"I'll hold him, Doc," the officer said.

"Hold him down firmly while I give him the shot."

"Lousy bastards! Leave me alone!" Lachlan yelled.

"All done, Doc?"

"Yes. Let's get out of here—I don't like suspected rapists much."

The two men left the cell and walked away. Lachlan could feel the effects almost immediately: his mind was becoming clearer, and the truth of his situation was set to haunt him.

Outside the cell, the officer asked, "What's the drug, Doc?"

"It's for a mental disorder. If we don't keep up the medication, he will slide further into his psychotic condition."

"Are you saying if he doesn't get the drug, he could get off?"

"No, his psychotic problem is bad. But his lawyer might try."

"Can't have that, can we? I must get back to the front desk. See you next time."

With that said, the officer walked away from the doctor and returned to the desk. Once there he had time to reflect on what he had said. What a travesty it would be if he got off. Surely the jury would hear all the evidence, and the insanity defence wouldn't fool them . . . But then, maybe they would.

A voice interrupted his thoughts. "Constable, can you hear me?"

"Of course. How can I help you?"

"I would like to see the officer in charge, please."

"Why? Can you tell me what for?"

"My daughter is missing. She was due home a few days ago and hasn't arrived."

"What is her name, ma'am?"

"Sandy Davies. We live in Laton, and she hasn't called—that's not like her. I would like to have her posted as missing."

"Wait here for a moment. I'll call the detective who is in charge of missing persons."

Jan was reading over the last batch of medical evidence from the forensic lab. There was a wealth of evidence for them to work with, but the phone interrupted her thoughts.

"DI Hastings, can I help you?"

"It's the front desk, ma'am. There's a lady here who says her daughter is missing."

"Did she give a name?"

"Yes, she did—her daughter's name is Sandy Davies."

"Keep her there; I'm coming out."

Jan took a deep breath as she walked to the front entry. She could see the resemblance to Sandy immediately. This was the part of her job she disliked, but she had to be the one to do it. Approaching the woman, she said, "Hello, Mrs. Davies, could you come with me?"

"Something bad has happened, hasn't it? I can see it in your face. Is my daughter dead?"

"No, she isn't dead, but she is in hospital. I think we should go into my office; it's more private there. Harry can you have two coffees sent to my office? It's this way, Mrs Davies."

The two women walked toward Jan's office, and on the way they passed Kelly. "Everything okay, Jan?"

Jan nodded and continued toward her office.

When they reached the office, Jan said, "Take a seat. I'm Detective Inspector Hastings. What I have to tell you will be a shock, but in saying that, Sandy is in very good hands."

"Just tell me," Mrs Davies said nervously.

"Sandy was raped and beaten a few days ago. We have been trying to find her family ever since. She will recover, but it will take time."

A knock on the door stopped the conversation. The young officer entered with the coffees and placed them on the desk.

Sandy's mother sat staring at Jan, as if she didn't believe her. "You are sure she will be all right? She isn't going die?"

"She should be all right, and no, she will not die. She is in hospital, and her doctor is the best in her field. We can go and see her now, if this is what you want."

"Is she badly hurt?"

"I can't lie to you: she's in a bad way, and you will have to be prepared for a shock."

"Can we go now? I want to see her."

"Well then, let's go. My car is parked out front, and the hospital isn't far."

The two women drove to the hospital. Jan hadn't been able to warn Rachel of their arrival but knew she could cope in any situation. They walked in the front door and stopped at the front desk.

Jan asked where she could find Rachel. "Can you page her for me, please?"

"Yes. Dr Scott, you are requested at the front desk."

Jan and Mrs. Davies sat in the lounge waiting for Rachel. The door opened, and she stepped inside.

"What's up, Jan?"

"Rachel, this is Mrs Davies, Sandy's mother."

"Oh! Thank goodness, we have been trying to find you since she was admitted."

"Can I see my daughter now, please?"

"Of course. Let's go to her. Mrs Davies, please be prepared for a shock—your daughter has been severely beaten."

"Just take me to her."

"Very well. Please follow me."

The three women walked to Sandy's ward in silence. Jan glanced at Rachel, who nodded. The nod said, "Be ready for the mother's reaction." They reached the ward and walked in.

"Oh my God! Who did this? My poor darling, you don't have to worry now; I'm here." Turning to Jan, she asked if there was a suspect or someone in custody. Tears flowed a little at first, but then there was a flood. Through her tears she asked again, "What kind of man could do this?"

"All I can say at this time is that we do have a suspect, and yes, he's in custody. The case against him is very strong and will be more so when Sandy recovers."

"Tell me, Doctor, will my daughter recover fully from this ordeal?"

"I cannot say that with any certainty at this time. But with good medical care, and people around who love and understand her, everything is possible."

"Can she stay here? I don't have much money or insurance, but I do want her to have the best of care."

"Don't worry about the cost—Sandy will stay here until she has recovered. The hospital will cover the cost."

"Thank you, Doctor! Can I just sit with her now? I will need to find accommodations, but I can do that later."

"Stay here as long as you wish. I will pop in now and again. Sandy is receiving morphine by infusion drip, and this keeps the pain at a minimum, but she does wake periodically and is able to talk. If you need anyone, just press the buzzer twice. Now we will leave you alone with your daughter for a while. Come on, Jan, let's go and have a coffee. I can bring you up to date on her progress."

Jan and Rachel headed for the café; their conversation started about the case, and as they drank their coffee, they talked about the arrest.

Mrs Davies sat at her daughter's bedside holding her hand. She had trouble taking in the injuries she could see, let alone those hidden from sight. Sandy stirred and murmured something that her mother could not understand. Leaning closer, she whispered to her, "It's me, darling. Do you need anything?"

"Mum? Oh, Mum, is it really you?"

"Yes, sweetheart, I'm here. It took a while to find you, but I am here now."

"Please don't leave, Mum. Please stay with me. I sleep most of the time, but when I wake I will see you, and this will make me feel safer." Sandy's voice tailed off as she once again fell asleep.

My poor darling. Who could do this to you? A tear fell onto Mrs Davies hand, and then another, and before she knew it she was sobbing. She let her head rest on her arm very near Sandy's head. This was how she remained until the two nurses entered the ward.

"We're sorry, but we must give Sandy a sponge bath. You can stay if you like, but we need to get near the bed."

"That's okay, I'll sit over here until you've finished."

"Thank you. We won't be long."

Jan returned to Sandy's ward to ask Mrs Davies if she needed a lift back to the station.

"That won't be necessary, I'll stay here with Sandy. The nurses have made up a bed for me, and I can stay here all the time if I want."

"That's good. Well, I'm off home, but I will see you tomorrow."

As Jan entered her apartment, the phone rang. She dropped her files and lifted the phone. "Hello?"

Clarisse said, "It's me, Jan. Just ringing to remind you about Saturday. Be here at 2.00 p.m. sharp."

"Giving orders now, are we, Clarisse?" Jan joked.

"Yes, I guess I am. Surely you wouldn't miss your cousin's wedding, would you?"

"No, I wouldn't. By the way, can I bring Rachel?"

"Most certainly! I sent her an invitation; you need only to pick her up."

"Everything else okay? All the plans are going well?"

"They sure are, Jan. Mum made the most beautiful wedding cake today, and the rest of the food is being catered. This will leave Mum free to enjoy herself. Well, must go for now. See you Saturday."

"See you then, Clarisse. Bye for now."

Jan wondered how fate could play such terrible games. For her cousin and Clarisse, it was wonderful, but for Sandy it was not so good. In one of her lucid moments, Sandy had told them she had never hitch-hiked before; the only reason she had accepted it this time was the car had her home town plates. Jan had noted this information in Sandy's file, knowing it would enhance the evidence against Lachlan.

Sitting in his cell, Lachlan was not as brave as his ego made him appear. He now wondered about the time he had been in the cell and how many years he would spend, if convicted. These thoughts at first made him angry; from there it was easy to blame everybody except himself. *These bloody women begged for my advances. Why, then, have they turned on me? Surely, the jury would see them for what they were. Yes, they will acquit me in time, and then it's goodbye to this cell. There are more women to beg me again for my advances.* They would try though and he started to realize his part in what he believed was consensual sex wasn't. The action when he knocked them out was just to keep them quiet; perhaps it would have been better just to hit them but not knock them out.

This of course was a lunatic talking to himself; he fully believed it was just a wonderful sexual experience. The fact that he left these women bruised, bloodied, and traumatized did not enter his mind. He sat back on his cell bunk, curled his knees toward his chin, and wrapped his arms around them. Then he started to rock gently back and forth. He felt all the world was against him—they all spoke to him to like an animal, and polite conversation never happened. Even in the short visits from his mother and new lawyer, there was no laughter or general banter; all was stiff and sterile.

Through the atmosphere and the roughness meted out to him by the police all the time, they really made him feel his actions were disgusting,. *Mum will visit today.* It seemed an age since he had seen her, but then, she too was a woman. *Should I trust her? The bloody cops have got to her. They will get her to make me confess. Next time she comes, we won't talk about the case.* Lachlan sat back against the wall and smiled. He had their number.

Clarisse had been watching the clock ever since she woke. Time seemed to drag, and it took an age before she could leave for the airport. Finally it was time, and she set off. It was an easy drive and the time went quickly now. After pulling into the car park, she stopped, locked the car, and walked to the terminal. Jackson's plane landed, and before she knew it, she was in his arms.

"Hello, princess, how are you?"

"Great now. It is so good to see you."

Jackson lifted Clarisse off the floor as he hugged her, and a long lingering kiss followed. *I am in heaven in his arms,* as she thought as she squeezed her arms around him a little tighter.

"Let me breathe, darling! You're strangling me."

"Sorry, but I have to hold you tight. Want to know why?"

"Yes."

"Because I love you so much."

Jackson laughed, picked up his bag, and held Clarisse's hand as they walked out of the terminal. Upon reaching the car, Jackson asked about going to his new flat before going home.

"Of course we can, but why now? We could go later."

"I want to go now. I need to hold you close and make love to you, and this is the only chance we will have before the wedding."

"What if I said no?"

"Well, I'd cry. You don't want that now, do you?"

With a smile Clarisse squeezed his hand and nodded. Clarisse drove off toward the flat, and it wasn't far away. Soon they drove into the car park, not bothering to take the luggage out, and they walked into the building. Jackson unlocked the door and stood back, letting Clarisse enter. There on the table was the biggest bunch of roses Clarisse had ever seen.

"Oh, Jackson! They are lovely! But how?"

"Got a mate to get them for you. See, I can do things you don't know about."

Holding the roses in her hand, Clarisse lifted them to her face; the scent was just as lovely as the roses, and she turned to Jackson with a smile. "I love you so much. I wish it was tomorrow already."

"Do we need to wait for tomorrow?"

Clarisse held out her hand to Jackson, and they walked to the bedroom. They sat together on the bed, and Jackson began removing her clothes. He kissed her on the neck, ears, and mouth as Clarisse removed his shirt and undid his trousers and belt so they could fall to the floor. All this happened with no embarrassment. They lay back on the bed, wrapped in the arms of seductive love and its power, for the first time since Clarisse's rape. This would be, for Clarisse, a complete and wonderful sexual experience. As the waves of emotion flowed over them both, it melted them into a couple who loved each other completely.

Afterward, they lay in the comfort of each other's arms and talked about the island and their planned honeymoon. They had already made the reservations for later in the week. For the present, though, their lives were in the here and now, and the love affair that had begun so long ago on their island had won a battle over disaster.

"Jackson, wake up. It's late, and Mum will be in a state."

"No, she won't. We could come home at midnight, and she would just smile one of her knowing smiles which tell us everything is great."

After dressing, they quickly made the bed, picked up the roses, and left the apartment to drive home.

"Hi, Jackson, it's lovely to have you back," Flora said when they arrived. "Is the flat all right?"

"Yes, Mum, it is," Clarisse said. "How did you know that's where we've been?"

"A little bird told me."

Everyone was happy as they all walked inside. Jackson took his luggage into Clarisse's room while Clarisse found a vase for her roses. After dinner they discussed the plans for the next day: the wedding was at four and the breakfast at five; all the tables were set up on the veranda, ready for the food and drinks. When all was in order, Flora and Earnest went off to bed, leaving the two lovers together. Jackson suddenly remembered he hadn't rung Jan, and he picked up the phone. There was a slight delay before she answered.

"Hello, who is it?"

"It's me, cousin. Sorry about the lateness of the call. I arrived back just about lunch time."

"Cutting it fine, eh? Well, I'll see you tomorrow. Give Clarisse my love. Bye for now."

Jan replaced the phone and walked back to the table, where she had been sitting and talking to Rachel. Her thoughts were on Rachel, and she found herself asking what her true feelings were. Did they go beyond friendship? *Should I just tell her? But what would she say?*

"You're quiet, Jan. Was it bad news?"

"No, it was Jackson; he is at Clarisse's."

"The wedding is tomorrow, isn't it?" Rachel asked.

"Yes at two sharp. It should be a wonderful day."

Are you picking me up?"

Jan replied, "Would 1.30 be all right, that will give us plenty of time."

"Okay. Well I must go now, I want to call in and see Sandy before retiring. See you tomorrow."

Rachel left and drove to the hospital. As she entered Sandy's room, she noticed Mrs Davies asleep on the bed set up for her. Rachel sat on the chair near the bed and carefully placed her fingers on Sandy's pulse, waking her.

"Who is it?"

"It's Rachel. I just wanted to see how you were before I went home."

"My mum's here. Did you know?"

"Yes, I did. Tell me how the pain is. Are the drugs still effective?"

"They are, but I still can't move much; the pain then is very bad. How long will I have such pain?"

"I can't give you a definite answer yet. I will do a full medical on Monday; this should give us a better insight of your injuries and tell me how the internal injuries are progressing. I must leave now, but I will see you in the morning."

CHAPTER TWELVE

ALICIA WAS WONDERING WHY PAUL hadn't been in touch. She had rung his number many times without result. Deciding to try it again, she dialled the number, and to her surprise, there was an answer.

"Hello, this is Detective Smith. How can I help you?"

"Why are you answering Paul's phone? Has he been hurt?"

"Who are you? Do you know him?"

"Yes, he came to my house for dinner one evening."

"Oh yes! I remember, we were following him then. He is now in custody."

"Why, what for? He is a lovely man. What could he have done to be in jail?"

"I can't say anything much on the phone. I would suggest you go into the police station; there we can tell you what has happened."

"I don't believe that is necessary. Can you just tell me when he will be released?"

"If we have our way, it will be many years."

"I don't believe you! Just tell me what he has done."

"As I said before, if you want that information, you should visit the station. I am quite busy at the moment. Just believe me when I say that you are a very lucky woman. Bye for now."

The phone clicked in Alicia's ear. What had he done? Perhaps she should go to the station and find out. What made the detective say she was lucky? Surely, Paul hadn't done anything so bad. As these thoughts played in her mind, she wanted to know why he was in jail. Later that day, she decided to visit the police station and find out the truth. She drove to the station and made her query at the desk.

"Can I speak to someone about Paul Johnson?"

"Sorry, we don't have a Paul Johnson, only a Lachlan Johnson."

"Well, that must be him."

"I'll call the detective in charge. Jan, can you come to the front desk?"

A tall woman approached them and nodded to the desk officer while addressing the woman. "Hello, you wanted to talk to me?"

"Yes. Why is Paul—or Lachlan—in jail?"

"He is a suspect in several rape cases. I am sure we followed him to your home at one time. Sadly at that time we missed him."

Paul, a rapist? What a joke!"

"It is no joke. He has been charged with beating and raping several women. All I can say is you were very lucky."

"That's what the officer in Paul's flat said. He really is a rapist? How does such a gentleman do that?"

"He is no gentleman, I can assure you. It would be better for you to just forget him."

"It is still hard for me to imagine, but I guess I will have to."

"That is my advice. Go home and thank your friend—the man who ate with you that night. It was his presence that saved you."

"Thank you, Detective. I'll do just that."

Alicia left the station and drove home. Once there she sat and reflected on what might have been. *Thank goodness Kyle called in unexpectedly. I must tell him that he saved me that night. Thank goodness all men are not like Paul.* Holding that thought, Alicia decided to close all thought of Lachlan and then told herself to be more careful in the future.

Saturday dawned with the promise of a lovely day. All the plans were made for the wedding, and there was little rush.

Clarisse woke and looked at the man by her side. How handsome he was—and in only a few hours' time, he would be her husband.

Jackson's eyes opened, and he smiled at Clarisse. "Not long to go now. Not feeling like backing out, are you?"

Clarisse smiled back and then slipped out of bed, making for the shower.

"Am I invited?" Jackson yelled.

"The door's open."

Jackson stepped into the shower alongside her, and the water played over their bodies. Jackson picked up the soap, using the lather to massage his fiancée, and then they turned to face each other. The love they shared showed in their eyes; it was going to be a long shower.

"Are you two awake yet?" Flora hollered from downstairs.

"Yes, Mum, we're in the shower."

"Well, hurry up! There's a lot to do, you know."

They looked at each other and reluctantly stepped out of the shower, dressed, and joined Flora and Earnest at breakfast. After eating, they walked out to the back veranda. All the chairs were set out in rows, and a long buffet table was ready for the food.

Everything was perfect. It was a lovely sunny day, all the food was ready, and the clothes were laid out ready to wear. They only needed to wait for the afternoon; it was then that family and friends would surround them as they took their vows. How wonderful fate was—not only had Clarisse taken a holiday and met the best man in the world, but it was the one she would marry later that day.

He was the reason my ordeal at the hands of the Lachlan were bearable. His acceptance of my incapacity to have intercourse, when he came to find me—all of these things he understood, and he still loved me and wanted to marry me. This day is my day, the day all my dreams come together. Thoughts of the bad times were now past, and a new life beckoned.

Jan had gone to the station to check on the status of the case. While sitting in her office, her boss came in. "What in blazes are you doing here?" he said.

"Just needed to make sure the last few days weren't a dream."

"They weren't, so get out of here and get ready for your cousin and Clarisse's wedding."

"Yes, sir."

The two officers smiled at each other, nodded, and went their separate ways. Jan drove home, and once there she checked that her outfit for the wedding was all in order. As she was making a cuppa, the phone rang.

"Hello, Jan here."

Rachel said, "It's me. What time will you be picking me up?"

"I thought we had decided on 1.30?"

"Is it okay if I come over now?"

"Of course; you can dress here if you like."

"Thanks, Jan. I'll be there soon."

Jan hung up the phone and went back to her cuppa. She sat at the table, puzzled as to why Rachel was coming early. *She'll tell me when she gets here; it can't be anything to worry about, surely.* Her mind then turned to the afternoon and her friend's marriage. Fate was strange at times. Would this kind of romance happen often? Once here, even the rape made no difference to his feelings—in fact, it made them stronger. As she thought, Jan became even more proud of Jackson.

A knock on the door stopped her thoughts, and she opened it. "Hi, Rach, come in."

"I hope this isn't a bother."

"Of course not—you are welcome here any time. You know that."

"Thanks, Jan. I was feeling a little down. I called into Sandy's room, and her mother was there. The hurt and anguish on her face was terrible. All the questions she asked sent me back to Clarisse. I didn't have the answers she needed to hear. I told her and Sandy that I would be doing a full internal on Monday. Oh, Jan, I am frightened of what I might find. Even though we have done a short examination and have treated everything we thought of, Monday could tell us much more."

"Come on, let's enjoy today and face whatever comes on Monday. You will know what to do, as you always have."

Jan hugged Rachel, and the tears flowed and wet Jan's shoulder. This was a doctor who felt the pain of others, so her friendship with a no-nonsense cop gave her a feeling of a loving and compassionate relationship.

"Want a cuppa, Rach?"

"That would be great, thanks."

Jan turned back to the stove, replacing the kettle. She needed the time to compose herself. What were these feelings and, what should she do about them? The question at that time had no answer. With the cuppas made, the two friends sat at the table and discussed the coming wedding. Glancing at the clock, they started to dress for the wedding. When ready, they drove to the Stewart house for the coming wedding.

Clarisse was already dressed, and Jackson had disappeared into the spare room with Earnest. Both men dressed in the rented suits, tied their ties, and put a little more polish on their shoes. Jackson's closest friend, Phil, had arrived late the previous night, had booked into a hotel, and had taken a taxi to the house; he was already dressed for his part as best man. The job of bridesmaid fell to Jan, a job she relished. Clarisse's friends from the office started to arrive, plus the police officers and nurses who had helped her so much. After everyone had arrived, the house was quite full, and a buzz filled the air. Jackson and Phil took their place near the arbour in the back yard. Earnest, with Clarisse on his arm, began the walk down the carpet toward them; Jan followed them, and soon the wedding began.

Clarisse wore a short white dress and carried a posy of white roses. Jan was dressed in blue, which complimented the bride in every way. Flora sat in the front row with Rachel, Kelly, Mary, and John behind her. The celebrant began the ceremony, vows and rings were exchanged, and a long, lingering kiss sealed the joining of two people who loved each other very much. All took their places at the tables, and the wedding breakfast began, speeches were made, and a few jokes were told. From wherever people sat, this was a day to remember, but doubly so for Clarisse and Jackson.

Jackson stood to give his speech. "Today I married the most beautiful woman in the world. This wedding should have happened earlier, but I didn't realize how much I loved her, for almost a year. However she is now mine, and I am hers forever. Could you all stand and toast my wife? To Clarisse."

All stood and said, "To Clarisse."

Clarisse rose and repeated, almost word for word, what Jackson had said, but she added all the officers, Rachel, Jan, and her parents. She then for a toast to all of them. This ended the wedding but not the fun; everyone stayed for the evening and complimented Flora for the organization and the wonderful wedding cake. Jackson had held Clarisse's hand almost all of the time, and as it grew later he looked at her with a look that said, "Can we leave now?" She nodded yes.

"Okay, all of you, Clarisse and I are about to leave," Jackson said. "I don't think Flora and Earnest will throw you out, but we are going. Thank you all for making this day a wonderful one full of memories we will always keep. Goodbye for now."

Every one cheered as they left. Flora cried, and Earnest told her not, which had no effect. Jan and Rachel followed them out to the car.

"Have a wonderful week, you two. We'll see you when you get back."

They said thanks as the car drove off.

With the happiness of the romance and marriage behind her, Jan had to look ahead: she had a brutal rapist to convict. Monday morning would be the beginning of the concentrated effort of the rape crisis team. It would

ELIZABETH BLACKMAN

be work and more work for the foreseeable future. Even though they had two of the women ready to give evidence, the third was still gravely ill. With these thoughts in her mind, Jan drove to her flat, and here Rachel said goodbye and left for the hospital.

After parking her car, Rachel entered the hospital, opened her office door, and sat at her desk. There were three files there. The top file was for Sandy, and she read the entries from the day. From these entries; Rachel knew the girl was a long way from any real recovery. She left her office and walked to Sandy's room. Sandy's mum was still there, sitting and holding her daughter's hand. Rachel placed her hand lightly on her shoulder.

"Oh! It's you, Doctor. You gave me quite a start."

"Sorry, I didn't mean to frighten you. How has Sandy been today?"

"We had a short talk, but mostly she sleeps. Is that all right?"

"The drugs she is receiving are for just that purpose; it is essential she rests, both mind and body. I will leave her this way until Monday, and then I will have to perform a full external and internal examination. Her chart shows she hasn't developed any infections, which is good news."

"What will you be looking for, Doctor?"

"Please, call me Rachel. I like an informal atmosphere. As you know, Sandy was injured severely internally, and I need to know if the operation has been successful. I can only determine this with the examination."

"You are quite wonderful, Doc—Rachel. So is your staff. I know Sandy is in good hands, and you all give my daughter the fighting chance she needs. I cannot express my thanks adequately."

"We take a great deal of pride in our work. That work now is Sandy, and believe me when I say, if it is in my power, she will recover fully. I must go now, but I will see you tomorrow."

Rachel left the room and returned to her office. Her thoughts were on the newlyweds and what a great day it had been. Just seeing the love between the two made her think of Jan. *I guess she wants an early night after the excitement of the day.* The phone rang, startling her.

"Hello, Dr Scott here."

"Hello, Rach, it's Jan."

"I was just thinking of you! Some sort of telepathy, you think?"

Jan laughed. "Want to take in a movie tonight?"

"What a great idea. Where will we meet?"

"I'll pick you up at six, Will that be okay?"

"Sure, I'll see you then."

True to her word, Jan arrived right at six. Rachel was at the curb waiting, and she waved as Jan stopped and opened the door.

"What movie will we see?"

"Would you mind if we just have dinner at a nice restaurant?"

"Dinner would be fine."

Upon reaching the restaurant, Jan parked the car, and as they walked to the front door, Rachel reached out and took Jan's hand in hers.

"What's up, Rach? You're not yourself tonight."

"I went and saw Sandy before I rang you. Things are not good."

"She will recover won't she?"

"Oh yes, but her injuries are extensive. It is her mental state that is my biggest concern."

"I can't wait to get that bastard in jail, but he won't suffer like his victims have. The only way he'll get his just desserts is if he is housed with the lowest and nastiest prisoners in the jail."

"Why do you say that? Are they likely to hurt him?" Rachel asked.

"You bet. He is a bit of a pansy, and the others will think nothing of sorting him out."

"Really? Well, that would teach him a lesson. But what if the court thinks he's crazy?"

"We have to make sure that doesn't happen. Can we not talk about him now? It has been a lovely day, and I would like to finish it that way."

"Sorry. Let's order something extravagant for dinner. My treat."

The two women ordered and managed to laugh as they remembered the wedding and the look of love between the bride and groom. Everyone was so happy, there were jokes aplenty, and laughter rang out the whole time. Jan thought about her cousin and how life could be at one time sad, and the next so wonderful.

She knew he and Clarisse would be happy, and she was glad that Jackson wouldn't be far away from her now. His flat was quite near, as was Flora and Earnest. Her thoughts flowed, and Rachel called to her.

"Hey, you come back and talk to me!"

"Sorry. I was just thinking of the newlyweds, and how I would have Jackson close to me. Let's forget it all and eat."

"Suits me."

With that said, they ate their meal and talked about the day. After finishing their meal, they walked to the car, and Jan drove Rachel home, dropping her off before she drove home for some much-needed sleep.

D-C John Barton was once again on duty at the hospital, and he sat in the chair outside Sandy's door. Each time he was on duty, he looked to see if Sandy was asleep. If she was, he stood looking down at her. *She is so lovely, with her curly blonde hair spread out over her pillow. How could anyone hurt her? Only that depraved bastard we have in custody. I wish I could just give him a thumping, just as he did to his victims. When they convict him, they should hang him. That will not happen, though, with all the goody-goodies saying he is sick. His lawyer will say he didn't know what he was doing. What a load of garbage—he is not sick. If he was, how could he so carefully plan what he was going to do? Surely that in itself is enough to prove he is normal and knew exactly what he was doing.*

John felt a hand on his shoulder, and turning, he saw Mrs Davies. "I'm sorry I'll leave now," he said.

"Let's talk in the passage," she suggested.

"You have a lovely daughter, Mrs Davies."

"Thank you for that, John. You care for her, don't you?"

"Is it that obvious?"

"I'm afraid so. It must be hard in your job, when dealing with men like the one responsible for my daughter's condition."

"I hate him. He is evil, and the sooner he is put away, the better."

"I understand, but you must not come into Sandy's room—you know that."

"It won't happen again. It is enough for me just to be near, making sure nobody else hurts her."

John took his seat outside the room, Sandy's mother sat in the chair near her daughter's bed.

Monday came slowly for Rachel, and all she could think of was Sandy: what would she find, and was she healing as well as expected? She walked to her office, and the duty nurse gave her the report for the weekend, everything seemed in order.

"How is Sandy this morning, Nurse?"

"She still sleeps a lot, but her temperature is normal, and she is resting comfortably with the aid of the drugs."

"That's great. I will be giving her a full external and internal examination today. If all is well, I will start lowering the morphine dose. Rachel went toward Sandy's room, where she noticed John outside the door.

"Do you ever go home, John?"

"Yes, I do, but only for a quick sleep, then a shower and shave before I come back."

"Why?"

"If I had noticed his car was gone, and there was no note of it in the log, this wouldn't have happened."

"Oh, John, you are no more to blame than any of us. It was not your shift, so please don't blame yourself."

"I'll try, but when I look at her, I feel so helpless."

"We all feel that way, but we aren't. All we can do now is to make sure Sandy gets well, both in mind and body."

"What you say is a comfort, but I will still put in guarding her."

"Very well. Would you like to come in?"

"No. Sandy doesn't want me in the room. I'll stay out here."

Rachel nodded to John and then walked in to see Sandy. Mrs Davies rose from her bunk as she heard Rachel come in.

"How is she?" Rachel asked.

"She slept well—or should I say, the drugs allowed her the rest she needs. This is the big day, eh? What exactly are you looking for from the examination?"

"During the first operation we had to suture the vaginal wall, plus some damage to the neck of the cervix. I want to make sure they are healing. While Sandy is under the anaesthetic, it will be easier to observe the other injuries, like her broken hand and dislocated elbow. To make it plainer, we can do all of the invasive examinations while Sandy is asleep. In this way we can save her a lot of pain and embarrassment. Anything we can do to alleviate this, both mentally and physically, can only aid in her recovery."

"Thanks for that, Doctor. She really has suffered enough."

"Please call me Rachel; it makes life much easier, don't you think?"

"My name is Allison."

Rachel let her hand rest on Allison's shoulder in acceptance of her wishes. She stood at the bedside and looked at Sandy, who still slept peacefully. *What will I find today? Will all be well and improving as the days pass?*

Sandy stirred and opened her eyes. "Where's Mum?"

"I'm here, sweetheart."

"Have I been asleep long?"

"Yes, quite a while. Dr Scott is here and wants to talk to you."

"Hello, Doc. Is this the day for my examination?"

Rachel said, "Yes, it is. A nurse will give you your premed injection in about thirty minutes. Shortly after that, they will bring you to me in the theatre. Here the anaesthetist will put you to sleep, and the examination will take place. Please don't worry—I'm sure all is healing well—but it is necessary to make sure."

"I'm in your hands and know you will look after me."

Rachel smiled at Sandy and her mother, and then she returned to her office. While sitting at her desk, she wondered how the case against Lachlan was going. She didn't have time to ring Jan, so the question would have to wait until later.

CHAPTER THIRTEEN

THE RAPE CRISIS TEAM WAS in full swing. They had charged Lachlan with three counts of aggravated rape and one of attempted murder. His cries of innocence went unheard; no one who heard him could care less, and in fact in most cases it was music to their ears.

Jan was in the main squad room surrounded by her colleagues. All the files were on the table in the centre of the room, and Jan picked them up and handed one to each of the officers. She looked at them and began to set out her orders.

"I do not have to tell you how important the time between now and the trial is. You can't leave a stone unturned or a page unread. His guilt must be unquestionable. Every piece of clothing, any DNA evidence securely—it must be kept in the evidence locker. Log everything from his flats; nothing is too small, and you must miss nothing. If you need help, then asked for it; don't think, it's not important. Believe me when I say everything is important. Kelly and Mary are working with the forensics team, and there is a wealth of evidence from the last rape. The last victim came very close to death, and though much attention must go to her, please do not forget the others. Each and every victim has been traumatized for life, so we must convict him. He mustn't be given any latitude to mount a defence. Do I make myself clear?"

A loud yes from all convinced Jan she had the right team. The witnesses would bring to a close this most horrific spate of crimes. Lachlan could not slip away—she would make sure of that. Each officer in the group knew that their boss meant every word; they, too, had a stake in this conviction, because many of them saw how Clarisse and Sandy looked after the attack. If they needed incentive, that was it; they were prepared to work day and night until they convicted their prisoner.

"Mary and Kelly, come with me," Jan said.

"We are right behind you, Jan. Where are we going?"

"Just to my office—I need to talk to you alone. Kelly, I want you to go and see Alicia; she could be a prospective witness for the defence, and she believes Lachlan is a man who couldn't rape anyone. It will be your job to convince her otherwise; show her the photos and any other evidence that could change her mind."

"Got you, Jan. I'll start right now."

"Mary, you and I have the job of going through all his effects. By this I mean we need to search the other flat. If you're ready, we will go now."

Jan and Mary drove to the address of the other flat. They walked up the stairs and reached the landing on which the flat was located. They stood in front of the door for a while, just looking, and then Jan slipped the key in the lock and opened the door. The cleanliness of the flat surprised them: this flat spoke of a person everyone had said he was—before he attacked them. Jan went into the bedroom to search while Mary stayed in the living area. Upon opening a drawer, Jan gasped at what she saw.

"Geez, Mary, come in here!"

"What's up? Bloody hell, what are all these for?"

"I know what they are, but I hope he never used them."

Both police officers reluctantly picked up each item and placed them in an evidence bag. They felt disgust for the man who had such weapons in his possession, the only purpose of which was to inflict extreme pain. Working as one, they soon had all the evidence from the flat bagged and ready for the forensics team.

Jan sat at the table, removed her gloves, and turned to Mary. "Have you ever seen such an array of items made for violence in your life? Everything in this flat shouted sadism. That's what he is, a bloody sadist."

"You're right. Half of the stuff I've never seen before, let alone know they existed. He really is a monster, isn't he?"

"Yes, he is. Well, let's get out of here—it makes me sick just knowing he lived here."

After locking the door behind them, they walked out to the car and drove back to the station. Jan took the evidence bags to the forensics lab and told them where they came from. "Give them your full attention. If they show signs of use, there may be some DNA evidence left on them."

Staying only a short time, Jan went back to her office, and once there she began going through all the other evidence from the flat. In one of the bags she found a diary. What it held would shock her more than she knew: every detail about what he would do to each victim was written in graphic detail. Jan found it necessary to stop reading and take a deep breath, but eventually she closed it all together. Leaving her office, she went to the lunchroom and made herself a coffee. As Jan sipped her coffee, what she had seen and read filled her mind. The horror of what he had done—and what he would have done, if he had he not been caught.

Why are people born with such terrible flaws in their character? Are all deviants born, or do they consciously become what they want to be? If this is so, is there a cure, or are they just content to get their satisfaction any way they can? Does it become necessary for them to make others suffer, in order for them to exist. Police officers face this kind of sadistic behaviour forever; their duty to protect will always be put to the test, because of the Lachlans of this world.

"You okay, Jan?"

"Geez, Kelly, why don't you make a noise when you come in?"

"Sorry, didn't mean to scare you."

"You didn't scare me, just startled me."

"Whatever you say, boss. Why the deep thoughts, anyway?"

"Have you seen the latest exhibits from his flat?"

"No. That bad, huh?"

"You bet. Well, I'm off to the hospital. Rach should have finished her examination by now. See you, Kelly."

"Sure, Jan. Do you want me to do anything while you're gone?"

"No, just carry on."

Jan made her way to the hospital and saw Rachel was at her desk. She entered. "Hi, Rach, everything okay?"

"Oh! Hi, Jan, you startled me. Come in."

"How did the examination go?"

"I am happy to say it all went well. Everything is healing, and I'm sure she her ability to have children has not been affected."

"That's wonderful. I needed some good news today, after what we ran into at the jerk's flat."

"Don't tell me—I want to hang on to my happy news for a while."

"I won't, love; I'll just let you take me to see Sandy."

Jan and Rachel shared a joke as they walked, and they still had a smile when they reached Sandy's room. Allison put her finger to her lips, and Jan and Rachel nodded and beckoned her out into the corridor.

"How is she, Allison?"

"She has only woken once; she spoke to me for a short time."

Jan said, "We'll leave her to sleep. I see her devoted doorman is back on duty?"

"He makes me feel safe—you should be proud of him, Jan."

"Proud of John? Yes, I am. It was his work that gave us the lead to capture our rapist."

Rachel chimed in. "You could include yourself and the other team members in that."

"Thanks, Rach. It was our job to get him, but I wish it had been sooner."

Rachel said, "I must go now, Allison, but I will be back again soon. Come on, Jan."

"Right with you, Rach."

They walked away, talking about the case and speculating on how long it would it be before the trial. Their conversation also included the honeymooners, and if they were having a wonderful time. Jan's thoughts turned to Jackson and his new wife. *Fate is a funny thing sometimes. Who would have thought these two would be together after such a trauma-filled eighteen months?*

Clarisse and Jackson were enjoying their time together. Again they walked the beach, their feet crunching on the sand. Jackson loved to hold Clarisse close, to remind him she was his. *I must be the luckiest man alive. What luck it was to meet her. But I was an idiot, because of the time it took to face my true feelings.*

Their lovemaking was perfect, starting with a shower together. After drying, he lifted her in his arms and placed her on the bed. Silken kisses moved from lips to breast as the power of love engulfed them in its passion. They were as one, and their love for each other brought them to a sensual climax that never seemed to end.

Clarisse also felt privileged to be in the arms of the man she had married. He was so wonderful. *Never does he ask for anything I can't give. If the memories intrude, he whispers in my ear and holds me close.*

At these times he would not press for a sexual encounter, just comfort in the embrace of his arms, letting her know at this time there would be only comfort.

"Good morning, my love. We didn't get a great amount of sleep last night."

"We didn't? Well what were we doing?"

"Making love, I guess. Did you mind?" he joked.

"Oh, Jackson, what can I say. Of course I didn't. How anyone could mind—but then, you're mine now, so I needn't worry."

"Should we get up now and have breakfast? I really would like to go for a walk with you along the beach to our secluded cove."

Clarisse smiled at him and nodded. After eating a leisurely breakfast, they set off on their walk. It was a beautiful day, and tomorrow they had to leave for home. Neither wanted to go, but Jackson's new posting had come through, and he had to report on the Monday. Clarisse had also decided to resume work; she felt more confident now and was able to face whatever happened. Jackson told her she need not work, but she wanted to, even if only for a short time. Their cove came into sight, and they looked at each other and smiled. Here they could lie on their towels and let happen whatever was to happen.

Lying on his back, Jackson looked up at Clarisse. How beautiful she was. How did he get so lucky? *She loves me. What could be better than that?* His thoughts were interrupted by a long, searching kiss. His body came alive, and the kiss returned. The lotion they had applied made their body's slide, and the kiss lingered as Jackson let his hands explore his wife's body. Slowly he unlaced her top and let it fall. Her breasts fell into his hands, and he massaged her nipples them until they rose and hardened. Clarisse let her hands slide down and remove his trunks while he removed hers; they each lay naked beneath the warm sun. Once again their lovemaking began. His movements were slow and deep, and his kisses searched her very soul. He rolled her over and lifted her upright on his lap, and it was in this position that their mutual climax came.

Clarisse moved her hands in sensual movements over his chest and back, massaging his body until he was ready to make love again. Jackson let his arms slide around her, and he gently pulled her down until their lips locked in a kiss that tasted of liquid nectar. Their lovemaking over, they lay looking at each other, and a smile played on Jackson's lips as he looked at Clarisse.

"Have I done something wrong?" she asked.

"What could you do wrong, you are like a vintage wine, one that I would like to drink, but am content to just sip, one drop at a time."

"I'm like wine to you now? Well, please drink me slowly, so I can savour you also, to the last drop."

"I will, and it will take a lifetime. Now, let's go for one last swim before we dress and leave our cove."

Their swim over, Clarisse kissed him gently and then pulled on her bathers. Jackson watched every movement, and his eyes told the story of the love he had for her. Again he felt the need, but he clasped her hand in his, and they walked back to the bungalow.

After dinner, they started to pack ready for the next morning. Neither spoke, because it wasn't what they wanted. Why had their time gone so quickly? It seemed only yesterday that they had arrived. Cases packed and dinner over, they retired for the night in each other's arms. The story of their love was played out again before sleep overtook them.

With the morning came the time to leave. Jackson picked up the bags and put them in the car. Clarisse stepped into the car, and after a long look back, they set off for the city and home. Arriving at the flat, Jackson carried the cases upstairs, opened the door, and entered. "Will you come and see what they have done?"

"Well, I'll be. What a homecoming!"

They were both looking at the large bunch of flowers on the table, and a bottle of champagne with glasses ready for them to drink. In the kitchen they found a cooked meal, ready to heat and enjoy.

"What a family we have. Who do you think is the culprit?"

"Probably all of them—Mum, Dad, and Jan. I wouldn't put it past Rachel either."

"Well, Clarisse, we will have to amuse ourselves. Now, what can we do?"

"I have no idea. Do you have a suggestion?"

"Hum, let me think . . . Yes, I know—but I won't tell you until after we've eaten."

A smile played on Clarisse's lips as she looked at him. She knew what he was thinking, and it was definitely on her mind.

The following morning, Jackson kissed his wife and went to report at his new office. Clarisse went to the hospital to see Rachel.

Rachel greeted her with a smile and beckoned her into the office. "Is everything all right, Clarisse?"

"I am a little puzzled, and I don't know how to begin."

"I always say at the beginning is best. So tell me, what's wrong?"

"I can't understand why I can be so intimate with Jackson, but I find only disgust at the thought of any other man. Does this sound silly? Should I feel the way I do about Jackson? Don't women who have been violated find any sexual intimacy abhorrent? If this is the case, why is it so easy to be intimate with him?"

"You are right about the women who are attacked as you were; they can suffer with an inability to become intimate. However, in your case I believe your love for Jackson was there, and it had been deep so for many months. When he came back into your life, he pushed the ordeal into the background. I must say the love between you two is palpable; it is there for all to see. To me, this is the trigger: Jackson is love, and Lachlan is evil. Your feelings toward him and other men is quite normal. I think as your life continues, these thoughts will go away. And please, my dear, don't think your love for Jackson makes any difference to what you suffered at Lachlan's hands."

"Thanks for that, Rachel. You are right about our love: it is warm, gentle, and sensual. Jackson is the perfect husband and lover. By that I mean he never demands but waits for me to want him."

"Two people who are meant to be together always make me happy. In your case, I am ecstatic."

"Thanks! I must go now. Oh, how is Sandy?"

"I shouldn't discuss it, but she is getting better every day."

Clarisse nodded to Rachel, left the hospital, and made her way to the office. She noticed every head come up as she entered. Her boss came out of her office and was smiling as she neared Clarisse.

"Do you want to start work again?" she asked.

"Yes, I would. Will next Monday be all right?"

"That's fine. We will see you then."

All the staff members came up to Clarisse, offering their congratulations on her marriage, and their happiness at her return to work. As she left, Clarisse was very happy. She had a wonderful marriage, and now she knew her workmates would welcome her back. Life felt good, and there was only one dark cloud above her: the trial to come.

CHAPTER FOURTEEN

KELLY STOPPED OUTSIDE ALICIA„S HOME. and stepped out of the car. She made her way to the door, pressed the buzzer, and waited for the door to open. Kelly heard footsteps, and then the door opened, but only as far as the safety chain would let it. She held out her police identity badge to Alicia.

"I am Detective Sergeant Smith. I would like to talk to you about Lachlan Johnson."

"Why? I don't wish to be involved."

"I'm sorry, but you are already involved. Please let me in; we could talk more privately."

"Oh, all right, but it really is an inconvenience."

Kelly entered and followed Alicia to the dining room, and they sat at opposite sides of the table.

"We are concerned that the defence could call you as a witness," Kelly explained.

"I won't be appearing for anyone. As I said, Paul was a friend and a gentleman, but if I believed the police, he is a monster. I only had the one date. If what you say is true, it was fortunate another friend had dropped in. I asked him to stay for dinner, which he accepted, and he and Paul talked together like old friends. Not long after Kyle left, Paul left also, saying he would ring me about another date. I waved to him and then came back inside. This is the extent of my friendship with him. I fail to see how I could give evidence."

"I do have some photos of the women he attacked. Perhaps they could change your mind."

"I have no desire to look at anything to do with the case, so please don't say any more. Just leave."

"Thank you for listening. You will hear from the prosecution team, and they will urge you to make a decision. Please listen to the evidence and make the right decision. Goodbye for now."

Kelly rose and walked back to the front door. Alicia followed her, opened the door, offered a begrudging goodbye, and then slammed the door. While driving back to the station, Kelly thought about Alicia. Why was she so defensive? Had the defence approached her already? Jan would have the answer—there must be some way to inform her of the complete facts of the case, and perhaps a chat with Clarisse would change her mind. *Don't be silly, Kelly, that would be against the law.* All she could do was report about the interview to Jan.

Kelly returned to the station, parked her car, and went straight to Jan's office; she knocked, entered, and sat in the chair.

"Well, how did it go?" Jan asked.

"She won't co-operate at all—says she hasn't been approached by the defence. I don't believe her."

"Did you show her any of the photos?"

"No. She refused to look at them."

"Well then, she will change her mind quickly when served with a summons to appear for the prosecution. We will leave her for now—she really is small fish, anyway. It's almost lunch. Shall we go together?"

"Where's Mary?"

"She is with John at the lab looking over the evidence. It seems they find more every hour they work. They will probably be there for a few hours. Come on, let's go."

With all the evidence coming together, it was time the rape crisis team and the defence began working together. The job before them may have looked easy, but no rape case ever was. All the witnesses had to be informed and their statements gathered; it was essential that both sides worked in harmony.

The completed forensic evidence was ready; this included DNA from the victims and from the perpetrator, done with the aid of a warrant. Clarisse and Sue had given a full description of the defendant even though he had dyed his hair and changed his eye colour. Clarisse was in no doubt that it was him. Sandy's statement could wait until later; she could write it just before the trial began. Rachel had also submitted a written affidavit; of course, she would be the chief medical officer to present evidence in the court itself. The scientists from the forensic lab would also give their evidence in court, even though their written statements were on file with the police evidence.

The scene was set, all the hard work almost at an end, but still the team worked tirelessly, making sure there were no loopholes for the defence lawyers to exploit. Jan was happy: the work of almost two years was slowly coming together. The happiness didn't only come from work—seeing Clarisse and Jackson together was a factor. Both of them were working now, and life for them was complete. Jan then thought of Rachel. Their friendship had also progressed, and they went to movies and had dinners out. On the odd occasion, Rachel stayed over at Jan's flat. All Jan wanted was to see Lachlan convicted and jailed for a long time. If justice was done, it would be life.

John still took his turn guarding the door at the hospital, even though the rapist was in jail. Sandy still needed to know she was safe. She was recovering extremely well; the fighting spirit she shown when attacked was now helping her get well. Jan visited as often as she could, and of course Rachel and Allison spent a lot of time in her room. Allison quite often went to Rachel's office to ask questions about her daughter.

"Hello, can I come in for a while?"

"Of course," Rachel said. "What can I help you with?"

"I know Sandy's bruises and cuts that are visible are healing, but is her broken arm going to be all right?"

"All of these things will heal with time. But that is not what you want to know, is it?"

"Is it that visible? Doctor, you are right. Will she recover from the internal injuries, and will the mental anguish she has suffered lessen over time?"

"The internal injuries have responded to medication; the sutures have dissolved, and they only do that when healed. Her mental state at this time is not so easy to diagnose. I have spoken to a psychiatrist I know, and when I feel Sandy is ready, I will bring her into the case. This is all I can do at the moment."

"You have done so much, and so have the police. If Sandy can stay here, I'm sure she will recover fully. I can't thank you all enough."

"You are right. The police and I do work together in these cases; we trust each other completely, and if we have our way, Sandy will recover both mentally and physically."

"Thank you for all that. I had better get back to Sandy now."

With those words, Allison walked back into her daughter's room. Outside the door was her faithful guardian. He had started a new shift and sat relaxed, nodding his head as Allison walked past.

John knew he had strong feelings for Sandy, but he could never say it. Jan would relieve him from the hospital team. Although if he had the opportunity, he would stand in the doorway and look at her.

"Get out of the doorway, John." John would whisper these words to himself, but it was hard to go back to the chair. He wondered if, when she was completely well, things would be different. He could tell her his feelings, and maybe she would love him, too. But deep down he was afraid she might never recover. He prayed that she would return to the woman she was before a vicious rapist took her innocence and confidence away, just to satisfy his own deviant desires. *The trial cannot start soon enough. How great it will be when he's in prison, at the mercy of his fellow inmates. He will not be so smug then.*

Jan had talked to all of the rape victims, asking if they would give evidence at the trial. Many had said they would be happy to appear for the prosecution. All the files about the rapes were at to the prosecutor's office, with the forensics safely locked away. They charged Lachlan with seven cases of rape, with violence and two of attempted murders and aggravated assaults. Now there was time to relax a little and await the coming trial. Lachlan's mother had been to the station again, saying that her son could not do such a thing. She had hired a lawyer, and Lachlan was examined by a psychiatrist; his report was with the defence, with a copy sent to the prosecution.

The prosecution lawyers kept Jan updated as to what the defence intended to do. It was their intention to use an insanity plea because they felt this was his best chance of winning. Jan knew her team must have their testimonies expose the true picture of the events: all that had happened must be unquestionable, and they had to give their evidence about the crimes in their own words.

With all of the material evidence pointing toward Lachlan, the forensics team was also ready. Their testimony was overwhelming and was in itself enough to convict. The prosecution also had a psychiatrist who had examined Lachlan, and his findings were positive: he believed Lachlan knew exactly what he was doing. He had planned with precision each rape; he wined and dined women until they trusted him, and then with controlled aggression, he raped and beat them until they could no longer fight back. His evidence would be damning—he stripped away the insanity plea so all they needed now was a jury that believed in truth and justice.

Jan sat in her office staring at the papers in front of her. She was deep in thought when a voice broke her reverie.

"You okay, Jan?" Rachel asked.

"What?"

"I just asked if you were okay."

"Of course I'm okay. Why would you think otherwise?"

"Come on. You were about a hundred miles away, or at least your mind was."

"I guess it was. I was going over what is going to happen from here on."

"Thought that might be it. Feel like a break?"

"Sure, what do you have in mind?"

"Lunch, before visiting Sandy. She wants to ask you about her testimony."

"Sounds great, but are you sure she is ready?"

"It was her suggestion, so let's go."

Jan called to the staff, telling them she would be out, and to ring if they needed her. The two women walked to a nearby café, sat, and read the menu. They decided on ham sandwiches and coffee, when finished they went back to the hospital.

They made their way to Sandy's room; she was lying back on the pillows as they entered, and a smile played on her lips. Rachel and Jan sat on the chairs while Allison sat on the end of the bed.

"Thank you for coming, Jan," Sandy said.

"That's all right, how are you feeling?"

"Much better now. I couldn't run a marathon, but I'm okay. Mum told me the trial is getting closer."

"Yes, it is, but we have time. Don't feel you have to push yourself."

"I won't, but I should start. Would it be okay for me to write my memories down? This way if I get upset, I can stop."

"Oh, Sandy, I'm not sure you should do that,"

"Why not, Rachel?"

"You need someone with you while you write."

"I'll be here Rachel. I can watch. If I leave, I'll take the book." Said Sandy's mum.

"In that case, it will be all right but, Sandy must not be alone."

"Are you all sure about this? There really isn't any hurry."

"Please, Jan, let me do it. I want this deviant to get what he deserves."

"Okay, sweetheart but don't push yourself, I want you to get better."

"One other thing, Sandy: you have heard me speak of Clarisse. Well, she wants to visit you. I have stopped her until now, but if you agree, I'll tell her."

"I would like that; from all I hear, she is really nice. Please ask her to come. I would love to see her."

"Isn't she just wonderful? I'm the proudest mum around, and I love her so very much," Allison said.

A chorus in the positive from Jan and Rachel made Sandy blush. "You have all been so great to me, and I care for you all. I am in Mum's loving hands at all times, the nursing care is wonderful, and my guardian is always near."

With that Rachel and Jan left the room. Jan nodded to John and then placed her hand on his shoulder and gave it a friendly squeeze. John felt a warm glow; he knew his boss was happy with him and his work.

Rachel went on her rounds. Jan returned to the station and was pleased to see her team hard at work. As she sat down in her office, she thought back to the first rapes. Could they be encouraged to give evidence? If all the women came forward, the result of the trial would not be in doubt. With these thoughts she reached for the phone and dialled the first woman on her list.

"Hello, can I help you?"

"This is Detective Inspector Hastings. I am calling all the women who have been attacked by the same rapist. I'm asking, once again, would you appear in court when the trial begins?"

"No! I won't do that. I am over it now and have a new boyfriend; he doesn't know anything about it. I am sorry, but I have the rest of my life to think of. Please don't contact me again."

"I understand your hesitancy, but we have him in custody, and with your evidence we will help convict him".

"My answer is no. Goodbye."

The phone clicked in Jan's ear, giving her quite a start. *Well, she could have been a little less nasty.* Finding her file, Jan traced a red line under her name, all the while thinking, *If needed, you'll be there.* Jan rang each of the women from the earlier rape cases, and they all had the same answer: none of them would give evidence or a statement. Sitting looking at the phone, Jan had trouble believing that these women, who had been so badly traumatized, preferred to stay anonymous.

Could it be they were afraid of the publicity? Yes, this was what it must be. All she could do was shake her head in disappointment. From the reaction of all the women, it was obvious that her squad could only rely on Clarisse, Sue, and Sandy. Would this be enough? There was abundant forensic evidence; the only thing troubling Jan was the intended plea of insanity. An independent court psychiatrist should examine him before the trial., Jan's thoughts were slowly showing her the way she must go to get the conviction she desperately wanted. It was her job to make sure the three women would see their tormentor convicted and jailed for a long time.

Lachlan's lawyer had visited him, and he had asked for time to bring himself up to date and to have Lachlan examined by a psychiatrist. The plea, as Jan expected, was to be one of insanity. If a person was insane and not in control of their senses, could he plan the dates and set up the scenario for the beating and rape of these women? In addition his ability to play the gentleman and then disappear after each attack indicated his sanity.

Lachlan still believed he had every one fooled. He had disdain for the police officers and very open dislike of Jan and her team. *They don't have the evidence to convict me. Freedom will be mine soon, and then I will exact punishment on these inferior people.*

He spent time making up these plans; at times he would laugh and snicker. What fun he would have—the snotty Jan first, then the others. Clarisse he would save for last. Hers would be the most agonizing rape and death. He knew this would need careful planning.

The cell door opened, jolting him out of his reverie as his mother came in.

"Hello, son, how are you today?"

"What the hell are you here for?"

"I just wanted to see you. Is that a crime?"

"Just make sure I have the best lawyer. I haven't done anything wrong, so bloody well get me out of here!?"

"I can't, son. You have to stay in custody until your trial."

"Has that bum of yours left the house?"

"That bum, as you call him, is now my husband."

Lachlan stood up, and leaned across the table. He grabbed his mother by the front of her blouse, pulling her close. "He's what?"

"Guard, guard! Please let me out!"

"You're not going anywhere! Just sit down and shut up," Lachlan growled.

The door opened, and two guards entered. They grabbed Lachlan and flung him back into the chair. They warned, "Move again, and we will cuff you."

"I'm leaving, and I won't be back," his mother said. "I know now just the type of man you are. I hope they convict you, and you get what you deserve!"

"No, Mum, don't go! Please don't go!"

"Just shut up," the guards said. "Your mother has gone, and you have probably lost the most important person and witness in your life."

The two guards left the cell and walked to the front desk. Jan was there talking to Lachlan's mother, and they stood behind the desk and overheard Jan ask, "Are you okay?"

"Yes, thank you. I can see what he is like now. How could I have been so blind?"

Jan slowly walked with her to the door, saying her goodbyes. Then she returned to the officers. "Was the camera running?"

"Sure was. We have it all on tape."

"That's great. See you later."

With that, Jan walked toward her office and the pile of files on her desk. After sitting down she picked up one of the files, leafed through it, and pulled out one specific page. This was the statement from Clarisse. Reading slowly, she internalized each move Lachlan had made and how he had so viciously attacked her.

Now that Clarisse was a relative, she would have to pass this file to one of her team, but which one? Kelly would be best able to handle the job, as she had written down Clarisse's full story. This decision made, she picked up the phone and rang Rachel.

"Hello, Dr Scott here."

"Show off! You really like saying that, don't you?"

Rachel laughed. "Come on, I did earn my degree you know."

"Okay, now what are you doing after work?"

"Nothing. Do you have a suggestion?"

"Perhaps dinner and a movie."

"Sounds good to me. Can we make the movie a take-home one? That way we can be alone to discuss the case, and you probably need some veg out time, like me."

"I sure do, but we had some luck today: our prisoner chucked a real whammy and actually attacked his mother. We have it all on tape."

"That's great Jan, can you pick me up from the hospital?"

"You bet. I'll be there about six thirty. Bye now."

Rachel placed the phone on its cradle, left her office, and walked to Sandy's room. Clarisse and Sandy were talking to each other in quiet tones; it was as if their conversation was for them alone. Rachel coughed at the door and then entered, and the two women stopped their conversation and looked toward her.

"Hi, Rachel, how are you today?"

"I'm fine, Clarisse. You two seem to be getting on well."

"Oh yes, it's great: we talk, and at times we only need to look at each other to know the answers."

"How are you, Doc?" Sandy said. "I'm so glad Clarisse came to see me; we are becoming good friends. Don't you think that's great?"

"I certainly do, Sandy. I must say, you are looking better with each passing day. We may be able to send you home soon."

"No, Doc! No! Not for some time—I can't face the outside yet."

"I'm not going to throw you out, Sandy. You can stay as long as is necessary. I would never put all our hard work in danger, so rest easy. Well, I must go. Jan and I are having dinner and a movie tonight. I'll see you tomorrow."

Clarisse had to leave also; she wanted to be home to greet Jackson, because they liked to cook dinner together and then sit and enjoy their meal. After they washed dishes, it was time for them to curl up on the couch and watch television. With Jackson's arms around her, the world held little fear for her now.

Jackson yawned and then looked at his wife. "Time to get ready for bed, don't you think?"

"Yes, it is. I hadn't noticed the time before."

"Let's shower together; that way we can save water and time," he said with a grin.

"Do you really believe that, or are you playing with me?"

"Would I do that?"

"Yes, you would."

Laughing, they walked to the bathroom and undressed for their shower. Jackson loved to watch as the water slid over his wife's body: it gave her skin a silken look, and he would massage her body with the body wash they used. Kisses exchanged and words of love passed between them, and after showering, they dried each other and slipped into bed.

The passion they discovered on their island was still as intense now, and their lovemaking was a slow and sensual act. Their love for each other brought them to a mutual climax—a feeling that, once found, is hard to let go. Two people who had come together in such an unusual way could see nothing but love in the years ahead.

"I love you so much, Jackson."

"Not like I love you."

These words spoken, this loving couple slowly slipped into a dreamless sleep.

At home, Clarisse's parents sat discussing their daughter and son-in-law. They marvelled at how their love for each other had survived all the trials and trepidations that had come their way.

"I think our daughter is safe now. When we are no longer here, Jackson will keep on loving her."

"What are you on about, Earnest? We are going to be around for a long time—we have to be, because we have grandchildren to look forward to and spoil! All I see in our future is happiness for us and for our children. I can say that now Jackson is truly one of our family."

"Yes, Flora, I guess you're right. Goodnight, love, see you in the morning."

Rachel and Jan had reached the restaurant and ordered their meal. While eating, their conversation did not contain any mention of the case. Jan looked at her companion and felt quite blessed to have such a wonderful friend. They were never short of subjects to discuss, jokes to tell, and laughter that was infectious. Slowly Jan learned why Rachel had studied medicine and had developed an interest in psychology, hypnosis, and forensic medicine. Rachel wanted to know what had led Jan into the police force. They each wanted to make a difference in the field of sexual predators. Jan looked only to apprehending the perpetrators and making sure they went to prison, and she saw to the initial care of the victims of these horrendous crimes. She spent many hours talking to them, always trying to ease their fears in this most devastating of times.

Rachel chose medicine, and the road was long and hard. After graduating, she worked in a large hospital. By chance, she had served time in the emergency room; it was there she saw firsthand the pain and mental anguish suffered by victims of sexual crimes. Deciding to study further, she left work and dedicated all her time to study in the field of sexual deviancy and crime. It was necessary to learn other subjects because these would then tie in to make a package. She had an understanding of traumatized people, and patients could gain full trust in their doctor.

Their dinner over, the two friends picked up a movie and headed home. Still laughing, they walked up the stairs and into the flat.

"You put the kettle on, Rach, and I'll put the movie in the player."

"Okay, Jan, won't be long."

Soon they were watching their movie and drinking their coffee. The movie was hilarious, and both laughed until they wept. It was a truly wonderful evening. Jan had to leave, but before she left, she looked long and hard at her friend. "From here on, Rach, the work gets more important. Talk to Sandy and help her come to terms with the trial and having to face her attacker."

"I'll do my best, Jan. I really will. See you soon."

"Thanks. I'll see you soon. Have a good night."

Jan drove home, her mind racing ahead of the car about how her witnesses would react when faced by their attacker. Even Clarisse would need to be ready to face Lachlan. Would she be able to, or would she freeze on the witness stand? All these questions were unknown. Jan would need to speak to Jackson alone and warn him, if there was a problem when the court case began.

Knowing how level-headed Jackson was, she hoped he would be a steadying factor for his wife. She knew Sue would have no trouble—she was so angry about her clothes that she was likely to just mouth off at him right there and then. Jan chuckled at this thought. Prostitute or no, Sue's feelings had been hurt. She stopped in her garage, stepped out, pulled down the roller door, and then walked inside.

After placing her bag and keys on the table, she made her way to her bedroom, undressed, tossed her clothes to one side, and then slipped into bed and was soon asleep.

In her office the following morning, Jan called all of her team together. "Good morning. Are you all ready for the next phase of this operation?"

"I guess you could say we have been ready since this all began."

"Okay, Kelly, but does she speak for all of you?"

"You bet," answered Mary and John.

"All right, then let's get to it. Mary, you and John can take Sue's file; Kelly you have to take Clarisse's. I can't do it because she is now a relative. It will be my job to work with Sandy. I must impress on all of you that not one witness is to be neglected. If you need help, ask; there is too much to lose if we slip up. Do you understand?"

"I certainly do, and I think Mary and John do as well. The conviction of this devious psychopath is paramount for us all."

"Thanks for that, Kelly." Jan looked at their faces and she knew by their expressions they understood just how important the next few weeks would be. She had the best detective team in the city, and they wouldn't let her down. All she needed do was let them know just how good they were.

The officers took the relevant files and made their way to the operations room—the work to convict for them had just begun. They had caught him, but now they had to jump the hurdle of conviction.

CHAPTER FIFTEEN

JAN PICKED UP THE PHONE and dialled Caroline's number.

"Hello, Caroline Hunt speaking."

"It's D-I Hastings here, from the rape crisis team."

"Oh, how are you? Is this about the trial of that awful man?"

"Yes, it is. The trial isn't far away. Could you come into town so we can run through your statement? It is very important that all the witnesses for the prosecution have all their statements set to memory."

"Like you, I'm anxious to see that awful man convicted. I am at your disposal; just give me a date and time, and I will be there."

"Thank you, Caroline. Would next Friday be all right?"

"Let's see . . . next Friday is the tenth of May. Yes, that will be fine. I will see you then! Bye for now."

Jan felt a sense of relief. Caroline was a very important witness for them: her evidence of how she found Sandy and the terrible condition she was in would paint a picture for the jury.

After the phone call, Jan drove to the hospital to see Sandy. She met Rachel in the foyer of the hospital and exchanged a greeting as they passed. Upon entering Sandy's room, she startled the woman.

"Who is it?"

"It's only me, Sandy. Don't be afraid."

"Where's Mum?"

"I don't know; she wasn't here when I came in. Perhaps she is in the café?"

"You're probably right; it doesn't take much to startle me. Sorry, Jan."

"You don't need to apologize to me, love."

As they were speaking, Allison came back into the room carrying a mug of coffee and a sandwich. "Hello, Jan, have you been here long?"

"Not long. I'm glad you're here—I need to talk to Sandy about the trial."

"Oh yes, the trial."

Jan looked at Allison and noticed a fleeting look of fear; she knew this would not be easy for her. Once again, the nightmare of her daughter being beaten and raped would be just as devastating as when it first happened.

"Will it be really horrible in the courtroom?" she asked.

"I won't lie to you, Allison. When Sandy is on the stand, she will be asked the most intimate questions. His defence will try to throw the blame back onto her. This is why we are helping our witnesses handle any questions put to them."

"Do you think I can do it, Jan?" Sandy asked.

"Yes. I will personally make you ready. I am handling your case, so you will only have to talk to me. Your mum and Rachel will help as well. Rachel is the medical witness for the prosecution, and her evidence is very important, but she will talk to you later."

Allison asked, "So everything is coming together? How long do you think we have?"

"Probably a month or two, Allison, but both of you shouldn't worry too much. All of us will be there. I must leave now; I want to see Clarisse about the trial."

"Please give her our love, will you?"

"Sure. Bye now."

Jan left the hospital and drove to Clarisse's flat, knowing it was her day off and she would be home. As she drove, the details of the case kept running through her mind. As head of the team, she had to make sure the case was ready for the prosecution lawyers to present in court. Pulling up outside of the flat, she quickly entered the building and knocked on Clarisse's door and waited till the door opened.

"Oh, hi Jan, come in."

"Thanks."

"This is a nice surprise. I hope nothing's wrong."

"No, everything is fine. How is Jackson?"

"Wonderful as always. I know he would like to see you more, but we both realize how busy you are. How about you?"

"The team is putting together all our evidence for the trial. I have given your file to Kelly."

"But why?"

"We are to closely related now, and the defence may use that fact in court."

"I guess that's all right. Will you be near when I am on the stand?"

"Yes, I will be as close as I can get. The team will give evidence first, and we will be with you in a small room away from the actual courtroom. After our evidence is given, we can stay in the courtroom. It will be after that you and the others are called. I will stay with you until you till then."

"Will Jackson and my parents be allowed in the room with me?"

"No, but I will make sure they are seated just behind the prosecution lawyers' table. Don't worry; we will all look after our witnesses."

"Will Jackson get the time off for the trial, do you think?"

"In a case like yours, the federal police will give him all the time he needs."

"Well then, I guess it's up to me to stay calm. I hope I can do that."

"I have great faith in you, and I know you won't let us or yourself down, so cheer up—it's going to be over soon."

"Won't that be a great day? Jackson and I will be free of him, and our lives will be even better than now."

"Is that possible, love?"

"I guess not, but the fear will be gone. Jackson won't have to sooth the fears in the night. He's so wonderful, but I guess you have known that for a long time."

"He's a little rat, really. The tricks he pulled on me and our other cousins when we were younger . . . You wouldn't believe."

"I know about the tricks, but he is truly wonderful to me."

"I'm glad about that—and yes, I love him, too."

Both women laughed at the joke about Jackson, and their conversation continued for some time before they heard the key in the lock, which told them he was home.

"Where are you, sweet?"

"In the kitchen. Jan is here, and we are enjoying a cup of coffee."

Jackson dropped his briefcase as he walked to the kitchen. "What are you doing here, Jan? If you'd warned me, I would have stayed at work!"

"Please, Jackson, don't say that!" Clarisse said.

He grinned. "Sorry, sweetheart, but I want you all to myself."

"Well, you can't, and I will stay as long as I want," Jan joked.

"Okay, Jan, don't get mad. Just make me a coffee, and all is forgiven."

"Cheeky little fellow, aren't we?"

"Why not? I have my wife to look after me, and she won't let you hit me."

All three burst into laughter at this remark. They continued to enjoy their coffee and conversation for the next hour, and then Jan jumped up, saying, "I'd better go. I'm late for dinner at Rachel's. See you soon."

With that, she flew out the door and was gone, leaving the two lovers to cook dinner and spend their usual evening together.

"Will I be all right?" Clarisse asked Jackson.

"Yes, you will. With Kelly and I here, we will get this excuse for a man."

"Having you in my life is so wonderful. You are my lover, friend, and husband, and I cannot imagine life without you."

"You will never have to. I am yours for life! Come on, love, let's cook dinner."

Clarisse held out her hand to Jackson as they walked to the kitchen to begin cooking.

Lachlan was in the interview room waiting for his lawyer; his mind in turmoil about what would happen in court. Surely the jury would see he was not responsible—only psychopaths did the things they say he has done. He had to convince them that as a psychotic, they should send him to an institute for the insane; once there it should be easy to escape. *Why isn't the idiot here yet? He's late again. How can we have time to talk about my defence when he is always late? Bloody useless piece of work. Shouldn't have had that argument with Mum; she really does love me, so maybe writing to her would help.* The door opened, startling him. His lawyer stepped in and sat down opposite him.

"Hello, Lachlan, how are you?"

"You're bloody late again. How the hell am I going to beat these stupid charges, when you're always late?"

"I'm not late, Lachlan. In fact, I am a few minutes early."

"Oh, to hell with you. What bloody law school did you go to, anyway?"

"Listen, mate, if you continue to swear and shout at me, I'll do exactly what your last lawyer did."

"No, don't do that. I'm sorry, but we do need to make these sluts look just like they are: all of them came on to me, and it's not as they say."

"Lachlan, they are telling the truth. I have read their statements, and I know you were responsible. If you want to minimize your sentence, you should plead guilty, thus letting the judge know you are remorseful. If you don't, you will be jailed for a long time."

"Plead guilty? You must be mad! I'm pleading not guilty by reason of insanity, you idiot."

"That won't wash. Even I don't believe you are mad; it shows in your every action. You knew exactly what you were doing, and you enjoyed it."

Lachlan jumped to his feet, letting the chair clatter onto the floor. His face was red with rage, and as he leaned across the table, he spat the words to his lawyer. "Get out, get out! You know I'm mad! You are against me as well—everyone wants me in jail, but I won't go!, I am innocent, I tell you."

The lawyer looked at him and shook his head. "You are not mad, but you want everyone to think you are. "Well, I have given you my advice. If you take it, you may get out of jail before you are an old man. If you maintain this nonsense, you will have no one to defend you I'm leaving now. When you calm down and want to talk, the police will let me know."

The lawyer walked to the door and knocked. An officer let him out, and he went to the front desk and informed the officer of what had transpired before he left the building.

Once again, Lachlan found himself alone. *They should know by now that the psychosis is real; they will send me to an asylum. My lawyer will be responsible for my defence.* He sat back on the bunk and slowly began to realize that not all who knew him liked him; even his mother had abandoned him. Lying back on his bunk, he thought of what was going to happen. Was he so bad? The women wined and dined by him enjoyed it in every sense. Lachlan's psychosis returned: of course he wasn't bad. He gave his women the full treatment, they could never get his kind of attention from anyone else, and he loved them. *Is it so strange that giving them pain and this extreme pain brings on a climax they have never had before? When I leave them, they don't yell or shout at me; they are usually very silent, content with the level of satisfaction I gave them.* His conscious mind was content with the idea he was not guilty, that he did not rape or attempt to murder any of them.

Rachel entered Sandy's room, and Allison was with her daughter. Both greeted Rachel with warm smiles. "Good morning, Rachel, how are you?"

"I'm fine, Allison. I need to talk to Sandy alone, please."

"Something's wrong, isn't it?"

"Yes, unfortunately there is, but I need to talk to Sandy alone. Don't be too alarmed."

Allison looked long and hard at Rachel, thinking, *What is wrong with my daughter? Why won't Rachel let me stay? It must be bad news.*

"Don't worry, Mum, it's all right," Sandy said.

At her daughter's urging, she left the room.

"What is it, Rachel? What's wrong?"

"There is no easy way to tell you this. During the rape, I believe he used some sort of device to injure you. What it was, we don't know, but we need to take you back to theatre. You need an anaesthetic; this way we can find and repair the damage he has done."

"Am I pregnant, Rachel?"

"Oh no! No, sweet, we took care of that when you first went into theatre. It is compulsory to make sure there is no sperm and blood, then look for any sign of STDs. I must find the cause of the pain you continue to have, and see if there is an infection, so I have to examine you again."

"Okay. I trust you. Can Mum come in now?"

"Yes, I'll let her in, and then I must go and make arrangements for theatre."

Opening the door, Rachel stood to one side and let Allison into the room. "Sandy will fill you in. I have to go and get ready."

That said, Rachel walked back down the passage and out of sight. As she walked, she hoped she hadn't frightened Sandy too much. Now it was up to her to find and cure this problem. She arrived at the theatre and asked a nurse to get Sandy ready. She then walked into her office and rang Jan. The phone rang for a time, before she heard the voice of her friend.

"Hello?"

"It's me. I'm just ringing to let you know we have to examine Sandy again. I am taking her back to theatre to find what it is."

"Oh damn. Is it bad, Rach?"

"I won't know for a while. I'll ring you when it's over, okay?"

"Sure, but make it quick, can you? Poor kid has suffered enough. make it right, Rach, please."

"As always, I'll do my best. See you later. Perhaps I could cry on your shoulder."

"Any time, love. Bye for now."

Jan sat back in her chair; her thoughts once again turning to all the women this man had made suffer. She did not understand how he could do these things and still give the presumption of innocence. They should just lock him away for the remainder of his life. This was not the case, though—the raped and beaten women had to bare their souls in a courtroom to receive the justice they deserved. Rationality came back to Jan, and she turned the thoughts of Lachlan to where they were concerning the trial. These took her back to the few men arrested and who were not guilty; she knew that justice had to be done in all cases.

Jan realized she was too close to the case now because of Clarisse, and she could not let her own hate for Lachlan jeopardize the case, a knock startled her

"Who is it?"

"Good God, Jan, it's only me," Kelly said. "What's up?"

"I was deep in thought. Is everything okay?"

"Sure. Just wanted to get any updates for the case. Is there anything new."

"Rach just rang, and they are taking Sandy back to theatre. There is a major problem, and it needs to be investigated."

"Poor kid. Did Rachel tell you what it was?"

"I don't think she knows—hence the need for another operation."

"I hope it isn't really bad. It's enough to be so brutally raped, let alone have some permanent injury."

"That's what I'm afraid of. I was thinking about it when you knocked."

"No wonder you snapped at me, Well, I must get back to the case; Clarisse is coming in for her lesson on how to keep calm in court. I'll see you later."

Jan watched as Kelly left the room. The gloom which had surrounded her from the time of Rachel's phone call was a little lighter now, and knowing she would see Clarisse later brightened her day considerably. She decided to look over the evidence and went to the locker where it was kept, pulling out the box that contained all the items taken from his flat.

She lifted the box that had been in the drawer of his cupboard, and its contents again sent a shiver through her. Did one of these cause the injury to Sandy? Just the thought that a human being could find satisfaction by using implements like these left her quite numb. How could he do things like this?

Placing the small box to one side, she started to read some of the correspondence in the large evidence box. There was a pile of letters tied with string. Untying it; she opened one of the letters and began reading aloud.

"Dear Sue, sorry I haven't written for some time, but I was waiting for you to tell me if you enjoyed our last sexual encounter. I couldn't ask you when I left, as you were asleep. I can still see you lying on the floor, and you looked so peaceful. Do you now know it is much more exciting to be raped and beaten, than just normal sex?"

Jan could not read on, were these letters going to help or hinder? It really didn't make any difference. If the prosecution intended to use them, the defence was entitled to see them. As Jan looked again at the letter, she realized they hadn't been posted; this meant what he had written was all in his head.

She decided not to tell anyone at that time and wait until the prosecution lawyers perused the evidence in the box. She returned all but the small box that held the unusual items, which she wanted to show Rachel, and pushed the box back into its slot.

Leaving the evidence room, she ran into John and noticed he looked quite agitated.

"Hi, John, are you all right?"

"No, I'm not! Have you heard about Sandy?"

"Yes, I have. You love her don't you?"

"How do you know that? I haven't told anyone."

"I'm experienced at reading people's action, and when you are near Sandy, it is reflected in your eyes, I have known for days, but I won't tell anyone."

"Do you think the operation will be a success?"

"I don't know. We just have to wait. Rachel will let us know as soon as she can. When are you on duty again?"

"Tonight at nine. When I am there at night, I can stand at the door and watch her sleep. She is so lovely."

"John, don't do that! We don't know how it will affect her."

"I know I shouldn't do it, but the compulsion to look at her is very strong."

"Please don't do it again. Maybe in the future, but not now. Do I make myself clear?"

"Yes, Jan. You won't take me off the detail, will you?"

"At this time no, but if you break your promise, I will. I must go now; please heed my words."

With that Jan walked away toward the front door of the station, and as she reached the door, Clarisse was opening it. Both women balked and then acknowledged each other.

"Hi, Jan, where are you going in such a hurry?"

"I have to go to the hospital. Are you seeing Kelly about your testimony?"

"Yes. Are you going to see Sandy?"

"I am, but I will be back in time for our lunch date."

"Okay, I'll see you then."

The greetings over, each went her own way. Jan drove to the hospital and entered the front door; she then made her way to Sandy's room, where Allison was sitting on the chair by the bed.

"Hello, Allison. Is it all right if I wait with you?"

"Of course. I guess all of us are waiting for the results of the operation."

"Yes, we certainly are. Would you like a tea or coffee? I can go to the café, if you like."

"Not now, thanks. I want to sit quietly and wait."

"Well, let's do just that."

The silence was palpable in the room, each with her own thoughts, and they were very different. For Allison, the fear for her daughter's future showed in her demeanour; she constantly wiped her eyes as they filled with tears. Jan's thoughts were on what she had seen in the box; they made her shudder like when she first saw them, and it filled her with apprehension.

Time seemed to go extremely slow, and Jan felt every second. She had the knowledge of what was probably the cause of Sandy's injury.

After his conversation with Jan, John went to the lunchroom, poured a cup of coffee, and then sat at one of the tables. All his thoughts were with Sandy. Would she ever want a man in her life? Would he ever be able to tell her how much he loved her, or would he have to watch as she lived a loveless life?

The love he could give her would be one of tenderness and understanding, and he'd make sure no one could hurt her again. His thoughts went on as he imagined being married to her, and what a wonderful life that would be. Having finished his coffee, he went back to the evidence room and continued to log all the relevant statements to copy for the defence team.

CHAPTER SIXTEEN

CLARISSE LEFT THE POLICE STATION and went to the café across the road. She was meeting Jackson for lunch, and she chose a table and sat down to wait. Jackson arrived soon after; he walked toward her with the cheeky smile he saved just for her.

"Hello, my love, I hope you haven't waited long."

"Yes, I have—I've been here for at least five minutes."

Jackson leaned over to peck her on the cheek and sat down at the table. His smile was broader now: his wife was returning to the lovely woman he had met and loved on an island in the middle of the aqua sea. *We must go back there soon.* He wanted to make love as they had for first time, all those months ago.

"Hey, Jackson, come back to me, please?"

"Sorry, love. I was on an island making love to a beautiful woman."

"Who was she?"

"My wife. We must go back there, don't you think."

"Yes, we should, but we have just come home. why the urgent need to go again?"

Jackson didn't answer, but he reached across the table and held her hand. As he looked into her eyes, he spoke a million words to her without a sound. Clarisse was also on the island, and her thoughts were the same—but for her, it was the first time she had made love, so the memories were even sweeter. They continued their meal with small talk, and after lunch Jackson had to return to work. Clarisse made her way home, thinking of a special meal for them that evening.

Lachlan sat in his cell all alone. He had no lawyer to defend him. Perhaps it was time to apologize and take the man's advice? No—why should he? They were here just for him, weren't they? He had to get out of here.

His urges were getting stronger, even with the police forcing him to take his medication. He rested his head in his hands. His life was over if he couldn't get out. He needed a woman—it was not enough just to dream about the pain he must inflict it; he had to see the pain and the fear in their eyes. He lay back on his bunk; he would wait for the officer to come. *I wonder why they never send a female officer? They're afraid I might attack her.* A smile swept across his face: even confined as he was, he could still inflict fear.

He could hear footsteps coming toward his cell, and he hoped it was his mum. *No, it won't be her—she hates me now and believes all the lies they told her.* The footsteps stopped at his cell, and the slide window opened. An officer asked if he wanted to see his lawyer yet.

"What do reckon, idiot?"

"By your tone, I'd say no, you don't."

"Yes I do, you jerk! Let him in now."

"I'll phone him. If he wants to come, he will be here after lunch."

"Bloody idiot, just get him here!"

"I don't like your tone; just remember who is the prisoner."

"Shut up and get my lawyer."

Lachlan heard the footsteps retreating, leaving him with no idea whether he would get a lawyer.

As the police officer walked away he smiled to himself: it was fun to torment this individual. When he reached the desk, everyone there saw the grin, and knowing where he had been, they joined in the joke without him having to say anything.

"Set him up again, mate?"

"Doesn't take much. He wants his lawyer. Could you give him a call? It's up to him if he wants to come."

"Sure, George. You off duty now?"

"Yep, I'm on my way. See ya."

Later that day the lawyer entered the police station and asked the way to Lachlan's cell. One of the officers led him to the cell, and before opening it he made sure Lachlan was not near the door. Satisfied, he opened the door and followed the lawyer inside; this time he didn't leave.

"Can you leave us alone, please?"

"No."

The officer angered Lachlan. He looked long and hard at him and then spat out his feelings. "Get out now, you bloody excuse for a copper!"

"Calm down, Lachlan. If he has to stay, he has to stay," the lawyer said.

Standing at the door, the police officer listened to the conversation between the two men. He heard the lawyer tell Lachlan he would be better off pleading guilty. This suggestion did not please him. From then on, the words became a whisper, inaudible to anyone but them.

The police officer leant against the wall, waiting for the time limit. He glanced at his watch and broke into the conversation.

"Time's up, let's go, sir."

"All right, I will see you tomorrow, Lachlan. Think about my suggestion, please."

"I'll think about it."

The lawyer and the officer left the cell and walked to the front desk. The lawyer hesitated for a second and then left the station.

At the hospital Sandy was coming out of the theatre, and Allison was by her side as they reached her room. The transfer from trolley to bed was made with quick precision. The staff placed a blanket over Sandy and then left the room.

"Isn't she pale, Jan? Oh, my poor girl, why did he do this to you?"

"He's an animal, that's why!" Jan could not hide her hate for Lachlan. It was visible in every part of her being, and tears welled up in her eyes as she looked at Sandy. A small moan came from Sandy, and then she tried to move. It was easy to see that this movement hurt her. Allison stood and wiped her daughter's brow, murmuring soft words of love in her ear. With this soothing, Sandy fell once again into the safety of morphine-induced sleep.

"How long will it be before Rachel can come and tell us the results of the operation?"

"Right now, Allison," Rachel said as she walked in.

"Do want me to leave, Rach?" Jan asked.

"Oh no, what I have to say to Allison is important for the case, so please stay."

"Is it bad news?"

"Will both of you sit down and listen? There is good news, but unfortunately some bad. I located the problem. It was a small puncture in the vaginal wall very near the cervix. It is almost certain, he used some sort of sexual implement to cause the damage, which is the bad news. Now the good news. I have been able to stitch the wound and clear the site around it. The infection can be controlled with antibiotics."

"She will be all right, then?"

"Yes, Allison. It will take more time, but I'm sure she will recover fully."

"Thank you, Rachel. You are one in a million! Don't you think so, Jan?"

"I have known it for a while now, and yes, she is the very best," Jan said with a smile.

"Enough of the flattery, you two. We have all done our part, and soon the perpetrator of this misery will be in jail."

"How far away is the trial, Jan?" Allison asked.

"Not long at all, but the sooner the better."

As the three women talked, Sandy opened her eyes and looked at her mother with the hint of a smile. Allison saw the look and held her daughters hand.

"How do you feel, darling?"

"Am I going to be all right, Mum?"

"Yes, you are, but I'll let Rachel tell you all about it."

"As your mother said, you are going to be okay, but I will expand on that later. Do you have much pain?"

"Yes, it feels like a burning fire inside me."

Rachel pushed the buzzer, and in a short time a nurse arrived with an injection, which she administered before leaving again.

Rachel said, "Now I want you to sleep. We are going to the café for a coffee."

"All right." Sandy's voice tailed off as the drug took its effect. She fell asleep, and the three women left the room and went to the café.

Jan stopped at the counter, ordered the coffee and sandwiches for them all, and returned to the table. All the conversation was of Sandy's prognosis, and they were happy at the outcome. Allison returned to Sandy's room, and Jan and Rachel went to the sanctuary of Rachel's office.

"I have something to show you, Rach. I believe you will discover your torture weapon among these."

Rachel could not believe what she was seeing: laid out on her desk were the implements Jan had found in Lachlan's flat. "What the hell are they?"

"You may well ask. These are what Lachlan used during some of the rapes. Can you tell me which one you think he used to cause Sandy's injury?"

"Do I have to, Jan? I feel sick just looking at them. What sort of man uses these things to find sexual gratification?"

"I have seen other sadistic items rapists have used, but these beat them all. This creep is the most savage and dangerous rapist I have caught."

"Thank God you caught him. Will it be long to wait for the trial? I want this madness to end. Please, Jan, stop it now."

"Once he faces the jury and they hear the evidence, I have no doubt they will find him guilty."

The small talk continued until it was time for Jan to return to the station, to make sure all the evidence was ready for the trial. Jan replaced the items she had shown to Rachel. One, however, she kept. Jan took it to her office and phoned the forensic lab.

"Hi, Jan, what's new?"

"I have an interesting item for you. I want you to turn it inside out—do as many tests you can. I believe he used it in the last rape. If you could match it to Sandy's DNA, it will close the door on any defence he may have."

"Okay, Jan. I'll send a team member over to pick it up; can you give me two days?"

"Sure, just make it happen, and I'll kiss you."

"In that case, I'll have it ready tonight!"

Jan closed her office door and then walked out of the station to her car. All she wanted now was a long night's sleep—one without the nightmares caused by the case. Once inside her flat, she threw her brief case on the lounge, went into the kitchen, and grabbed a can of soup. It took no time to heat, and after pouring it into a soup bowl, she sat and began to eat. The door buzzer sounded, disturbing her meal and thoughts. She stood and walked to the door. "Who is it?"

"It's John. Can I come in?"

Jan opened the door and let him into the flat. He noticed she was eating her dinner. "I'm sorry. I'll go, and we can talk tomorrow."

"Talk to me now, John. I may not have time tomorrow. Sit down, and we can talk as I eat."

"I think it would be better if I don't stay on hospital duty. It is too hard. All I want to do is hold her and tell her she's safe. I can't just sit outside the door anymore; while I'm there, I can hear her breathing, and it is slow torture for me."

"You are sure about this?"

"Yes, I am. I will help sort out the evidence for court, and maybe one day I will be able to tell her how I feel. But for now, I will stay in the background."

"I knew I'd picked a good copper. I will put another officer in your place, and down the track things could be different."

"Thanks. I'll go now. See you tomorrow."

Jan let John out and returned to the kitchen, making herself a coffee before she sat on the lounge to watch TV. *Yes, he is a good officer. I wonder how many could do what he has done. Would they be able to put a witness and her feelings before his own?*

As John walked away from Jan's flat, he wondered if he had done the right thing. He knew it was right for Sandy, but in doing it, would he lose her? He satisfied himself by holding onto the feeling that at some time in the future, he would be able to approach her again.

Lachlan's cell door opened, and his lawyer entered and took the chair opposite him. "You asked to see me. Does this mean you have come to a decision?"

"Yes, I have. I can't beat all of these lying bitches, so I will plead guilty—but only on the understanding that it is by reason of insanity."

"Well, I will try, but I don't believe it, and I don't think a judge will, either."

"You don't believe me?"

The lawyer didn't answer him; he sat silently as Lachlan ranted and raved about the unfairness. Lachlan stood up and paced the cell back and forth; he railed about what he considered an injustice. He stopped very near his lawyer, looking at him with a dark frown. "You did you say you don't believe me? Why don't you believe me? I'm innocent, I tell you. Those bitches are lying. Can't you see that?"

"Whether I believe you or not, the evidence against you is overwhelming, and more is added every day, so how can I believe you are innocent?"

"Get out! Get out, you blithering idiot! What sort of lawyer are you?"

"Idiot or not, you are stuck with me, and unfortunately I am stuck with you, so sit down and bloody well listen. If you don't, I will leave."

The lawyer's words stunned him into silence. He slowly sat down on the chair, remaining silent for quite some time. His thoughts spun as he tried to grasp that they had truly caught him, and he had no real defence. *They are going to win, those bloody lying sluts! They are going to be responsible for me going to jail!*

His lawyer sat looking at him, and what he saw was a man who had just realized there was no way out. This gave the lawyer hope that there wouldn't be a trial. His thoughts were on the victims of his client: would they be happy with him pleading guilty? Alternatively, would they rather see a judge and jury convict and sentence him, using the full weight of the law? In addition, the fact he would do this, but only due to insanity—this would never happen, and it was plain to all that he was sane enough to plan and carry out each rape.

"I can't win, can I?" Lachlan finally asked.

"I can't answer that. It has to be a decision you make. If you throw yourself on the mercy of the court, you may lessen your incarceration time."

"I won't go to prison. I can't. Surely they will put me a facility for the insane."

"Do you ever listen? You are going to prison. The evidence against you is damning. Take my advice and plead guilty."

"Get out! Leave me alone. I'll represent myself, and I will get off, so just get out—I don't need you!"

The lawyer stood up, pushed the chair back, and knocked on the door; an officer let him out. At the desk, he informed them of Lachlan's intentions, and then he walked out of the station.

The duty officer rang Jan's number; it rang for some time before she answered.

"Hastings here, how can I help you?"

"It's the front desk. I thought you should know the latest about our rapist."

"What's he up to now?"

"Silly bastard intends to represent himself."

"He does? Well, isn't that great? Makes our job easier. But what a joke."

As Jan put the phone down, she burst into laughter; her team came to the door at the sound.

"What's the joke, boss?"

Jan couldn't stop laughing, let alone tell them what the joke was. Finally she gained her composure. "Our rapist is going to defend himself in court."

"He is?"

Now it wasn't just Jan, but the whole team that laughed; this news lifted the spirit of them all. Not having a crafty lawyer to grapple with meant less time in court, and the women giving evidence would not face the intense questioning of a shrewd defence lawyer. There was a downside though: Lachlan would be close to them, and this could cause them some anxiety. Would the women be able to look into his eyes without feeling threatened, and would the trauma be too much for them? These thoughts brought Jan back to reality. His schooling was of a high standard, and he would know courtroom ethics. This would enable him to build a web of lies. Would a judge and jury see through his lies, or believe his cry of innocence? Deciding this could be a threat, Jan decided to arrange for Sue and Clarisse to come to the station for an interview; she would also need to talk to Sandy at the hospital. After making the calls, she left the station and drove to the hospital, making her way to Sandy's room.

As she entered, Allison nodded in greeting. "Hello, Jan, is everything all right?"

"Yes and no. Our prisoner has decided to represent himself."

"What does that mean?" Sandy asked.

"It means, Sandy, that when you are giving your evidence; he can question you directly and will try to intimidate you."

"I will be safe, though, won't I?"

"Of course you will. You will be in a court of law and under its protection."

"That's okay, then. I will still say what I have to say. I won't let him get away with what he's done."

"Good for you, Sandy, but I had to let you know. He may change his mind, but we have to be ready for any eventuality."

Jan sat and talked for quite some time; she had to make sure Sandy and Allison knew what lay ahead. As she talked, a familiar voice broke into the conversation.

"Hello, all, are we having a party?"

"No we aren't, Rach, just bringing Sandy up to date with the case and the perpetrator."

"I will get the details from Sandy later, but now I have to ask you and Allison to leave—I need to examine my patient again."

"I have to go back to the station. Is our movie night still on for later?"

"Sure is. These nights are becoming the done thing, aren't they."

"Yep. Bye for now. See you later, Rach."

Jan waved goodbye to them and was on her way to the station. When she arrived, she could see that the witnesses had arrived: Clarisse was with Kelly, Sue with Mary. It had been a successful day, and as she walked to her office, her thoughts were on the night ahead, knowing it would bring a quiet meal and movie night spent with her friend.

Rachel arrived as expected with a movie for them to watch. It was a wonderful, warm evening, one to remember for them. Their feelings were explored, and they gave in to their love, it had always been there but not explored until now. Both knew their love would be accepted by some but not others. So these lovers would step out and embrace love far into the future.

Jan called at the hospital early; she had to tell Sandy about the change with regard to the police guards.

"How are you today, Sandy?"

"I'm much better today. Rachel thinks I can go home soon. Isn't that good news?"

"Still not worried about court?"

"No. I don't care where he is—he can't hurt me anymore, and I'm safe with all of you nearby."

"That's what I like to hear. Clarisse and Sue feel the same, so it's full steam ahead."

"By the way Jan, where's John?"

"You've noticed he isn't in the guard squad?"

"Yes, and I miss him. I liked him very much. Is that wrong, Jan?"

"Of course not, Sandy. If you want, I'll get him to come and see you."

"I would like that very much."

"I'll tell him to come later. I know he is a fine officer, and whatever you want, he will agree."

"Thanks, Jan. Do you have to go now? You've missed Mum; she is having breakfast in the café."

"I'll catch her later, sweet. Give her my regards, won't you."

Their conversation over, Jan left the hospital and headed to the station, to her office. There was a pile of files on her desk ready for her okay, and she read the first file. A sharp knock on her door jolted her from her task, and on looking up she saw Jackson outside her door. She motioned to him to come in and stood to greet him. "What brings you here, cousin?"

"Need a favour, Jan. I am working on a case and need to go to Sydney. I don't want to leave Clarisse on her own. Can you stay with her?"

"Of course I can. What sort of case is it?"

"The confidential kind—can't say more than that. I'm leaving later this afternoon. Clarisse knows I have to go, but I will ring her before takeoff. I'll see you later."

With this said he was gone, leaving Jan to resume reading the files. Kelly then entered her office with a cup of coffee in her hand. "Time for a break, boss."

"Oh thanks, Kelly. I do need a break."

The two officers talked as Jan drank her coffee. It was only three weeks until the trial, and everything needed to be ready.

Jan rang John to tell him about Sandy, and the happiness in his voice, made Jan feel she had set the scene for a likely romance. John heard the words he had hoped for and knew that the road ahead would not be easy, but he was determined to be in Sandy's life for a long time. Dressing carefully, he drove to the hospital, left his car, and walked to Sandy's room. He knocked gently on her door.

"Who is it?"

"It's John, Sandy. Can I come in?"

The door opened, and Allison stood in the doorway looking at John with a smile. "Hello, John, of course you can. Sandy mentioned you might be coming to see her."

"I won't come too close, and if Sandy wants me to go, I will."

Sandy said, "It's all right, John. Please come in, I've missed having my guard on duty."

John entered the room and sat next to Allison, and the three of them talked for what seemed like hours. John asked if he could come again, and Sandy said she would like that. She would be going home soon, and Allison would then invite him to dinner.

"You do remember I live at Layton, don't you, John?" Allison said.

"Yes, I do. Is Sandy going to stay with you for a while?"

"Yes. The hurt and fear will take some time to heal, so she is staying with me until after the trial."

"That's a good idea. I will be in court all day, so I will see you then. Sandy, when you feel comfortable about me being around, I will accept the invitation for dinner."

"Thanks, John. I look forward to a time when I'm not afraid to be alone with a member of the opposite sex."

"I'll leave now but will visit you again tomorrow, if that's okay."

"Yes, that would be great. I'll see you then."

John left the hospital feeling an exhilaration he had not felt before; it was as if he could see into the future and picture a life together with Sandy.

At last the time came for the trial to begin. Lachlan had not changed his mind about representing himself. The jury each took their place in the jury box. The judge first outlined the charges against Lachlan and then the jury's purpose during the trial. The prosecutor began his speech to the court; he listed the crimes against the accused, also telling them it was his choice to defend himself.

Lachlan stood to give his rebuttal speech to the jury about his innocence and the charges against him. During his speech he became belligerent toward the women who were to give evidence against him, and the judge was quick to say, "You are out of order, sir. You must not make derogatory remarks about any of the witnesses." Lachlan nodded his understanding to the judge and continued his speech.

With all the introductions done, they called the first witness. Jan took her place in the witness box, ready to answer the questions. The clerk of the court placed a Bible in Jan's left hand and asked her to raise her right hand.

"Do you swear that the evidence you give is the truth and nothing but the truth, so help you God?"

"Yes, I do."

The prosecution lawyer stood and began his examination of the witness. He asked if Jan held the rank of detective inspector, was the officer in charge of the case, and made the arrest, taking the accused into custody.

"Yes, sir. I have been in charge of this case from the beginning."

It seemed hours to Jan as she answered each question in turn. Finally the prosecutor had completed his examination.

Lachlan stood and approached her. "You have just lied to this court, haven't you?" he said.

"No!" was Jan's swift reply.

"How did you apprehend me? It wasn't just you, was it?"

"It was a team effort—of course it wasn't just me."

"So you *did* lie, didn't you?"

Here the judge decided to educate the accused as to what he would allow in his courtroom. "Please approach."

When the prosecutor and Lachlan stood before him, he began his objection of Lachlan's behaviour. "It is plain you have no idea of the law as it is applied in a court. You cannot tell a witness she is lying. If this is the best you can do, you should think again about a lawyer."

"I thought this was a free country. If I wish to defend myself, it is my choice."

"It is, sir, but you are doing yourself an injustice by carrying on this way."

The prosecutor interrupted. "Sir, if we go on like this, the trial will take the next four months."

"I am inclined to agree. Sir, keep your questions relevant, or I will order that a legal aid lawyer take over your defence." Both men went back to their respective tables, and the trial continued.

Lachlan kept his anger hidden until Clarisse settled into the witness box. The prosecutor only had a few questions for her to answer.

"Can you see the man who raped and beat you in this court room?"

"Yes, sir. It is that man sitting at the other table."

"Could you point him out, please?"

Clarisse raised her hand and pointed to Lachlan. It was here Lachlan lost all semblance of dignity. He stood and pushed the chair back, making it clatter to the floor. With viciousness in his voice spat out the words aimed at Clarisse.

"You're a bloody liar, a vicious slut! If I get my hands on you, you're dead! Do you hear? Dead and cold! Then I can laugh."

At these words, the police and court staff tackled and handcuffed him. Jackson flew out of his seat and ran to his wife—this was not easy because the courtroom was in an uproar. He bent over and placed his hand on her arm, and this startled her for a moment, but when she recognized him, she threw herself into his arms. "Oh, Jackson, I'm so glad you're here! He really is mad, isn't he?"

"Only so he can make the jury think he is. But it won't work—they will convict him."

Jackson stayed close to his wife as the court returned to normalcy. The judge banged his gavel on his desk and ordered everyone to calm down. The court police soon had Lachlan back into his seat, and the rage he felt toward Clarisse had left him exhausted.

Jackson took a seat closer to the witness box; here he could get to Clarisse, and she could see him and gain the courage to go on.

The judge had retired to his room, awaiting the restoration of order in the court. The clerk informed him as soon as it was ready. On entering and resuming his seat, he gave orders to both the prosecution and defence. "The accused will be provided a legal aid lawyer, and he will remain restrained for the duration of the trial. Do you understand me?"

"No, I don't! You have no right to do this to me, and I can defend myself!"

"Young man, I have the power to sentence you right now, but I won't, so please heed my words."

"If it's an order, I will, but I don't like it."

All in the court were appalled at this answer, and the judge glared at him long and hard before saying, "You, sir, will do exactly what I say, or for the remainder of the trial, you will be segregated from the court, I hope you understand this."

Lachlan sat pouting as the appointed lawyer continued the case for his defence. As each witness spoke, he became more morose. He sat glaring angrily at the judge and muttering under his breath. The trial continued without further upset, until they asked to read Sandy's statement to the court.

"Why isn't this young lady in court?" the judge asked.

"She is still in hospital, Your Honour. Her wounds have not healed, and it will be some time before she is well enough to give her verbal evidence in court."

"Did you gain permission for her statement to be read out?"

"Yes, sir; I have it here."

"Bring it to me, please."

The clerk of the court carried the letter and handed it to the judge.

"Does the defence have a copy?"

"We have, Your Honour."

"All right, you may proceed."

The prosecutor began to read the statement. The contents were harrowing, and the jury was transfixed; they heard the words but tried not to show emotion. The prosecutor showed the graphic photos of Sandy's injuries to the jury.

When the evidence from the letter was finished, the prosecutor introduced Caroline Hunt. After swearing in, she was prompted by prosecution lawer to tell the court how it was when she found Sandy.

"I was driving home, when I noticed someone walk out onto the road, then disappear. I thought this strange, and slowed the car, Sandy walked out onto the road in front of me. It was if she had accepted the fact that it might be her attacker, she was in a bad way."

"What do you mean; she was in a bad way?"

"Her clothes were torn, there was blood on her face, it seeped from many cuts and abrasions, both eyes were black, her legs and arms were scratched and bruised. I was afraid she might not live, getting her into the car was very painful, and she lost consciousness twice. Once in the car I drove to my home, rang the police and ambulance, then I wiped her face with a cloth, all the while soothing her, and telling her she was safe. The police and ambulance arrived quickly, Sandy was unconscious again, the paramedics tended to her, while the police officers talked to me about finding Sandy."

Caroline broke down in the court and placed her head in her hands as the tears flowed. Finally she could continue. "I have never seen such injuries as those Sandy suffered. They will never be erased from my mind."

After Caroline's evidence was finished, the prosecution rested its case. The crimes listed, proven by the DNA tests, were considerable and undisputable. Now it was time for the defence lawyer to present evidence to the court.

"Your Honour, I will now present the defence case. There is not a lot—we have heard cross-examination of all the witnesses, and they have presented a damning case. My client has asked me to change his plea to one of guilty whilst insane. I would ask the jury to keep this in mind as they consider their verdict."

He then returned to his seat, Lachlan whispered to him again, but it was inaudible.

The prosecutor stood and outlined all of the case. He told of the trauma suffered by the victims and that they could not feel safe until the conviction and incarceration of the accused. It was the defence lawyer's chance to outline his case, but as he had nothing to add, he declined.

The last speech was from the judge. "Members of the jury, you are charged to bring in a verdict. You must look at the evidence from both defence and prosecution. You will retire to the jury room and discuss the evidence. You must come to a unanimous decision. You must take all the time necessary for this decision. We will convene tomorrow morning at nine o'clock. If you come to a verdict before then, the court will reconvene. You may now leave the courtroom to consider your verdict."

The jury retired, and the witnesses with their friends and partners left the court; they were all heading to a restaurant for a well-earned meal.

Lachlan felt the opposite, he was not happy—he was now feeling a sense of extreme depression. He was going to jail, he knew he was. *That bloody jury believes those evil bitches.* In his fear, he began to talk aloud, his voice echoing back from the cell walls.

"I don't deserve this, I am innocent. Why don't these people understand? All the money I spent wining and dining these hateful bitches . . . Surely the payment I took wasn't extreme. They enjoyed it, I'm sure they did! Was it so bad, and am I the evil monster they print in the papers?"

The clang of the cell door startled him. Who would be coming to see him? He looked up, and his mother stood before him.

"Why are you here?" he said.

"I wanted to see you. I am your mother!"

"Just get out. I don't want you here—you deserted me, didn't you?"

"No, I didn't. I tried to help you, but you threw it back at me. I still would like to help. You must know the jury will find you guilty. You will need me then."

"You are just a whore, like those who gave evidence against me!"

"No, I am your mother, and my heart aches for your future. Jail is not a nice place, and you will suffer in many ways. Let me be there for you."

"Just get out! I don't need your help now, and I will never want it."

Without an answer, she called the guard and motioned to the door. She felt a terrible sense of loss; it was as if her child had died, leaving her with the certainty that her son was indeed guilty.

The happy group at the restaurant had laughter ring out from their table.

"This is a wonderful day! If we get a guilty verdict, we will find closure from this nightmare," Earnest said.

Clarisse replied, "Oh, Dad, you have never said a truer word. But I don't think I could go through that again."

"Clarisse, my love, life is all wonderful from here. Our life together will read as a romantic novel," Jackson said.

"You're biased, cousin?" Jan joked.

"Come on, Jan. Let's enjoy our lunch and probable victory."

The conversation remained happy as Clarisse, Jackson, Jan, and Clarisse's parents finished their lunch. A young man approached them and told them the jury had reached their verdict.

What did this mean? The judge had told the court to convene in the morning, and the jury had only been out for a little over an hour. The now puzzled group left the restaurant and made their way back into the courtroom.

The court came to order as the judge entered.

"Ladies and gentleman of the jury, have you reached your verdict?"

"We have, Your Honour."

"Clerk, can you deliver the verdict to me, please?"

The clerk took the folded paper, and handed it to the judge. As he read the verdict to himself, a silence descended over the court. Looking up, he asked the jury, "Have you taken sufficient time to reach this verdict?"

"Yes, Your Honour, we have."

"Is it a unanimous verdict?"

"Yes, Your Honour."

"Would the prisoner and council stand to hear the verdict?"

As asked, Lachlan and his lawyer stood and faced the judge. When all was quiet, the judge began reading the verdict to the court.

"The jury has found you guilty of aggravated rape, occasioning bodily harm with regard to Mrs Clarisse Hastings and Miss Susan Jones, also of the attempted murder and rape of Miss Sandy Davies. It is now time for me to pass an appropriate sentence upon you. I have listened to the evidence from both council and witnesses, and their verdict allows me to sentence you appropriately. I sentence you to a term of twenty-five years in prison, with no possibility of parole. You will be taken from here and be placed in a place of incarceration. Here you will remain until your sentence is completed. This brings to a close these proceedings. I thank the jury for their time and effort during this trial. You are now excused."

As the judge spoke his last words, Lachlan leapt to his feet, shouting, "Liars, liars! They don't have the right!"

His outburst brought a quick rebuke from the judge.

"You will take your seat now, or I will have you further restrained!"

"Why? You don't have the right to order me to do anything!"

The judge motioned to the court officers, and they quickly restrained him and sat him back in his seat.

"In this courtroom, I can order you to behave, or I can find you in contempt. This would certainly lengthen your sentence. Now sit!"

The victims of Lachlan slumped in their seats. They were at last free of threat—their torment was now at an end. Jackson held his wife close, and her head fell onto his shoulder as she sobbed with relief.

Jan held Sue's hand, thanking her for her testimony. Sue accepted Jan's good wishes and announced she had left the game. "I should be thanking you. Giving evidence has put me in the public eye, and a well-known author wants to write a book about my experiences. He's going to pay me while he writes, and then I get a percentage of the sales."

"That's great, Sue. If I don't see you again, good luck."

Jan then pulled her phone from her pocket and dialled Rachel.

"Dr Scott here."

"It's me, Rach. He's been found guilty on all counts! Is that great or what?"

"Oh, that's wonderful! It's the best news I've had since this all started. How long did he get?"

"Twenty-five years without parole. Can you tell Sandy and Allison for me? I will be tied up here for some time. You know the drill—forms to fill in and arrangements for him to be transported to jail. I will see you tonight, okay?"

"Certainly! I'll be at your place at eight thirty."

Rachel made her way to Sandy's room, and at the door she saw John there. He, Sandy, and Allison were in a deep discussion.

"I am so glad you are all here. The trial is over, and he has been found guilty on all counts!" Rachel announced.

"Oh, how wonderful! How long did he get? Come on, Rachel, tell us, please?"

"Steady there, Sandy. I don't want you to harm yourself."

"Well then, just tell us! This waiting is torture."

"He has been sentenced to twenty-five years imprisonment, without parole. Isn't that great?"

Allison said, "I don't think I have heard sweeter news in my life! Now Sandy and I can go home to Laton. There she can heal mentally and physical. Thank you for everything, Rachel. I must see all the police officers and thank them."

"John, why are you in here?" Rachel asked.

"Sandy and Allison gave me permission a few days ago. I know the rules, and you can be assured I would not do anything to harm either of them. I just visit, and when Sandy goes home, I have to wait for an invitation to Layton. Is that okay with you, Doctor?"

"Yes, John. Thank goodness there are still some gentlemen around! They keep the scales level, don't you think?"

The three people in the room nodded their approval to Rachel, who then left.

"Mum, you still look apprehensive. Do you still fear he will be freed?"

"Yes, darling, I do. Only when he is firmly behind bars will my fears be calmed."

John interjected at this time, saying, "Will both of you trust me? It is time to look to the future, not the past."

"Yes, let's do exactly that."

Clarisse and Jackson went home after the trial. Once inside, Clarisse fell into Jackson's arms, and he slowly eased her to the floor. He sat and held her, and then lifted her head and placed it on his lap.

"What is it, darling? Are you sick?"

"No, I think it's just sheer relief from the tension, which has been with me night and day for what seems an age."

"You are safe now, my love. I am here, and my friends will make sure he will never be in a position to hurt a woman again. Let's get dressed and go out with our family and friends."

Lachlan was in a different place. His smugness was gone, and fear filled his very being. His home for many years to come was a ten-by-ten cell. He only glimpsed one or two of his fellow prisoners, but it was enough to heighten his fears at their appearance. "Why am I here with these thieves and murderers? I'm not like them—my education alone is far higher than these animals."

A guard yelled, "Lights out!, have a bad night." Lachlan's punishment began.

Jan, and the rest of her division arrived at Rachel's flat at 8.30. When they were all gathered, they drove to Earnest and Flora's house for the post-trial party. Rachel had given Sandy permission to attend, but she must use a wheelchair. John picked up mother and daughter and then headed to the Stewart home.

The other guests had arrived when John pulled up outside the house. Rachel came out to help Sandy into the wheelchair.

"How was the trip, love?"

"It was great; just to be out in the open air is wonderful."

"I'm glad about that. Now, let's get you inside. Mr and Mrs Stewart are waiting."

"Hi, Jan. It was a great verdict, don't you think?" Said Sandy

"Yes, it was. Now women can feel safer with him behind bars."

The house was lit up like a Christmas tree—coloured lights, streamers, and balloons were everywhere. Happy people talked and laughed; this was a celebration of relief. With the verdict, they could all begin to live again. Sandy stayed close to John and her mother; Clarisse sat beside her and talked for a while. There were many people for Sandy to meet, and all of them understood her feelings.

The night went on until Rachel had to return to the hospital. She took Sandy and her mother. John and the remainder of the rape crisis team had to leave. Jan spoke to Rachel before she left; through their gestures, they had agreed to meet later. Clarisse and Jackson were the last to leave, and they bade her parents goodbye and drove back to their flat.

For Clarisse and Jackson, it was now time to take a long-awaited holiday. Their flight and accommodations were booked. The flight seemed to go slowly; it took an age for their island to come into view.

"There it is, Jackson. Isn't it beautiful?"

"Yes, it is. Will you make the same meal, the one we had on our first wonderful night?"

"Do you think I will have time to plan a meal?"

"Maybe not . . ." As he spoke, Jackson raised one suggestive eyebrow at his wife.

The plane had landed, and the happy couple made their way off the plane and into a taxi, which whisked them off to their bungalow. They carried the cases into the bungalow—the same one in which Clarisse had surrendered her love to Jackson.

After a small meal they sat on the swing, which still hung on the veranda. Jackson eased his arm around his wife's shoulders. "Do you know how much I love you?"

"As much as I love you, I hope."

"Oh, Clarisse, you are my life. I feel my heart thump whenever I see you, and my life would be nothing if you weren't in it."

As they gazed into each other's eyes, the unspoken question was answered. Jackson lifted his wife and walked toward their bedroom. Their love was open, not hidden; if one saw them it was obvious that their feelings were as a twine, which wrapped around them and made them one.

Their love making over, they decided to walk along the beach until dinner. After picking up their towels, they left the bungalow; the sand was soft and warm underfoot, and they held hands as they walked. Time and distance were not a problem; they talked as they walked hand in hand.

"Jackson, how do you feel about children?"

"I love them. Maybe we should have a child. What do you think?"

"I'm so happy you said that!"

"Come on, Clarisse, don't tease me. Are we going to have a baby?"

"Yes, we are. I didn't want to tell you until we were on our island."

Jackson wrapped his arms around her. He wanted to be close as he placed his hand on her abdomen. "When will he arrive?"

"Hey! How do you know it's a he? It might be a girl."

"Oh damn, who cares? Boy or girl, it's ours—when is our baby due?"

"Rachel says about mid-October."

"Rachel knows? You told her first?"

"Of course—she is my doctor. I had to be sure, before telling you, that I wouldn't have trouble during the pregnancy."

"I'm sorry, my love. I'm just a bit jealous."

He pulled his wife down onto the sand, and they sat side by side, looking into each other's eyes. From the beginning, their love had turned a full circle, and now for them, it was complete. They would tell all their family and friends at home, but not until this holiday, which they had looked forward to so much, was over.

Back at home, life had lost the madness that had engulfed them for more than two years. Jan and the rape crisis team had time to catch up on their paperwork and their personal lives. Earnest and Flora's lives were almost back to normal; they visited the hospital to see Sandy and Allison and entertained Rachel and Jan with the occasional meal at home. The conversation always light hearted and away from all their dark days.

Jan and Rachel still had their movie and dinner nights; their friendship gained strength, and they talked for hours, exploring all that had happened since they first met—and of course, they wondered whether another rapist raise his head. This was a real fear. Jan led the team, and Rachel was in control of the forensics and the care of victims.

Rachel was on her way to see Sandy when she bumped into John.

"You visiting again, John?"

"Yes, Doc. Is it all right?"

"Sure—we can walk together."

They talked as they walked, Rachel was glad that Sandy had the comfort of a nice man. Life hadn't been kind to her, but all was going well now. They reached the door to Sandy's room, and Rachel spoke. "Good morning, Sandy. Where's your mum?"

"Mum had to go home; all her pets were being looked after by a neighbour, and she wanted to thank them and buy more dog and cat food. I'm expecting her back later today."

"Tell her to come and see me when she returns. We need to talk."

"Is there something wrong?" Sandy asked, concerned.

"No, love. We need to make arrangements for your care when you go home."

"Will it be soon?"

"That is why I need to talk to your mum. It's not bad news, Sandy, so don't worry. I will see you when Allison gets back."

"Okay, Rachel. I am a little tired."

Rachel left John with Sandy and returned to her office. Her mind was on the meeting she would have later in the day. What she had to discuss with Allison was something that may not happen, but she still had to tell her. Sitting back in her chair, she thought back to the beginning of the hunt for the rapist. Her mind was full of the different women who had been involved, first the victims and their families, then the great team of professionals who had finally brought to an end the vicious rapist's reign of terror.

Later in the day, Allison knocked on Rachel's door. Rachel stood up and beckoned her in.

"Come in and sit down, Allison."

"What's wrong? Is it about Sandy?"

"Yes, but I am hopeful it can be dealt with successfully."

"Please tell me just what is wrong."

"During the rape, he used an object of some kind; it penetrated the cervix. The wound has healed now, but I cannot be absolutely certain it will not become a problem when Sandy wants to have a child."

Fear filled Allison's mind as she took in the news Rachel had told her. "Have you told her, Rachel?"

"Not yet. I needed to tell you first."

"Do you want me to tell her now?"

"No, I will do that. We will do it now—come on, let's go."

The two women walked the short distance to Sandy's room in silence. John was gone; he had returned to the station.

"What's wrong, Mum?" Sandy said.

"Rachel will tell you, sweetheart."

Rachel took her time explaining all the things she had told Allison. Sandy lay very quiet, but she took in everything she heard. When Rachel had finished, Sandy remained silent. It would take time for her to acknowledge all she had been told.

"Would you like me to leave, Sandy?"

"No, don't go. I need to ask more questions. You aren't saying I will *never* have children, are you?"

"No, I am not saying that, but it is my duty to tell you what may happen in the future."

"So everything could be all right? I could have children?"

"It could go either way."

"Mum, you have always told me to look on the bright side, so let's do just that, eh?"

"When put like that, we will take whatever comes in the future."

Rachel nodded her approval and wondered at the strength Sandy possessed, knowing what she had been through. This lovely young girl could still remain positive. "I must leave now, but I will come back later. If the tests come back soon, I will be able to tell you when you can go home."

"Doc, are Clarisse and Jackson still away?"

"Yes, they are, but they should be home in about a week."

"Thanks, Doc. Mum and I will see you later."

"Bye for now."

Earnest and Flora were at the airport waiting for Clarisse and Jackson; they wanted to hear all about the holiday. The plane landed and people disembarked.

"There they are, Earnest."

"Yes, I see them."

Clarisse and Jackson were pleased to see them and headed in their direction. With greetings all around, they made their way to the car. Upon arriving at the flat, they parked and went into the building. Good-hearted banter passed between them, and after a cuppa Earnest and Flora went home, leaving the kids alone.

Rachel walked to Sandy's room. She was very happy: the tests had come back, and all was well. As she entered, both women looked at her.

"Well, Doc, what's the verdict?"

"They all came back negative. All the infection has gone, and your blood work is fine. I am very happy that now I can let you go home."

"That's wonderful, Rachel! How much longer does Sandy need to stay?"

"Just a few days, perhaps the weekend. However, I will have to keep seeing her for a few months. I would like to keep up with Sandy's hypnotherapy; Clarisse has benefited from her sessions."

"I will keep seeing you for our sessions," Sandy promised. "Thanks for your all your care, Doc. I was lucky to have you. Coming to see you will be like visiting a friend."

"I must go now, but I will see you tomorrow."

Jan and Rachel visited Clarisse and Jackson that evening; they rang for take away, and the company was light-hearted and warm. There hadn't been an evil case for a while, so the doc and the cop were able to take it easy for a while.

"How was the holiday, you two?"

"Wonderful, thanks Jan."

"What did you do on the island?"

"That's our secret No more questions okay!"

Sandy had been at home for two weeks when an invitation arrived: it was from the Stewart family requesting her and her mother's company at a celebration party the following Saturday. Caroline received the same invite; the explanation for the party was to celebrate the end of a nightmare and the beginning of love and happiness.

The night of the party arrived, and all of the people who had been involved in the case were present. Smiles and laughter filled the night air. John sat close to Sandy and her mum. Jan, Kelly, and Mary arrived together, with Rachel just behind them. The last to arrive was Caroline.

Sandy wheeled slowly over to her.

"I haven't had the chance to thank you. I dread to think what would have happened if you hadn't stopped."

"Fate is what we call it. However, just seeing you now looking so well is payment enough. I am so grateful I took that road; it was not my usual route, but somehow I felt I should. When you are completely well, you and your mother have an open invitation to come and visit."

"That would be great! I'm sure Mum would agree. If John is at our home, can I bring him as well?"

"Yes, my dear, that, would be fine."

When all were present, Earnest stepped up on a chair, and called the group to silence.

"I'm sorry to break up you happy people, but there are things that must be said. First, to our gallant police officers, then to a doctor of exceptional qualities Rachel has been instrumental in bringing both Clarisse and Sandy back to health." Applause rang out for the people named. "Also, Flora and I went from absolute despair to happiness, as our daughter went through the most horrific experience, then to the love of her life. Every person here has been through this journey with us. Now to Sandy: our home is your home, if you or your mother ever needs it, and of course so is John.

"Finally yet importantly, I must now talk of our son-in-law. It was his strength and love which gave Clarisse the confidence she needed. Will you all raise your glasses and drink a toast to everyone here?"

With the toast over, Earnest stepped down from the chair. As he did, Jackson took his place and beckoned Clarisse to his side.

"Clarisse and I have some news for you all, but first I must thank everyone here as Earnest did. This party is to tell all our friends that we are expecting a child in October."

The small group exploded with congratulations to the young couple. If the party had been noisy before, it was now almost bedlam. The group crowded around them, and best wishes from them all made it impossible for Jackson to step down; he had to recognize all of them.

As the friends left and made their way home, the Stewarts and Hastings sat and quietly talked.

"Did Rachel know our secret, Clarisse?"

"Yes, I had to tell her, to ask if I night have trouble with the pregnancy or the birth."

"By the look on your faces, she must have been positive."

"She was, Dad, and we are very happy, aren't we, darling?"

Jackson nodded and said, "Some people say that a love is meant to be. It certainly was. I don't want to be a drag, but I would like to go home with my wife. Is that okay, Dad?"

"Sure is. Off you go! We'll see you later."

With all that said they went out to the car and drove home.

This small group of friends remained close. The disastrous way they met now was a friendship which would last for a lifetime. Jan and Rachel moved hand in hand, and John and Sandy celebrated their engagement. Caroline visited often, and Allison looked at her daughter and knew bad things could turn to good with time. The friendships were still very close. Soon they all got the call: Clarisse and Jackson had a new baby boy.

Jan and Rachel still had their movie nights. Their relationship had turned to love, they spent as much time together as they could. All the friends and relations accepted them as they were, so their feelings could be open to all.

One such night Jan's phone rang. She picked it up, listened as she looked deep into Rachel's eyes.

"Okay. I will be there soon. Sorry my love, it's on again."

Rachel knew exactly what that meant. Both prepared for what was to come next.